MW01061336

Solving
FOR
THE
Unknown

Solving

FOR

THE

Unknown

LOAN LE

SIMON & SCHUSTER BFYR

NEW YORK   AMSTERDAM/ANTWERP   LONDON
TORONTO   SYDNEY/MELBOURNE   NEW DELHI

SIMON & SCHUSTER BFYR

An imprint of Simon & Schuster Children's Publishing Division

1230 Avenue of the Americas, New York, New York 10020

Text © 2025 by Loan Le

Jacket illustration © 2025 by Alex Cabal

Jacket design by Laura Eckes

For information about special discounts for bulk purchases, please contact Simon & Schuster Special Sales at 1-866-506-1949 or business@simonandschuster.com.

Simon & Schuster strongly believes in freedom of expression and stands against censorship in all its forms. For more information, visit BooksBelong.com.

The Simon & Schuster Speakers Bureau can bring authors to your live event. For more information or to book an event, contact the Simon & Schuster Speakers Bureau at 1-866-248-3049 or visit our website at www.simonspeakers.com.

Interior design by Laura Eckes

The text for this book was set in EB Garamond.

Manufactured in the United States of America

First Edition

2 4 6 8 10 9 7 5 3 1

CIP data for this book is available from the Library of Congress.

ISBN 9781665917155

ISBN 9781665917179 (ebook)

For Amelia and Zoey

Solving
FOR
THE
Unknown

CHAPTER 1

VIỆT

All Vietnamese kids understood that the stork story could never apply to them. Sure, the idea was great. Việt even thought it was comforting that a majestic bird could have carried him in its secure beak before delivering him home. Unfortunately, Việt's real origin story, according to his parents, was that they found him in some trash can, with ants crawling over him—an embellishment they liked to add before uncontrollably laughing.

Việt's parents learned their jokes from *their* parents, which basically meant they didn't learn how to tell jokes at all.

As he grew older, Việt realized he was carefully planned, like everything else in his parents' lives. They waited to have him until their wholesale distributor business in Westminster was stable. But since that took years and years, his parents had more gray hair than other parents of classmates his age.

Especially the ones here. Việt's mom and dad never experienced college life or move-in day; they didn't know what to expect, so they looked unusually lost as they stood in the Tercero parking lot at UC Davis, surrounded by other incoming freshmen and their families rushing from their cars to the dorms.

"I'll get my welcome packet. I'll be back," Việt said just as his parents started whisper-arguing.

The minute he turned, he exhaled. He should be used to this—all their arguments. During the car ride, beneath the crooning of Vietnamese ballads, his parents blew up at each other after Ba took a wrong turn. Suburban areas turned rural, then back to suburban and then eventually, the town and the campus was a mixture of the two. When they finally reached the parking lot, his mom came out of their van scowling. A familiar, uneasy feeling swelled inside Việt. With him gone, how were they going to survive each other?

At the check-in table, upperclassmen Student Housing volunteers were way too peppy, but their energy was contagious, so Việt's wariness waned, and the excitement that started up last night returned. He was here, finally. A volunteer handed him a twenty-minute unloading pass and a thick folder containing plans for this week's Aggie Orientation.

Soon enough, other leaders redirected his father to park closer to the curb outside Laben Hall and helped them unload the trunk. The students were surprised when Mẹ also got to work immediately. His mom was barely five feet and might look like she knitted for fun, but in reality, she was weight-lifting crates of fresh produce all over Bolsa every day.

Laben Hall was sandwiched between Campbell and Kearney. Inside the dorm, the air was ripe with Lysol, flowery perfumes, and pungent cologne. The hallways were narrow, walls covered by flyers in serial-killer block letters. Scratch that; maybe Việt shouldn't have stayed up late watching reruns of *CSI: Miami.*

As they passed different rooms, he heard roommates and parents in conversation. Laughter exploded from somewhere at the end of the hall, but all was quiet on their end.

Việt and his parents stood before a door with a plaque reading ROOM 136. Hands full, Ba urged Việt forward with his hip, which was made of iron, apparently, because the next thing he knew, he was through the door, nearly landing face down.

His new roommate and his parents turned; they weren't what Việt expected.

Instagram stalking had easily led him to Wren's page. His posts showed off his chalk art and wall graffiti, but Việt couldn't find a clear photo of him.

Over boba at 7 Leaves, Việt had passed Wren's profile to Bảo and Linh. After checking out Wren's art, Linh, also a painter, said she'd love to meet him. Bảo asked if he should be worried about "competition," prompting Linh to steal back the strawberry boba they were sharing. He didn't even protest. Bảo was so whipped for her. They were sickening.

What Việt didn't expect to see was a kid wearing khakis and a polo shirt—but why was it buttoned up all the way to the top?

They exchanged poorly timed hellos. Wren's dad matched with his own pressed khakis, and his mother had on a white blouse, pink pants, and beige flats. She reminded Việt of a rich woman on *Law & Order* or *Criminal Minds*, the character who was always sure her corporate loves-golf-but-is-too-busy-to-uphold-the-sanctity-of-marriage husband or ~~her precious I-punch~~-holes-in-the-wall son were innocent of any crime.

Meanwhile, Việt's parents had on jeans and loose shirts so they could easily move around.

Well, this should be interesting.

"Now, tell me, how do you pronounce that name of yours?" Dad Khaki finally asked.

"Yeah, it's Việt," he answered, lowering his pitch.

"Wow, that's an *interesting* name." Oh, perfect. "Say that again, I want to try it."

"Well, in Vietnamese, the letter *e* in my name has an underdot, so the tone is lower. It feels like your throat is tightening when you say it," he explained. "But it might be easier for you to imagine saying the first half of the word *Vietnam*."

"Ah, well, I didn't think it'd be that easy! How's this?" The man tried to pronounce Việt's name but couldn't get the tone right.

"Um, well—"

"Dad, just pronounce it like he said and stop torturing all of us. It's *Việt*," Wren interjected. His pronunciation was close to the Vietnamese way. In the middle of folding cardboard boxes, his top

4

button had come loose, and he was brushing back hair away from his eyes. "I go by Wren because they had the bright idea of naming me Wrendell. Goes to show you that they shouldn't be naming *anyone*, like ever."

Wren's father shot Việt a sheepish grin, then busied himself with moving his son's boxes from the hallway and into the room. As they all unpacked, Wren's chatty mother pestered Việt and his parents with questions, which Việt answered himself. Ba and Mẹ weren't familiar with polite small talk with strangers; their work life and social life were deeply embedded in Little Saigon, where people looked like them, used the same language, and shared the same history.

After a while, Wren's mother switched over to voicing trivial observations—"This room is *so* small, isn't it?"—where his parents could nod their agreement. Việt felt bad for judging the woman earlier based on her impractical, well-to-do outfit; she was friendly enough.

Soon, Wren and his family left for dinner.

Ba checked one of the two wardrobes, scowling when he discovered one of the doors wouldn't close.

"Make sure you switch it with the other one," he said, and Việt had to laugh. He could be funny sometimes. But Ba's humor tended to come out at family gatherings, when he had four or five Heineken beers with the other men. Then there was no shutting him up.

Meanwhile, his mom parted the curtains of a window. Dust

motes danced in the air. She peered outside as if she was expecting someone.

Ba placed the last cardboard box onto his desk. It had most of Việt's books and DVDs—and some things he didn't want his dad to see.

"Uh, I can do it—"

But in Ba's hand was *The Forensic Casebook*, a rare title in English that was shoved into one of Tự Lực Bookstore's crowded shelves, forgotten.

Việt stilled.

Truth was, he had never intended to tell his parents about his idea to go into forensic science. But then he watched his best friend, Bảo—who never cared so much about anything—find his calling as a writer and an editor, and finally told his parents nearly a year ago. They proudly hung up one of his articles. Turned out they didn't care what Bảo did; they only wished he could find a passion.

Their reaction gave Việt hope. And he thought maybe *his* parents would want the same thing for him. He brought it up at dinner at around the same time—and found he was completely wrong.

Their meal forgotten, his father had started ranting about how much he and his mother sacrificed to give Việt a stable life, to pave him a path to *somewhere*, versus the literal and figurative dirt road they had to navigate when they'd landed in America. For their son to show interest in a "fake" science like forensics was akin to taking an ill-advised detour or a major wrong turn.

"Passion? What is passion, you Americanized kids all talk

about?" His dad had looked to his mother across the kitchen table, as if she'd have the answer. She showed confusion rather than share his father's anger. "We cannot afford to have passions."

Like usual, Việt let his dad rant. He picked at the rice in his bowl as his dad's emphasis on *afford* echoed in his head. He knew what his father was getting it. Việt had gotten into a couple of schools— big names, like the ones his parents' friends often name-dropped— but with little to no scholarships attached and knowing the number of loans he'd need to take to attend, they all agreed to choose a good state school. Because that was what they could afford to do.

It wasn't like he had his eyes set on Stanford or whatever big-shot school. Never did. He just wanted—

What Việt *really* wanted to tell his parents—

His mind returned to the present. Việt took the book from Ba and slid it underneath his other textbooks—for his "real science" classes.

"I think I can handle it from here," he said quietly.

His dad opened his mouth, but his mom interrupted them from a few feet away.

"This isn't working. Not cold." She was bent over, placing her hand inside the mini fridge. Ba went over to check on it himself. As Mẹ stood up, she shot Việt a tired, almost understanding smile.

"The school can't even give you a working fridge?" Ba complained.

Grateful for the distraction, Việt joked with Ba: "Do you want me to switch it with a fridge from another room?"

"Can you?"

Mẹ lightly slapped Ba's shoulder, telling him in Vietnamese that this would only get Việt in trouble. It was a familiar but rare move—that slap. Fun. They didn't seem to have any fun these days. Maybe work was getting tough; by the time they came home, they looked like they lost days of sleep.

Turned out the fridge worked; it was just the outlet that was bad.

When it was time for his parents to leave, Ba pulled out his wallet and offered Việt some money. "Nè. Take it."

"No, it's fine, I don't need any money." He'd saved enough from working at Bảo's family restaurant.

"Thôi, don't argue." Ba physically pried open his fingers, placing five hundred dollars in his palm. He must have taken it out just this morning because the bills were still crisp. "Use it on whenever con need it. Text Ba if con cần more."

Việt accepted it. "Cảm ơn, Ba."

If they were another pair of son and father, they would have hugged. But his dad always kept his emotions bottled up. So, Ba settled with a pat on Việt's shoulder, and Việt knew what he was trying to say.

His mother reached for his free hand. "Study hard. Be careful. Don't forget to call Mẹ. At least every weekend. Đừng lo cho Mẹ. And if con don't call, Mẹ will drive back up." The threat was undercut by the tremble in her voice.

Guilt washed over Việt. He thought about the emptiness of the house after his parents' explosive arguments—nasty words and insults worming through the air vents. He thought of his hesitant steps toward the kitchen, where his mom would often distract herself by washing the dishes. By then, Dad was always gone, driving to clear his mind. He'd come back later.

They had been three for as long as Việt could remember. With him six hours away this year, how would they function as two?

Who would be there for his mother when she needed someone to listen to her rant? His mother always told him not to feel buồn, but who would be there to soothe her sadness?

Yeah, a part of him was glad to be away. An escape from being his parents' buffer.

But the image of his mother in his head, in that kitchen, was heartbreakingly tiny.

Việt squeezed her hand. "I'll call. Promise."

Now he was alone. Việt sat on the bed, even though his duffel bag with his running shoes challenged him from across the room, urging him to move instead of remaining still. Because nothing good ever happened when he was still. The setting sun entered through the window, slicing up Wren's side of the room. Music blared from down the hall—some sort of gathering. He tried to will the earlier excitement from today to come back to him. To fight away the familiar sadness.

College was going to be good. Everything would be all right.

LOAN LE

Ali added Linh, Bảo, Việt to the Romeo & Juliet squad.

Linh: seriously ali?!

Bảo: 🖼️

Việt: ☺

CHAPTER 2

EVIE

It was five p.m. Jake had just texted to say he'd be at Toomey Field in ten, but knowing he was always late, Evie tacked on twenty more minutes.

Groups of first-years occupied pockets of the bleachers while Evie waited in the middle. Others sat on the grassy field, the all-weather track curling around them. Evie guessed they were still strangers because they were sitting politely spaced apart. If it were her and Lis and Kale and Tate sitting together, someone's feet would have ended up on someone's lap. Even so, the younger students were laughing and smiling, still high from their move-in day. They were excited for a chance to restart their lives, to explore the unknown.

Evie thought of her only sister, Linh, who was probably moving into Berkeley right now. She likely brought what she considered the essentials: her painting supplies. She easily imagined their parents scolding her for her haphazard packing, then giving up because her excitement wore them down. Story of Evie's life: being the youngest, Linh would eventually get her way.

Even Evie was impressed that her sister convinced their parents to let her major in anything creative. Well, Linh had to throw in a couple of lies before admitting the truth, and their parents gave her the silent treatment for a few weeks, but after clearing some misunderstandings, she was on her way to being a painter. She even got a boyfriend along the way—a boy whose family owned a competing pho restaurant that once tried to sabotage Evie's family restaurant. Their story felt like a modern *Romeo & Juliet*, without the tragic ending.

Yet Evie still hadn't told her parents about Jake.

Jake had been the athlete-scholar at his high school; Evie had always kept her head down, studying. If they'd gone to the same school, they wouldn't have gotten together. But Evie saw college as a clean slate, and while she didn't make over herself completely, she had a goal to make friends outside of her normally studious friend group, and eventually Jake and she became classmates, friends . . . and more.

Their similarities outweighed their differences. They liked order and routine and took school seriously. They knew the burden that came with birth order—all those expectations—and they felt responsible for more than themselves.

Jake and his family had a legacy here. Jake's first and third brothers and his father all graduated from here. His father had built a major pharmaceuticals company and was a longtime member of the Chancellor's Board of Advisors, and, when Jake was a first-year, he donated chemicals from his company that would otherwise cost a fortune for their school to procure.

Toomey Field was where they finally blurted out their feelings. Like silly kindergartners. That night, the stadium lights were dimmed, and they were, unbelievably, the only ones there. They shivered from a rare night chill, their hoodies doing little to help. They had bought the sweatshirts together, first-years duped into thinking school spirit actually mattered in the long run. After confessing her closely guarded feelings and becoming embarrassed, Evie made herself small by pulling the bottom of her hoodie over bent knees. She heard his quiet laugh—like he didn't want people to hear him—and she lifted her head to see him glancing at her so softly.

It'd been two years since that night.

Now a couple of runners dashed around the track. Some were at a nice jog, but there was one Asian guy who jumped out at her. His runner's pace was smooth, like he was just coasting along. Evie had never been a natural runner; she did it for exercise while others did it to clear their mind. The boy was oblivious to everyone around him, lost in his own mindscape.

Evie glanced down at her phone. 5:23. She was always looking at the time.

Jake Phan finally arrived. Evie heard him coming first. Some people down in the field called out his name. Used to this type of thing, Jake raised a hand before breezily walking up the bleachers in her direction. Evie took her time admiring him. And yes, maybe she felt a bit smug that he was approaching *her*. He was wearing a neatly ironed white button-down, and it contrasted against his recently suntanned skin.

Evie, respectfully, took in how well it clung to his lean torso. He kept up his workout routine over the summer.

Jake sat down. "Hey, you," he said, kissing her quietly. Evie intertwined their hands.

Staring up at him now, she felt lucky enough to know all the things about him that people might not see initially. The slight creases in his forehead, the ones she used to trace after lying in his bed, were from worry.

He was the fourth child in his family, following a line of three doctors—anesthesiologist, heart surgeon, and orthopedic doctor. He was planning to go into pediatrics, like her. No one else noticed the pressure that came with this pedigree because he carried himself well. That was what really drew Evie to him—he never buckled no matter what was thrown his way. Growing up, she too was burdened by her responsibilities, albeit as the eldest daughter.

"I'd like to continue our negotiation," Jake said playfully.

Before telling Evie he was on his way, they had texted about their dinner plans.

"Oh?" Evie arched an eyebrow.

"What if—"

"Non-negotiable."

He groaned. "I don't know how you can *live off* fast food."

"I'm not living off it. I'm treating myself. So, Raising Cane's?" Best chicken tenders ever.

"Promise: we'll do chicken tenders another time. But what if we grab tacos? Fish tacos? Healthier, right? And I haven't had it in ages." He paused. "Also, I have a coupon on my phone."

Ugh. He had her now. She could never say no to a deal. And that must make her parents secretly proud, especially her dad.

Evie finally nodded.

"But let me do one thing before we go," Jake said.

"What?"

"I have to stop by Spain's office."

Eli Spain wasn't the most hated professor in the science department.

He was the second. Every interaction with Spain was like an interrogation; a moment for him to ask trick questions to see if students were up to speed with the course materials. Everything he said was right, and even if you—the student—were right, you were still wrong. Evie was never his target, but she'd seen so many students switch majors because of him.

"Come on, he's an okay guy once you get beyond that strange *I'm better than you* complex."

"Jake, he loves *you.*"

Jake laughed shortly. Bitterly. "Only because my dad donated to the building."

Some of their professors were also his father's former classmates.

Being on their radar was both a good and bad thing; he was on a first-name basis with Spain, but Spain and other professors also talked to his father frequently, leaving little room for Jake to under-perform. Eyes were on him all the time.

Evie's parents didn't watch her as closely; even in high school, they knew they could observe her from the sidelines. She could take care of herself. She was like that the moment she was born.

Evie nudged her boyfriend by the shoulder. "Or maybe Spain recognizes that you're smart and hardworking, and he just wants to be your mentor."

Jake pressed another kiss to her forehead. "Well, I really should see him. But I'll be quick, I promise."

"Yo, Jay!" a voice among a group of boys called out to him.

"Oh, it's Brent," Jake said, standing up. "I'm gonna say hi to him first. Wanna come? Then Spain and dinner."

As a first-year prank this lovely gentleman named Brent had flooded one of the girls' communal bathrooms, beyond repair, so they couldn't use it for days. Multiple floors had to share the same, crowded bathroom.

Evie hated to be that person who held a grudge . . . but she was that person. So, she told *Jay* that she'd wait while he caught up with them.

They erupted with variations of Jake's name along with cho-ruses of "Bro!" Ugh. Yeah, she was not going anywhere near that.

Her eyes drifted back to the runner from before.

He had picked up speed. He pumped his legs and arms, and he

was breathing hard, racing toward an imaginary finish line, pushing himself to the edge. Then she noticed one of his shoelaces flying free, and she thought he might trip.

Occasionally her thoughts manifested into reality–like how a red light changed the moment she wished it was green. Or when the song looping in her head suddenly played on the radio.

Before the inevitable happened, the runner's eyes unexpectedly connected with Evie's. Or, from a distance she thought they did.

Then he tripped, tumbling repeatedly, before landing face down. Laughter erupted from one of the groups nearby.

Evie rushed down the bleachers.

CHAPTER 3

VIỆT

Việt tried taking a nap, but people were still moving in, playing music, laughing, and joking around. He heard everything through the thin walls. Việt eventually decided to go running.

Now that he was on campus, he didn't know what to expect. He didn't have siblings, so he mostly heard about college from his parents' friends who had older kids. Apparently, they were solving climate change and discovering cures to little-known diseases every single day.

"Alexander is so selfless and kindhearted," an auntie would brag.

Alexander? His childhood bully Alexander—who once poured a fistful of toothpicks into Việt's sneakers—contributing to the betterment of humankind?

Sure, Auntie.

Việt couldn't count on the tales of out-of-touch, oblivious parents. And he couldn't rely on books or TV shows—though, to be fair, someone always got murdered and the murders always got solved. Life wasn't that easy to navigate.

Most TV shows skipped over the quiet moments like now: him, walking across the campus in search of the track and field before the sun could fully set. Instead, more often shown were packed parties, red Solo cups, chugging challenges. College was where you met people. College was where, supposedly, you had the most fun of your life.

The thought of making new friends took a lot out of him. Việt didn't need that many. He had grown close to his cross-country and track teammates over the years. But they didn't really know him like Bảo did. With Bảo, there were no pretenses. He was just as weird as Việt—even though the other boy would deny it—and he never gawked at Việt's ability to memorize key plot moments from *Law & Order*, *CSI*, and *NCIS* episodes that replayed in his mind.

Now with his girlfriend, Linh, in the picture, Việt could let his guard down around her, too. Same went with Ali, Linh's best friend, because she had this weird ability to see through everyone. In a few years, when she gained control over some big newspaper, she'd make the most corrupt subjects fess up to their latest scandals. That was how good—and scary—Ali was.

But other people—sometimes Việt couldn't understand them. He was lonely in their presence.

That was why he liked watching reruns of Stokes and Sidle, Benson and Rollins, Reid and JJ doing their jobs. The two partners

saw a crime and they discovered irrefutable evidence, and no matter what the perp used as a shitty alibi, the evidence led to the truth.
Together they were strong. He wondered if he would ever find
someone to be on his side.

To Việt's surprise, the field was already crowded—friend groups
snapping together like magnets.

So Việt ran. Blocked out everyone around him. His breath
evenly flowing in and out of his nostrils. Core tight. He didn't
consider himself a nature person, but running made him feel like
he was part of the earth. The air, the wind, itself. Like, if he decided
to leap, he might take flight.

A half hour in, Việt was nearing his last lap. Then he heard a
clicking sound. The shoelaces on his left sneaker had unraveled.
Still, he pressed forward, knowing he was close to the finish line.
He didn't want to lose momentum.

Ahead of him, there were people scattered on the bleachers.
Right at the center, an Asian girl sat alone.

During high school races, whenever he was close to the end, he
abandoned all senses except for sight. He saw only the finish line.
He'd sprint and get swallowed up by the sweaty limbs of his cheer-
ing teammates and his coach who had screamed himself hoarse.

Việt decided, then, to focus on the girl. He saw her. Only her.

Breathe in.

Breathe out.

That was when she decided to look straight ahead.

Right at him.

Right as he tripped over his own shoelaces and tumbled over more times than he could count.

Việt rolled over to see the sky. It was an annoying pastel calm, which he might have enjoyed if his run had gone well. But level-ten pain shot up from his right knee to his thigh instead. He lifted his head and saw his left knee was scratched and bleeding. He blinked, and Linh, his best friend's girlfriend, was right beside him.

Wait, Linh?

How was she here?

And *why* were there three of her? The faces hovered, so he blinked a couple more times before the image solidified. Not Linh. This girl, the one who looked at him right before the finish line, had slightly wavier hair and short bangs that framed her worried face.

"Are you okay?" Her voice sounded far away.

Việt sat up too quickly; his knee burned. He bit back a swear.

"Hey, easy. You fell hard." She touched his arm. "Don't move if you really can't." Her voice was solid, all business. Like a doctor.

"No, I can move."

"Do you want to stay there, or need help getting up?"

"I'll try standing." Accepting her outstretched hand, Việt tried finding his balance. Blood dripped down his leg. He was close to crying. He hobbled over to a bench with the girl's help. Some people sitting in their groups now stared. Others snickered. He imagined their thoughts: *First-year who can't tie his shoelaces, am I right?* Great.

Việt said "Thanks" as the girl rummaged through a forest-green L.L.Bean backpack slumped by her feet. He was still trying to comprehend how he went from soaring to crash-landing.

He felt pressure on his knee, a quick sting, and then watched her apply a Pooh Bear Band-Aid.

"Sorry," the girl said, sounding embarrassed. "I worked part-time at a pediatrics hospital over the summer, and this was all I had in my bag."

Not wanting to seem ungrateful—she didn't *need* to use a bandage on him—Việt quickly said, "You couldn't have given me Tigger at least?"

She blinked in surprise before smiling widely. "I'll remember that next time I see you face-plant."

"I was going for a somersault."

"Guess you'll need to work on that, then."

Up close, Việt wasn't seeing Linh again, but his mind tried compensating for its initial thought. She was definitely Asian, and might be Vietnamese, and she *was* familiar. They had met before. They must have.

She noticed. "Are you looking for someone?"

"Wh—oh sorry. I just thought you were someone else. But it's impossible because she's at another school. . . ."

Conversations from a few weeks ago, that didn't seem important then, resurfaced in Việt's mind. Việt, Linh, and Bảo at 7 Leaves.

It was after they talked about Wren. Linh had said her sister was at UC Davis too, and maybe she'd connect the two of them before orientation, but she never did. Her sister's name—what was it?

"You wouldn't—I mean, you're not her sister, are you?" Việt asked.

"Whose sister?"

"Linh. Linh Mai."

The girl's face lit up, and that was when he *really* saw Linh. "Yes! She's my little sister. You know her?"

"I'm friends with her and Bảo. I'm Việt."

"Wait, *you're* the forensic-science guy? Bảo's told me you're obsessed with things like that, right?"

That was accurate, sure, but was that how Bảo planned to introduce him to every person he met?

"Ready, Evie?"

Evie. That was her name.

Evie stood up to face another guy.

Việt felt like he needed to do the same, so he disregarded his knee. The guy glanced at the Band-Aid, and he wished Evie could have left it bleeding. He was a building made tiny by a skyscraper.

"This is Việt. He's, well, someone from back home. Việt, this is my boyfriend, Jake."

He fixated on "back home." That was true. Even though they didn't know each other, they were from the same place and knew some of the same people. She was the closest person to home here.

The boyfriend didn't say anything, just gave him a *Sup?* nod.

"And I work at the restaurant right across from her family's place," Việt added.

"Yes!" Evie smiled. "Jake, remember that whole restaurant rivalry thing that I mentioned and how my sister ended up with her boyfriend?"

"Yeah, yeah, I remember," he replied. He glanced at his Apple watch. "Spain's not gonna be there for long. We probably should head out."

Was Việt the only one who felt awkward?

"Right," Evie said. She grabbed her backpack. "It was nice meeting you, Việt. You're okay to walk back by yourself? If not, maybe we can help you."

Việt envisioned these two strangers half carrying, half dragging him back.

"No, all good. I'll see you around campus."

Watching Linh's sister and her boyfriend walk away, Việt felt less antsy than he was an hour ago. Maybe it was because Evie, as much of a stranger as she was, knew of him. And that was more than the people sitting on the bleachers now, the ones who'd only laughed when he crashed. The same ones glancing over and smirking while a grown-ass first-year stood there with Winnie the Pooh on his knee.

Summoning his remaining pride, Việt limped back to his dorm.

CHAPTER 4

EVIE

The Paul Hom Asian Clinic had always existed at the edge of her world. Classmates and friends had volunteered at the clinic, which was founded in the seventies to provide affordable medical access to the nearby Asian community. Like Evie's dad, who only grudgingly went to his doctor's appointments—favoring herbal medicine over Western medicine or taking care of any small injury at home—so many people in the Sacramento community didn't have a kind opinion of or faith in the medicinal field.

They had a fair point: Sometimes there was a language barrier; Evie had heard from regulars at her parents' restaurants saying they were waiting for their son or daughter to get off work to bring them to this or that appointment. And honestly, many times—as one professor argued—the systems actively worked against people who weren't white.

That professor was Dr. Iona, who Evie decided to visit while Jake was with Spain. They chatted about their summers first—Dr.

Iona had explored the coral reefs of South Africa while Evie mentioned working at the restaurant and taking shifts at a pediatrics hospital.

Dr. Iona said she wouldn't be a good mentor if she didn't tell Evie about the clinic. Her grades were great, and she already had relevant working experience.

The application was due in about a month, and then qualifying candidates were invited to an interview. The deadline seemed far, but the first week on campus was a blur. It wasn't until the following Friday night, at Jake's apartment, that Evie was able to really look at the application and consider the opportunity.

Jake's roommate, Kerem, was elsewhere—he was part of the theater group, and they often had improv sessions or plans together. Out of all Jake's friends, Evie liked the lanky brown-haired Turkish American boy the most. He didn't get into nearly as much trouble as the others, and he was also STEM like her and Jake. One time, she spilled coffee all over her CHEM 2B notes, and he readily offered her his. Not to say he wasn't wild: Several emergency signs had gone missing when he lived in their first-year dorms. She wasn't sure what he intended to do with them—and if he kept them at all.

His absence gave the illusion that Jake had this apartment all to himself. Once inside, Evie sank into the farther end of the living room sofa and pulled out the clinic application to consider it.

Dr. Iona was right; on paper Evie looked like a promising candidate. If she were accepted, she could gain valuable experience

SOLVING FOR THE UNKNOWN

and even brush up on her Vietnamese, since volunteers were also encouraged to show proficiency in a foreign language. Evie didn't have plans to join other campus clubs either, so applying felt like a good next step. The right step.

Jake lingered nearby. He gestured to his phone between his ear and shoulder. "Mom," he mouthed, and immediately Evie understood the frown on his face.

Evie had met Jake's mother on a campus visit, when they were a couple for only a few weeks. Mrs. Phan was formidable, with her perfect posture, piercing eyes, and carefully ironed and tastefully coordinated outfit. Evie didn't have to spend much time with her since they were with a larger friend group. But since she and Jake had been dating for a while now, perhaps they would need to meet again soon.

"Okay, okay. I will," Jake was saying. A pause. "Yes, Mom, I know . . . I'll do it." He glanced up at the ceiling like it could save him from the conversation. "Look, I got to go. Can I please talk to you later?" His mother relented. He pressed end and quickly pocketed his cell.

He flopped onto the couch, and when Evie patted her lap, he crawled forward to rest his head there. She threaded her hand through his hair still damp from the shower.

"They're already nagging me. Make sure to send Dad's regards to this or that professor. Attend a university event on his behalf. Introduce yourself to a board member's grandson and become their mentor and friend." He moaned. "As if I wasn't already busy."

27

"That sucks. Do you really have to do all that?"

He sighed. "If I want my mom to be off my case."

Jake and his parents, especially his mother, had a tenuous relationship. She seemed to dote on the first son, Henry, and used him as the standard in their household. Evie had grown used to Jake's sour mood after finishing a phone call only because he recovered fairly quickly.

"Also, Henry might be proposing to his girlfriend," Jake revealed.

Henry had graduated at the top of his class, opened up his own clinic. Mrs. Phan's calls were also an opportunity to update Jake on Henry's latest accomplishments. It was pure luck that Evie and Linh had chosen disparate majors and interests; she couldn't imagine constantly competing with a sibling.

"That's great for your brother. Your parents must be happy."

"Nah, they hate her," Jake said. "She wears too much color, is into horoscopes, and owns a pottery shop, a small one in our hometown." He closed his eyes. "My parents think she's just after Henry's money."

"Do you agree with them?"

"I don't care, really. Can't see her being the breadwinner in the family since arts majors won't make any money—" Evie flinched, thinking of her sister, who wanted to paint for a living. "Anyways, me and Henry and my other brothers—we stay out of each other's business."

Knowing his family, she understood why he'd talk badly about an arts career. But she imagined Linh making a name for herself, in some way. Every time she showed her a new canvas, Evie felt her little sister's happiness, her freedom.

If anyone could support herself with creating the art she loves, she bet it'd be her sister.

"So you don't talk to your brothers about me?" Evie teased, tilting her head down.

"No." She frowned, then Jake raised his hand to cup her cheek. "I just want you all to myself."

Jake had it hard, in some ways, and she wanted to help him worry less, even if it was just by sitting here, stroking his hair while he aired out his frustration. "I'm here for you. You know that, Jake."

"Yep, and we'll get to spend even more time together, especially when we both get spots in the Paul Hom program." He pointed to the flyer on the coffee table.

"You're going to apply too?" Perhaps Spain encouraged him at their earlier meeting.

Jake shrugged. "My dad knows one of the preceptors. It won't be hard to get an interview."

Evie bit back her jealousy. As much as Jake complained about having to schmooze on his father's behalf, he never undermined or refused Leo Phan's immense influence. That was how he got away with missing a few lab report deadlines. She didn't want to fault anyone for being born into the right family, with the right connections. That wasn't up to anyone; Evie couldn't predict that she'd be born here, instead of Switzerland, or Australia, or France, or other countries that accepted refugees like her parents during the eighties. But Jake acted like it was normal to use his father's connections.

His advantages were different than hers. As the youngest, he had his brothers to guide him through each crucial period of his life. He had his rich parents as his defensive team—and, it seemed, his offensive team. Evie benefitted from the labor of her own parents so her worries would not be of war and poverty. Still, she was their first daughter who was launched into the world—with no instruction manual, no proper training. They were financially secure, but not well-off; academic scholarships and loans made college possible for her.

"I said something idiotic just now, didn't I?"

Jake had been watching her. She had stopped stroking his hair.

She sighed. "It's nothing."

"No, it wasn't nothing."

"Fine. It's just . . . some of us don't have parents with friends in high places."

Jake winced. "Okay, I deserved that. My brain caught up to my mouth. I shouldn't have mentioned my dad."

"I know that you don't need to use your dad or anyone else to make it through the program," Evie continued. "You already have—no, you already *exceed* the qualifications."

"I swear I'm gonna apply just like everyone else." He sat up and put his arm around her shoulder. "So I'm sorry, okay? I'd hate for you to be mad at me."

Evie softened, realizing his apology was genuine. "No. I'm not mad." At least, maybe not at Jake, but more at whatever entity that had created such disparate lives for him, for her, and for billions of people out there.

"We'll get in," Jake agreed. He kissed her temple. "Without any outside influence. Because we're us. And I believe in us. Wouldn't that be cool? The two of us volunteering together?" Evie snuggled closer to her boyfriend.

Us. Together. She liked the sound of that. In her mind's eye, she imagined driving to the clinic together in the early morning, ready with their coffees. Did they get to wear white coats? Well, in her imagination they did, and they looked great. Their work would begin the minute they stepped in. Their day might get hectic, Evie might grow tired from the rapid pace, but then she'd look up and find Jake across the room, just as focused as her, and she knew they would get through the day.

CHAPTER 5

VIỆT

Việt's first few weeks of college would make for a good film montage. He had orientation and Week Zero, when academics seemed to come second behind campus life. The school desperately wanted them to feel involved, so as part of their Fall Welcome, freshmen were thrown into events. Free food, free swag. There was a rally where everyone was plunged into darkness and at one point the freshmen had to put their arms around each other and sway to a chaotic beat set by the marching band.

Việt had looked at his neighbor—a mousy boy from his floor who looked even more out of place than him—and together they silently agreed not to touch each other.

There was also the Running of the First-Years—yeah, that was exactly what it sounded like. RecFest at the Activities and Recreation Center was all about the sports clubs, and Việt had gravitated toward the running club table. He didn't even think of trying out for the actual XC&T team, a Division I team; he wouldn't have time, and practice was likely brutal. But he knew he wouldn't stop running.

By the end of September, Việt had run with the club a few times. The club was coed, and its officers were either third-years or fourth-years. Việt's routes were led by a third-year named Tate, a tall guy with dyed blond hair and two streaks of dark brown running down the middle. *Chipmunk*, he had thought the first time Tate introduced himself. Việt liked the guy who chatted with members regardless of their year. He confidently led them from the front. He'd slow down if there was anyone struggling behind and let out words of encouragement: "You got this, man!" or "Nice stride!"

Their routes were intense, and Việt didn't know for sure if the club was for him in the long run. But they seemed eager to have more people.

After one practice, Tate announced he was throwing a party at his apartment at The Green.

Việt wondered whether Wren would want to go, though his roommate was never without plans. Whenever they were in the dorms at the same time, they talked about nothing and everything: classes, the food at the dining hall, plans for the weekend. Wren immediately ditched his khakis and wore jeans. He added a backward ballcap at some point. And he'd started coming home late, and judging by the chorus of voices shouting goodbye at him each night, he was fitting right in.

Some people could be like that—chameleons.

Việt showered after his run, then worked on his homework in his dorm until it was dinnertime. The door opened, and a mess of limbs and laughter sloppily piled through. Việt recognized a few in passing—on the way to the communal bathroom, to classes in the bleary mornings. Their names escaped him, though, and they already looked too pregamed-out and obliterated—eyes glazed, a manic energy to them—to know his. One guy boldly jumped on top of *his* bed to sit on the edge.

They only noticed Việt when Wren asked, "What are you doing? Studying?" He was searching through his drawers and pulled out some shot glasses. One of the guys removed a whole bottle of Svedka from under his sweatshirt—wait, *from under his sweatshirt?!* This didn't seem to faze anyone else in the slightest.

Wren poured it into the glasses and passed them around. "Reddy, Rodriguez, Jones—V, you want a glass?" V, that was a new one.

Suddenly all eyes were on him again, and Việt was reminded of his old middle school bullies who turned vicious when boredom hit.

"Uh, no, I'm good, man," he answered. But his answer was drowned out by Wren pushing his friends to drink at the same time, and they did it, just like that.

They all strategized their next plans.

"Okay, Palmer said we should meet at his dorm, then we can head over to the AEPi party—"

"And Taylor said she'd get some of her friends to come."

"Taylor and you playing matchmaker tonight!"

"Maria's going to be there too."

Somehow that settled their plans, and without another word, everyone started moving toward the door.

Wren said, "Okay, see you, V. I'm gonna be back late. Will try not to wake you."

The room was a disaster in their wake. The kid on his bed had left his shot glass tipped over on the comforter, but at least it was empty.

He wouldn't have felt anything but relief—to be alone again— if it weren't for what one of Wren's friends said next, just as the door was closing behind the group:

"You have the most boring roommate ever."

Everyone laughed, and the sound faded as they moved down the hallway.

Việt didn't hear Wren's response.

It finally hit him. He was doing homework while everyone was out partying. There was some truth to what the kid said—he was boring.

And then Việt got angry. Not because he was alone; he wouldn't have wanted to be invited to a frat party. But because Việt could have chosen differently. Tate, from the running club, had mentioned a party; it was for everyone and anyone to accept, so why shouldn't he go?

What could go wrong?

. . .

Việt woke up with a spoon in his left hand.

A spoon?

"Oh, hey, he's waking up. I guess the spoon worked."

"It was just a coincidence," another voice whispered. "The spoon had no effect."

"Nah, it was the spoon. Supposedly it's colder than your body temperature, so he must have sensed it and woke up."

A hand lightly tapped his cheek, and Việt raised his hand to brush it off.

"Don't *slap* him!"

"I didn't slap him."

So many questions. A tornado of them swirling in his mind, but the first sentence out of his mouth was, "It wasn't a slap." His voice was all scratched up; he cleared his throat, but it still felt dry. Inside his head, everything sounded as noisy as the crates of produce his dad would unload during his delivery runs.

The exclamation "He lives!" collided with this mystery person's answer, "See! Not a slap."

Then Việt was helped up into a sitting position. When he was somewhat at a ninety-degree angle, he heard: "You good?"

"Yeah, I'm just . . . I don't know where I am." Việt blinked and the tanned face of a guy came into focus. It was Chipmunk.

"Well, I guess it was a good sign that you *know* you don't know where you are. That shows you're conscious at least. Here, drink." He offered Việt an ice-cold Solo cup. "Water. Just what you need."

"Thanks."

"I'm taking food orders. You want anything? Might as well eat since you're here. Eggs? Pancakes?"

"Uh . . ." Việt's mind felt blank.

"Actually, maybe just drink your water." Chipmunk—no, Tate—clapped him on the shoulder before jumping off and bounding toward the apartment's open kitchen, partitioned by an island with four stools tucked underneath. "We'll just make something and hopefully you'll like it."

The first sip delivered a rush of crystallized wake-up signals through Việt, and he gulped down the rest in five seconds. He glanced at the state of the living room: A folded table used for Ping-Pong games lay collapsed in the middle of the living room. Crushed Solo cups, cans of White Claw and Truly, and one large bottle of Cîroc just begging for some hungover kid to trip over it. Bodies were on the floor, snoring away. Most were nestled in sleeping bags, from who knows where. A few were from the running club, and the rest were probably Tate's other friends.

Việt's chest was heavy. Someone took the time to essentially tuck him in with a fuzzy Aggies blanket. Last night's events seeped into his mind. Wren and his friends. The club invite. He got to The Green—somehow—and sat by himself mostly, and someone kept handing him drinks, and now—

Delicately, warily, like a newborn calf, Việt stood up. He walked over to the open kitchen's bartop, where Tate was washing dishes. He was now wearing a shockingly bright yellow apron.

"Um, need help?"

"*Someone* wants to help for once? Am I in the right apartment?"

A second guy—the one arguing with Tate as Việt woke up—carried in two bags of Hawaiian buns and placed them on the island. He was Asian, unlike Tate, and shorter as well. This new guy's pillowy brown bedhead contrasted his face, which looked severe and fully alert. Subconsciously Việt straightened up; his energy reminded him of Bảo's mother when she was controlling the restaurant's kitchen. Bảo would find that comparison hilarious, but this person . . . not so much, maybe.

"Can you handle a knife?" Bedhead ended up asking.

Việt wasn't an expert, but he'd watched Bảo's mother enough to know how to use one. Her temper was legendary, and she might have had a soft spot for him. Việt never dared push it, so he'd learned all his knifing skills from her and the line cooks who could cut at warp speed. "I'm not bad at it."

"Hmm. Promising. Unlike many firsties—Tate, where did he come from?"

Standing before the kitchen sink, Tate squinted, and Việt felt mortified thinking he probably couldn't even place him. Wouldn't even know his name. "Oh, that's Việt. La Quinta High School. Westminster. Runs a mile in 8.2 minutes."

Việt blinked. Correct.

But the Asian guy seemed unimpressed and walked over to the dish rack to grab a pair of kitchen knives. "Thanks for the robotic introduction. Most people say name, year, and major. Well, I'm Kale Thammavongsa." KAH-leh, got it. "And you apparently know Tate Galanos. He's taking care of the dishes because that's the extent of his kitchen skills." Tate started protesting, and Kale ignored him, then stood on his toes—being two or three inches shorter—to kiss him obnoxiously on the cheek. Tate lifted his shoulder to rub the kiss off.

Kale said to Việt, "How about you slice some of these buns and some green onions to garnish the eggs. I'll get started on them—some might want scrambled eggs, others fried . . . I have the SPAM and bacon going on the rear, but I don't know if that's going to be enough. . . ."

Việt wasn't certain if he was prattling to anyone in particular or just thinking out loud.

Eventually, they formed . . . an idea of an assembly line at the bartop. Next to Việt, Kale had four different sauté pans going. He ladled beaten eggs into one of them and started talking. This was definitely not his first time cooking—and maybe not the first time he let a blacked-out stranger crash at his place.

"So you're a runner like Tate?"

"Yeah, I've only been to a couple of club runs."

"You're not one of those who joined just for the parties, right? Because while these parties are fun—well, crazy and slightly illegal, maybe—the club's practices are pretty brutal. I joined and look what happened."

Still at his station, Tate added, "He fell in love with me and realized he didn't have a running bone in his body."

Ignoring his boyfriend, yet again, Kale squinted at Việt. "You don't look great," he said bluntly.

"This is the first time I've gone to a party like this. I can't remember much."

"Oh, you're such a first-year," the guy said, and sighed as if Việt had asked him for a favor at the most inconvenient time. "When you black out, you're not looking for fun. You're drinking away a problem you can't face."

"I wasn't really getting along with my roommate."

"Is he why you're not back at your dorm?" Kale asked. With a flick of his wrist, he flipped over a fried egg, solidly sticking its landing.

After Việt recapped what had happened, Kale had already finished the breakfast meats.

"Maybe we got off on the wrong foot," Việt said.

"Well, if you ever need to talk about it, just come by. I've had my share of troublesome roommates. Tate's the best one so far."

"Generous of you to say," Tate replied. He'd finished washing the dishes a while ago and was now going around the room, gently nudging his friends awake.

Which wasn't necessary since Kale had started shouting: "Breakfast is almost ready. Get up! We even have vegan eggs and vegan cheese because I don't want to hear anyone complain. Especially Beth at this godforsaken hour." With a spatula, he pointed to one of the girls in a sleeping bag.

A curly-haired girl stirred slightly, but remained there, except for her arm, which rose to reveal her middle finger.

"I love her," he told Việt, resuming his cooking.

He leaned forward to inspect the chopped green onions under Việt's hands, then nodded approvingly. "Nice knife skills." He asked Việt to toast the buns next.

Now Việt was wide awake—and it wasn't just the tantalizing aroma of greasy food. Kale was a talker. While Tate led the running club with quiet confidence, Kale's confidence was more apparent and unapologetic. He was a third-year food science major and food service management minor. His dad was a chef, while his mother was a pathologist—"she's not allowed to talk about work at the dinner table," he said. Kale had transferred from University of Hawai'i, in his home state, in the middle of his first year—"I knew I wanted to get out, just to see more places"—and eventually ended up here, where he found enough "idiots" to be his friends.

Kale only joined the running club to spend more time with Tate, "who was oblivious" to his crush.

"I eventually figured it out," Tate protested.

Now they were both grinning at each other, and probably forgot about Việt for a second, which reminded Việt that he was still not used to being around couples. To call his parents a *couple* would be an overstatement; *business partners* was far more accurate. The aunties and their husbands back home seemed to hate each other, yet refused to divorce. The only relationship he'd seen that was remotely healthy was Bảo and Linh's. They had a way of looking at each other; it was generally nice, maybe creepy after a while, since they were basically in their own world and Việt always felt like an intruder.

Soon enough, a few people who slept over, in all states of wakefulness, grabbed sandwiches as Kale left them out at the kitchen bar. Việt took a seat at one of the stools, done with his tasks. Tate went around, folding unoccupied sleeping bags, and cleaning up traces of last night's festivities.

Voices soon emanated from the entryway, a collision of "Hello!" and "Rise and shine!" and "We're back!"

"I hate it when people barge in like that," Kale grumbled.

"You're the one who always props the door open," Tate calmly countered.

More sounds of life. Unmindful of the remaining sleepers who groaned and cursed, the newest guests were cheerful and perky. Việt thought it'd be a good time to leave—clearly whoever was coming were friends of Kale and Tate—until he spotted a familiar face. Evie.

Evie threw her arms around Kale, clinging to him. "I missed your SPAM breakfast sandwiches."

"That's all you miss about me?" But he returned the hug with equal energy and gave one to a short Asian girl next to her. Việt heard him call her Lis. Turning around, Evie finally noticed him, and he wished he didn't have a stain on his shirt. Kale did tell him, "You don't look great."

Awesome.

"We meet again! Of all places. I never thought that you'd be here," Evie said.

Kale, having released the other girl who now went to hug Tate, curiously asked, "Oh you two have met?"

"We're both from Westminster. He's friends with my sister— she's dating his best friend, long story," Evie quickly explained. "Are you really surprised to see me and Lis, Kale?" she said, sitting down on the barstool next to Việt. "It's a Saturday!"

"What happens on Saturday?" Việt asked.

While Lis and Kale started conversing, and Tate was setting out more plates for everyone at the bar, Evie leaned closer to him, smelling like clean soap, the nice kind, not the overwhelming smell that made his dad sneeze. Her hair was wet, the end of her ponytail spotting the back of her oversized Aggies hoodie, gold with navy lettering.

"Saturday Sins started one morning when we wanted to erase all the things that happened on Friday night. We were *so* hungover and hungry, and we used to make a huge meal in our first-year dorm's common room. Anyone could come by." She laughed suddenly. "It used to be just breakfast, but now it tends to be dinners because of our different schedules. Kale's always the host because he's the best cook out of all of us."

"You don't cook?"

She paused. "I do, but not as good as my mom, unfortunately."

"This poor fellow," Việt heard Kale say to Lis, "I found him drunk and passed out on the couch."

"First time drinking, I guess?" Evie's friend asked gently as she joined in, leaning against the bar counter from the kitchen's side. "I remember those hangovers very well. That's kind of why I stopped drinking. Also, I have no palate for the taste of alcohol. You lucked out ending up here, since Kale's SPAM, egg, and cheese sandwich will *completely* wake you up."

She smiled brightly at him, and Kale, clearly touched, busied himself with the last of the food. Tate leaned closer to his boy-friend, teasing him in whispers.

Evie was looking at Việt with a frown. "Not to sound like a mom or anything, but be careful at the parties. They can get intense."

Lis snorted. "She's saying that now, but she got a bit buzzed quite a few times when she was a first-year."

Tate and Kale finished passing out breakfast sandwiches, and the attention moved away from him for a few minutes as the four of them started holding several conversations at once.

"So, Việt. Tell me about yourself. How are you liking school?" Lis asked while Evie asked about last night's party. If Việt didn't know better, Lis had turned into Ali. She was always straight to the point. Maybe that was how friends were made. Someone reminded you of someone else special to you, so you felt drawn to them.

"I can't believe it's been a month since I moved in," Việt answered, "and I'm still adjusting." Or finding where he belonged. Wren had found his group. Evie and Lis, Kale and Tate acted like good friends.

"What do you like to do?"

"Nothing much. I've only gone to the running club, so it's that, classes, then my dorm." He felt compelled to apologize then. "Sorry, I'm a bit boring."

Lis shook her head. "As long as you're happy doing what you do—no need to nudge. We all have different interests."

"For example, I like cows," Tate offered. "Something about them calms me."

Kale stood in between Lis and Tate. "He was in Tercero," he

said to Việt, like that sufficed as an explanation. Then he turned to his boyfriend. "I forgot about that. Or tried. Didn't you have a favorite cow?"

"Wildflower," Tate answered wistfully. "She always came when I called her. But she moved on to greener pastures," he added solemnly.

Việt almost choked on his breakfast sandwich. "Oh, uh, sorry. She died?"

Kale answered for his boyfriend. "No, she *literally* moved to another pasture, a different field!"

Evie, probably hearing the joke a million times before, threw a balled-up napkin at Tate, who ducked immediately.

"I wasn't obsessed with the cows, like *someone*, but when I ended up in Segundo, I was right by the garden. We were allowed to help, and I ended up pilfering all the veggies to feed these people." Kale gestured to his friends.

"I remember being a first-year and I couldn't believe all of the clubs on campus," Evie said.

"Besides the running club, I didn't see one that interested me. But if there was a forensic science club, I'd sign up. I watch a lot of forensic shows—"

The group froze, and Việt thought: *Should he not have said it out loud?*

Kale whispered. "Oh no, you summoned Lisbel." Lis all but shoved Kale away.

"You're into forensics?" she asked. She leaned so forward that

45

she might as well have climbed over to Việt's side. "We have a club!"

"But I didn't see it at the RecFest."

"Oh, our table was at the far end," Lis explained. "The club's agnostic; you don't need to be in any major to join. It's mostly grad students and a few third-years, and our advisors are from the graduate program."

It was a clear invite. A club for forensic science lovers like him. Well, if he couldn't pursue it as a career, it wouldn't hurt to join a club . . . right? "I'll check it out."

"We just found a new member!" Lis squealed.

"Let him attend the first meeting at least, Lis," Kale said. He added, "Though, we'd totally welcome you. I'm also in the club. An alternative slogan for this club is: *Welcome to every immigrant parent's worst nightmare. It's not that kind of science, but it's still science.*"

He wasn't off the mark . . . especially when Việt considered his parents. Việt remembered what Kale had said earlier. "Food science . . . and forensics?"

"Once you boil it all down, both my major and the club have to do with formerly animate objects. I still work with dead things—I just make them tasty."

Beth, the vegan who'd left her sleeping bag and had just started to dig into her breakfast at the end of the island, said, "Nope, I'm not listening to this—not at this hour."

"Sorry, Beth," Lis apologized sheepishly on Kale's behalf, before turning back to Việt. "I'll send you a few things. Intro packets and stuff like that. Take a look. Feel *free* to just look and not do anything with them. But it'd be cool for you to join. You'd know me and Kale at least."

Tate said, "Don't scare him away."

Evie gently nudged Việt's shoulder with hers. "Yes, Kale and Lis are like this without being caffeinated," she joked. "Already getting second thoughts about saying yes? I know Lis can throw a lot at you."

"Are you a part of it too? The club?"

"No, I never had the time for it. But I think you'll really like it."

Beth, the vegan, managed to finish her breakfast without further protest. She yawned at Kale. "Coffee?"

"Coffee? First, I'm the cook. Am I the barista now too?"

"You literally have a Keurig *and* Nespresso. Hand me a mug."

Kale refused. "Put some money in the jar, then. . . . This is not a charity!"

Việt disagreed; this *was* Kale's charity. Hosting people, including a stranger like him. This felt different from Wren's friends who invaded his space.

Here, Việt was still in the middle of chaos, but he'd never felt more rooted.

CHAPTER 6

EVIE

Once they got back from Saturday Sins, Lis hit the showers first, while Evie refreshed the whiteboard listing both her and her roommate's schedules, as well as the division of weekly chores. This weekend, she had to clean the living room. She cleared off their coffee table, putting their coffee mugs from this morning into the sink. She went to right a fallen throw pillow and spotted her tablet, which was opened to an email about the Paul Hom Asian Clinic.

Dr. Iona had sent around another reminder about the application deadline, and Evie only had a few more days. She wondered if Jake had submitted his already.

The page cursor blinked back at her as she read through the app's questions, which required long-form answers.

A freshly showered Lis appeared and crossed over to the kitchen, to the counter where they kept most of their go-to snacks: lychee jellies, Hi Chews, Oreos, peach gummies, and Goldilocks Polvoron. Evie guessed she would go for the jellies, her usual choice.

"I'm ready for nap time," she declared. "Kale's food always puts me to sleep."

"I wish I could do the same. But I better start the application for Paul Hom. It's due soon."

Her roommate made her way over, observing the clinic website. "I'm imagining getting my sixty-six-year-old auntie to an appointment. My mom would have to drag her, and if by some miracle my auntie went, she'd probably make a student cry." Filipino, Vietnamese, they were different but also the same when it came to stubbornness. "If you get into the program, you'll have to take weekend shifts, right?"

"Yes, it opens at seven in the morning." Evie was an early bird anyway; she was the daughter of long-time restaurant owners, after all. Her roommate was not.

"Here, let me help brush your hair."

"You don't have to," Lis said, even as she handed over the brush and moved to sit on the floor directly in front of Evie.

"But I like your hair."

Once dry and brushed again, Lis's hair was long and lush and glistened as if the sun was hitting it the right way. Evie's own hair was much wavier and didn't shine as much.

They watched a video on autoplay that documented the clinic's typical weekend. The patients looked relieved to hear their language being spoken. Undergrads calmly explained drug prescriptions and forms, and translated for the medical students who didn't speak the language. Everyone had a role to play.

"Look, it's a room full of different Evies," said Lis out of nowhere.

Evie laughed. "What do you mean?"

"Everyone's helping someone in this video. And you're a natural helper." Her roommate gestured at her own hair. "You're perfect for the clinic."

"Jake's applying too."

"Jake? I'm surprised his parents haven't already lined up other opportunities for him."

"Mm-hmm. I'm sure they have tried. It'd be nice if we could get in together."

Lis tilted her head. "Are you applying because of Jake, or because you want to?"

"Both, I guess. My advisor told me about it, and then Jake told me he was also going to apply."

Her roommate righted her head, and neither one said anything as Lis got lost in her thoughts. Or maybe she was falling asleep; she had planned for a nap. Evie continued brushing, finding comfort in the repetition.

"I haven't seen Jake in a while," Lis said through a sudden yawn.

Her roommate and her boyfriend had exchanged a quick hello and goodbye when Lis bumped into them at a café earlier this week, but that was it. As her boyfriend had predicted, he was busy fulfilling his parents' demands. Today he'd agreed to give a tour to a board member's son, a prospective UC Davis student. They had plans to study together at his place soon.

"I'm sure he'll come by when he's free."

Lis's response was delayed—she kept watching the video, now on mute. "Well, it'd be nice to see him soon."

CHAPTER 7

VIỆT

When Việt finally came back to the dorms from The Green, Wren was back, wrapped up in his sheets like a burrito. He was alone, though Việt half expected to find his new friends taking up the rest of the room, sleeping on the floor. The room smelled sweet, like spilled alcohol. He thought of opening the blinds to let all the light in, wake Wren up, but he wasn't at that level of petty yet. He just couldn't stop hearing the word *boring* in his head.

After showering, Việt went back in to find the room was spotless—Wren, nowhere to be found. It was easy to avoid him until later that day, when Việt was back at his desk. His roommate returned as Việt read through an email from Lis containing information about the forensics club, including a mock exercise.

"I didn't see you last night," Wren said. His voice echoed as he searched for an item under his bed. "I came back from the party, but the room was empty."

"I went out, then crashed on someone's couch." *Didn't really want to see you again.*

"I was wasted last night. Can't remember much. If me and the guys were being annoying, sorry." He nervously glanced around, a tell that showed Việt he did remember. "I'm going to head out to grab a bite. Need anything?"

"I'm good. Thanks."

Wren lingered, then left a second later. That's when Việt realized that his roommate had left the room empty-handed.

The next morning, Việt was back at Toomey after finishing a run. Guzzling water, he pulled out the packet that Lis had emailed.

Five students were accused of vandalizing a campus building. He had to figure out who the culprit was, using only the information given to him and the list of items each student had on them during the police search: their AggieCard, their apartment keys, and spare change.

The four possible vandals were all art students who had access to the kind of paint found at the scene: Hasan, who was from Chicago, was an only child, and liked to row every day. Ethan, whose mother was named after a flower. Jane, who had two sisters with *J* names— one of them a first-year—who was part of the recycling club. The other, Esther, had founded the UC Davis chapter of Habitat for Humanity and liked eating Oreos and peanut butter.

The facts seemed random, and Việt was sure they were meant to throw him off, but aside from their bio, and the items they each were carrying, that was all he had to go on to "solve the case."

Việt remembered Tate said he used to visit a cow for fun. When he needed to think.

Should he do the same?

Maybe he should finally meet the things responsible for the *wonderful* smell that drifted over to the dorms at random points in the day.

The cows at the Dairy Facility didn't seem pleased to see him.

(Okay, but were cows pleased to see *anyone*?)

Now a mile away from Laben Hall, Việt tried recalling what an orientation leader said about the facility. There were about a hundred cows and they used them for milk and for teaching purposes. Some were kept inside and others—the more gregarious ones? Việt wasn't sure—were outside. The cows were currently fixated on a newly delivered feed. The man who provided the food didn't spare Việt a look, which meant it wasn't odd for students to just hang around.

If Việt had wanted to find a worthy staring contestant, he'd found the perfect partner. But talking to them felt questionable. A second cow stared at him, huffed, then walked away, like it couldn't stand the sight of him.

A few minutes later, Việt ended up lying down on a patch of grass untouched by the cows. He was going to shower anyway.

It was nice. Staring at the sky, just watching the clouds pass. It made him forget about the weirdness back at the dorms. Classes piling up. This unsettled feeling he'd had since stepping onto the campus. Maybe it was just because he'd never been away from home this long.

His parents texted random tidbits of their lives back home, as would Việt. His mom sent a photo of a gigantic homegrown green opo squash a neighbor gifted her. She followed up with a pic— blurry, of course—of his dad enjoying said vegetable in a shrimp and squash soup. Meanwhile, his dad's texts consisted of weather updates at Davis. They were mostly unnecessary, since he had his own weather app, but once, his dad said it'd rain, which prompted Việt to grab an umbrella before leaving the dorms. It poured the whole day.

Now Việt crossed his arms, weighing down Lis's packet against his chest so that a breeze wouldn't blow it away.

A minute passed. Or maybe it was an hour. Suddenly he felt something touch him. For one delirious moment, he thought a cow had escaped and was nudging him—but this was not a nudge. He was being shaken. He opened his eyes, and saw the silhouette of—

"Evie?!"

"Việt, are you all right?! Are you hurt again? Should I get some-one?"

"I'm fine, I'm fine!" Việt shot up, then got to his feet, wiping off grass from his fitness shorts.

"Why were you on the grass? Here of all places?"

"I was . . . uh, napping?"

"Near the cows?!"

Her franticness made him laugh. "Yeah, I guess, near the cows. Just . . . following Tate's advice."

"Never do that."

"Uh, nap on the grass?"

"Follow Tate's advice. He's been corrupted by Kale and none of what he says should be trusted most of the time."

He took her in. She was dressed in running gear—a pair of light blue shorts and a pale yellow tank. "Did you run here too?"

"Yeah, it's a bit of a long run, but I stop by sometimes. To see the cows, and sometimes the goats too." Evie paused. "Are we destined to run into each other? With you on the ground?"

His head must still have been stuck in dreamland because he couldn't find the right answer. Just then, a cow *moo*'d loudly.

She pointed to the pages beside him, now on the grass. "Lis would be so happy if she saw you now."

"She'd be happy to know she's torturing me. I can't solve this case."

"You do know that this is not a real requirement, right? You're not going to be turned away if you get it wrong. Lis wouldn't do that." Evie smiled.

"Then why hand out a packet? Means she's expecting something from me." Việt narrowed his eyes at her. "Do you know the answer?"

"Lis tells me everything, and she's told me all the answers she's gotten over the last two years. Never the real answer, though. I guess just pick the most logical one and move on."

"But I don't have a theory yet."

Evie did a standing quad stretch. "Just don't put *We are all guilty of something*. Someone did that once. I think the kid was some smart-ass philosophy student."

"Lis reminds me of Ali, you know. Linh's friend," he said.

"Oh yeah, definitely. Maybe that's why we got along right away. That's how you make friends: you encounter people who seem familiar."

"You feel familiar."

Yes, he was definitely still not awake.

She tilted her head, the end of her ponytail brushing her bare shoulder. "Me? I'm familiar?"

He backtracked. "Maybe it's because you're Linh's sister. Maybe it's because we're from the same place." He glanced down at the grass. "You want to sit? Or lie down?" Evie checked her wristwatch. "Unless you are on a schedule?" he joked.

"Hmm . . . I have less than an hour to run back, then I have twenty minutes to shower and twenty minutes to make breakfast, but most of the time I can do it in fifteen and—" She stopped, smiling sheepishly. "Everyone has some sort of schedule," she finished somewhat self-defensively. "You must have one too."

"Yep. In my planner this morning was *Talk to cows*."

Evie laughed. Finally she admitted, "You *do* look comfortable."

Việt gestured to the patch of grass. After a second, she lay beside him with her knees bent. Her right ankle crossed over her left knee, it kept bobbing, didn't stay still for a second.

"I feel like a kid."

"Why?" Việt asked.

"I don't know. I haven't done this in so long. Lie down and just stare at the sky. Feels like we're . . . wasting time."

"You seem like you have your act together. Don't know why you can't 'waste time' occasionally."

She just shrugged. "I've been like this forever. I've always had something to do. Every time I wasn't needed, I felt guilty." Then, as if she didn't want to make herself sound serious, she sighed dramatically. "Classic eldest-daughter syndrome."

Việt remembered Linh used to be on the go too, but now that she was dating Bảo, she relaxed more. It was difficult to imagine a more intense version of Linh.

"Sounds tough," he eventually said.

A couple beats of silence passed. She probably didn't want to elaborate; they were still strangers, after all. Then she started talking again, and the sudden fatigue in her voice made him turn on his side to properly face her.

She continued staring at the clouds. "For years, being the eldest daughter feels like being an only child. And I don't mean it's because we literally *are* in the world for a few extra years before our siblings are born. We're expected to do something for the first time, then expected to do it well, no matter what. Being the most polite, get the best grades, things like that. And it's lonely to—"

"Carry that weight," he finished automatically. He felt that type of loneliness a lot.

"*Yes!* That pressure!" Now Evie had turned on her side to face him. "So, imagine that for years and years you carry that weight. Almost get used to it. Then there's this moment when you realize you don't need to carry that burden anymore. I went home this summer and saw that my parents were finally okay with Linh becoming an artist. Even proud of her. They looked happier, lighter, and it was so strange because that's totally not how it was when I went off to college."

Evie raised her hands, looking at them palm-first. She lowered her voice. "A weight has been lifted, but I don't really like that feeling."

She sounded confused. Hurt. And that made Việt feel . . .

"You feel empty, maybe useless," he said quietly. "When you were growing up, there was some comfort in knowing your responsibility. *I have to do this, I have to do that.* You're defined by it. You let yourself be defined by it because there wasn't really a choice. You were made to follow a path."

We cannot afford to have passions. That was what Ba had told him all those months ago, when Việt had first broached the topic of his future career.

It sounded like Evie was on a path and now reached a dead end or a block, and there was no one but herself to figure out an escape.

She was staring at him now.

"What?" he asked.

"Let me guess. You're either the oldest or an only child."

"Only child."

"Knew it. So you get what I'm talking about."

"Oh, believe me. I do. You feel guilty and guilt's not easily shaken off. But that doesn't mean you should sit with it because then you'll be stuck, forever unchanging. I think growth comes from realizing that you have the right to choose your own purpose, and if you have something to look forward to in the future, the guilt won't seem as heavy." He felt the urge to say more—dive into his parents' disapproval of the career he imagined for himself—but they didn't have all the time in the world. Plus, it felt easier to hear someone else talk.

As if reading his thoughts, Evie said, "This is way more than what I expected to talk about on a beautiful Sunday morning."

Việt wanted to change the mood. "I mean, if you want, we can go back to small talk for another"—he pretended to check a watch and threw out a random time—"seventeen and a half minutes. Does your *schedule* allow for that?"

"Ha ha. What about you? Let's talk about why you're here, alone, on such a gorgeous day. Trying to answer a forensic science question."

Well, that just sounded . . . sad, he wanted to say. Then Evie asked, "Do you really like forensics that much?"

This was what he had wished his parents would ask. But they never did.

Forensics wasn't what TV made it out to be, sure. And it wasn't like he'd gotten into it because of those shows—it only exposed a bit of it, and the rest of what he read online, in books, had tipped him toward the side of possibly pursuing the field as a career.

"There's this guy from the late nineteenth, early twentieth century," Việt said. "People think of him as the Sherlock Holmes of France because apparently he helped come up with how we study fingerprints and things like that, but his most important contribution was this idea that 'every contact leaves a trace.' At a crime scene, everything the criminal touches, they're leaving a piece of themselves. And they take a piece of the crime scene with them.

"We're lying here in the grass, leaving behind dead skin. As you were running, you were leaving footprints. Your hair—" It was splayed out on the grass, absorbing the sun. If he reached out, touched it, it might burn him. "While you were running, pieces of it fell out. Before, when you were brushing it too."

"You've really thought a lot about this, haven't you?"

"Twenty percent of my brain's reserved for forensic science. But the rest is empty. You know, just whistling wind."

The cows *moo*'d, like they were agreeing with Việt.

They both laughed.

"So, you like the idea of . . . what? Being able to trace something to its source," Evie asked.

"I like the idea of solving puzzles. Breaking things down to their simplest form. The things that don't seem significant but really are. Through forensic science, you're not only tracing the criminal, the person who committed the crime, but you're tracing the last moments of the victim, too. That's kind of reassuring, in a way. You want to comfort the victim's family members with the truth of what happened."

"The way you put it—it makes sense. That it all comes from a place of hope and want. I get why you like forensics so much."

"I mean, not going to lie. It also looks cool. I was Dr. Spencer Reid one time for Halloween."

"Hey, I was just watching *Criminal Minds* yesterday at my boyfriend's apartment."

"Romantic," he said. The skyscraper. What was his name again?

"Ha ha." Evie finally stood up and glanced around. "Want to run back together?"

"Right, your schedule," Việt muttered as he reluctantly went to his knees, then pushed himself up slowly.

Evie started doing butt kicks in place to get her blood flowing. "That too."

They took off. His limbs screamed, his heart begged for him to rest, but at least Việt wasn't alone in this feeling. Evie breathed in, he breathed out, and their feet hit the pavement at the same pace.

They stopped at another open field. The sun shone directly over people picnicking on green lawns—maybe that was where most of the room and board money was going.

"Hold on—I want to text a pic to my sister," Evie said, pulling out her phone. "It might inspire Linh's painting."

Sister. Việt stopped. The word appeared in his mind, and then images and more words rushed in.

The vandalism, the suspects, all art students, the things they had with them, Chicago, Ethan, mother named after flower, Jane had a sister—

"Of course." He dug the pages from his pockets and flipped to the page for the suspect, Jane. He scanned her biological facts again. Two sisters with *J* names—and one of them attended the school. What if only one of them had been caught?

He looked at the contents next, scanning Jane's AggieCard—and then he saw the answer. The name read *Jade,* not *Jane,* and there could be many reasons, but he bet it was because they'd vandalized the building together, and when they split apart, they somehow mixed up their cards. And Jane must have had Jade's when she was caught. The names were so close in sound, which no one had noticed.

"It's her."

Evie smiled at Việt. "See? The answer *was* right in front of you."

Việt: professor says lucky you, homework's gonna be light! Then prof assigns 50 pgs to read . . .

Ali: not bad

Việt: you liberal arts majors 😖

Bảo: didn't choose the liberal arts life, it chose me

Linh: ^^

CHAPTER 8

EVIE

"Why the hell are you smiling?" Lis moaned from her bed, covers over her head. But Evie knew her roommate; Lis had probably been up for at least an hour, and just refused to get up. Shoes off, socks on, Evie jumped on the bed, seating herself below her feet. Her roommate half-heartedly kicked at her. "Seriously, there's already enough sunshine in this room. And you smell like the outside. Did you go running?"

"Yeah, and I ran into Việt."

"Ah, forensics guy."

"Guess what? He was puzzling over your packet, *consulting* with the cows near the Dairy." Evie pulled out Việt's packet and placed it on Lis's duvet.

"That was an unexpected sentence." Lis sat up, lazily pawed at the pages, then flipped through his answers, squinting because her glasses were elsewhere. "Nice report. Got the right person. You didn't help him, did you?"

"No, I don't even know the answer. I just told him not to be philosophical and put *No one belongs* like that—"

"Ugh, I can't believe I dated that himbo for two weeks." The pages fell off Lis's bed. She stretched and yawned, not dwelling over her unfortunate dating history.

Evie made a mental note to brew coffee for them. "Remind me what's the point of the test anyway? It seems vague—there could be a ton of answers that people could spin."

"That's not the point—it's the intent."

"Intent?"

"Anyone who spends time figuring this out *really* wants to figure it out. We want someone like that in the club. Let's be honest—doing anything gets you invisible points. There's no money in it. There's no degree. It's really for fun. But, like, an intense sort of fun. So a person with intent would be nice."

Evie was pretty sure Lis meant *obsession*.

The moment she had spotted Việt this morning, she didn't even know it was him, that same boy from Saturday Sins. She almost missed him if not for his burnt yellow sweatshirt. He was so still; he clutched the papers like a person laid to rest with their bouquet of flowers. When she came closer, and he didn't move at the sound of her voice, that was when she panicked slightly and started shaking Việt.

Honestly, she didn't expect their conversation to go the way it did, but it was nice to have someone outside her circle understand her so well. He wasn't the eldest, but as an only child, he knew what it was like to live under a microscope.

Evie almost wanted to ask him more about being an only child, but a shadow passed over his face. And it wasn't from the clouds above them. Then he tried to make a joke, and even though she laughed, he sounded strained.

He had left his dorms, went all the way out there to be by himself. Not because he had to. Because he wanted to.

That was why she had asked about forensic science; she didn't want any more sad talk.

His face changed then. His lips curled up in a soft smile. His eyes shined, and he spoke with his hands. Whenever people used their hands, they were genuinely excited.

"I think Việt is exactly the member your club needs."

"Yeah, I like the kid," Lis said absentmindedly.

"He seems really into forensics."

"You talked?"

"Well, yeah. We ran home together."

"You ran together?" Lis wiggled her eyebrows.

"Oh shut up. He's nice. Someone who's a friend because they fit naturally in your life. Like you and me; it just made sense. And now I can't get rid of you—ouch!" Lis had launched a pencil from her nightstand, and it hit Evie's arm.

She smirked. "Be careful. You don't want to lead him on, or anything. Poor Jake."

"Ah yes, with all of my lovely sweat and BO."

LOAN LE

Mẹ: con, me moi coi TV. a robbery in sacramento.
Be careful

Việt: ?? i'm at school - nowhere near it

Mẹ: still it is dangerous

Việt: Ok . . .

Mẹ: con an chua?

Việt: not yet, but I'll grab some food later

Mẹ: do an o truong co ngon khong?

Việt: Yeah, food's okay

Ba: con miss rice?

Việt: Sometimes

Ba: Rice Is GOOD 👍👍👍

Việt: 😂

68

CHAPTER 9

VIỆT

Three days later, Lis hugged Việt the moment he walked into the first Forensic Science club meeting of the year at the Sciences Laboratory. He could tell she was a hugger—and noted that he'd have to prepare himself next time, if there was a next time, because she hugged *tight*.

The meeting room was cold like the labs Việt had been in for his other classes. The overhead lights were stark white. The club wasn't as small as he'd imagined it. There were about twenty people, and with Lis leading the way, he was pulled into intros. Sitting at the front desk were two preceptors, two mentors from the graduate program, regarding the members with friendly smiles.

The members had split off into two distinct groups—one group that distanced itself from everyone else, and another group that mingled with Lis, which usually included Kale, but he was missing because he was cooking. Cooking what, Việt didn't get a chance to ask.

"What's with the first group? They look friendly," he dryly remarked.

The group had three girls and two boys. They appeared taller, leaned against or sat on the tables, lounging like they belonged there and the rest of them were party-crashers. The tallest boy, dressed in jeans and a loose black T-shirt, was glaring at Lis.

Lis shrugged. "Ignore their weird vibes. They're fourth-years and think they run the club."

"Do they? Run the club."

"Well, they did—until I joined and made it clear that class years don't matter here. When they first joined, the club was way smaller. That meant they were always allowed to compete in the collegiate competition in the early spring."

At Việt's look, she explained, "Yes, we're not just meeting to geek out about forensic science. There's an actual competition that includes several colleges across the country, and Davis somehow gets enough donations that help us fund the trip."

"What do you win?" Việt asked.

One of the preceptors walked by, shrugging on a lab coat, and chimed in brightly: "Absolutely nothing!"

"Wrong! We get a shiny trophy and a boost in self-worth," answered Lis, ignoring the preceptor. "More members have joined over the years, and so last year was the first time the club had to hold a qualifying event to determine who'd go to the final competition. We lost last time because of—" Lis shook her head. "Just many reasons."

Việt wondered if that reason had to do with the tall guy. Did he and Lis know each other? She adopted her usual cheery tone and smiled at Việt. "But I'm convinced this will be our year. The fourth-years won't be ready for us."

At the boom of the preceptor's voice welcoming everyone tonight, the students parted and took their seats. Việt sat next to Lis in the back. The lights were shut off, and a PowerPoint presentation was projected on the largest wall.

Each club meeting, Việt was told, had lectures about different aspects of forensics: DNA, blood splatter, fibers. Then the members would apply techniques in mock investigations.

"The club preceptors have made it their mission to dispel the *CSI* effect—the stuff that's done wrong but is in a lot of the investigation shows you watch. Raise your hands if that's what got you interested in the first place."

No one raised their hands.

"Come on. Be honest."

Slowly hands went up, including Việt's. His parents were pretty lax with what he watched as a child, and while he shouldn't have been watching *CSI: Miami*, well . . . he was.

"Like I said, that's okay. How do you think I got interested in forensics? Anyway, the preceptors are here to show you how things are really done. It's way more interesting than most college courses, in my humble opinion."

"But let's start with the basics. What is forensic science?"

All around him—even returning members—had quieted and taken out their notebooks and pencils, their faces concentrated. It wasn't like they were here in class because they needed to fill the school's core requirements. No, everyone was here because they wanted to be. Việt settled in. Déjà vu washed over him—not from the moment itself, but from a sensation that he felt at Kale and Tate's place. The relief of finding an anchor to keep him rooted.

For the rest of the school week, Việt's mind buzzed, the energy from the forensic science meeting still flowing through him. It was the same type he used to fuel his running, but by Saturday morning he'd already gone for a run, and knew his homework was waiting for him. Unfortunately, Wren was thinking the same thing because when Việt returned, he was already at his desk.

Since the night with Wren's friends, they'd only had brief, neutral exchanges about the dining hall's food, how distant their classrooms were, and how much homework they had. Before long, Việt didn't really care what happened that night.

They sat with their backs to each other, lost in their assignments, and they continued in silence for two or three hours until the sun started setting and they were both yawning through the last of their work. Eventually Việt started to pack up, planning to grab a light snack or early dinner.

"Do you want to watch TV?" Wren asked.

"Sure. What do you want to watch?"

"National Geographic's having a special," he replied.

Việt was caught off guard. "You serious?"

Wren sort of flinched and looked away, and Việt realized it wasn't a joke. "Sometimes I just need to . . . chill, you know? And I like animals." He started to smile but raised one shoulder, like he wanted to brush it off. The move reminded him of Bảo whenever someone complimented his writing. That was what happened when you became used to being underestimated.

Việt realized he was genuinely trying to apologize. "Sure, I got some time."

It took him a good half hour to accept that the kid who led a pack of wild wolves, invading his space, was really the kid who was mesmerized by National Geographic and splitting a bag of popcorn with him.

He punctuated the silence with his random facts—like, this one: elephants are actually the only mammals, besides humans, to walk backward.

"Sorry. About the other night."

"You don't need to say."

"Yeah, but my grandma would give me shit if I didn't *really* apologize."

"Your grandma?" Việt smirked in the dark.

Wren sensed his reaction. "You know what—I take it back. Shut up." He threw a handful of popcorn at him. "Yes, Granny Ann Joseph can still kick my ass at age eighty-seven. She's always telling me apologies aren't words, they're actions. But it wasn't just that.

We were assholes. I was. They're chill—most of the time, I swear. But I wouldn't, you know, be able to watch this without them making fun of me."

"What makes you think I won't make fun of you?"

"I can't tell if you're joking or not," Wren said, shaking his head. "But I know you're not an asshole. And I think you probably know what it's like to be bullied." Wren quickly explained, "You're super quiet. Quiet kids always get bullied." Việt let him continue. "And I know that shit does stuff to you. Makes you want to take on a new identity, be someone else entirely."

His roommate knew more about him than he expected.

"You know, when nice people invite you to hang out with them, you should either accept or decline. But it warrants a response."

"Sorry, who's this?"

"The guy who was nice enough to cook you breakfast when you were hungover!" Kale. But how—

"How'd you get my number?" Việt asked.

"School directory."

"What a creep!" It sounded like Tate in the background.

"I said last week that my door would be open to you, and I meant it. Today happens to be a Saturday Sins dinner. You're totally welcome to join us."

"Oh." Việt glanced over at his roommate, whose eyes were beginning to close. They'd watched TV for three hours; it was nighttime now. "I didn't think you meant it."

"Get over here, Việt! And come hungry." Now it was Lis, and it sounded like she'd wrestled the phone from Kale. "I want to hear what you thought about the meeting!"

"Hurry up! We're getting hungry waiting for you." Now that was Evie, and if Việt was wrestling his decision before, her voice convinced him to go.

He made it to Kale and Tate's apartment, and slipped right in. There were more people than he expected; all of them appeared to be upperclassmen. They were seated at what looked like two folding tables pushed together. Việt was sure one of them was used for beer pong the other weekend. No one looked over at his entrance. A Spotify playlist played at a medium volume from a MacBook. He remembered the music at the party had been twice as loud, and the lights blinked along with the beat. Now the lights were dimmed, and the whole setup felt disarmingly and unfamiliarly too "adult." The tip jar that Kale mentioned when they first met was displayed prominently on the kitchen counter, and it had some cash in it, so Việt went over and pulled a few bills from his wallet.

"And Việt has arrived. Clap, everyone!"

To his utter horror, all the guests followed Kale's command, and Việt could only stare back, his hand in the jar, fingers clinging to a five-dollar bill.

"What are you doing?" the older boy asked, spotting his hand.

"Putting money in the tip jar?"

"What a gentleman." Kale grabbed him by the shoulders, like

a music teacher forcing their student to bow after a performance. "They don't make firsties like him anymore. Instead I have a bunch of freeloaders as friends."

"It's you who refuses the money," one guest said. "You didn't *want* me to pay, even as I tried to wrestle cash into your hands. In fact, if I remember correctly, you told me to shove it up my—"

Tate coughed loudly. He was seated at the far end of the table, and Evie and Lis waved Việt over, and he gratefully escaped everyone's attention. Passing by the other guests, he was given smiles and unabashed waves, before they returned to their respective conversation.

"Seems like a lot more people are here than last time," he said. "I thought it'd just be you four."

"The number dwindles over time," Evie said. He noticed her boyfriend didn't come. Jake, was that his name? "Once the weeks go on, it *is* mainly us four—and hopefully, five if you want to keep coming—but the first few Saturday Sins is almost like a celebration that we're all back on campus again."

Việt eyed the other end of the table, heavy with different dishes: roasted sweet potatoes, glazed carrots, roasted Cornish hens on a bed of lemon and rosemary. Dessert was Oreos and dark chocolate–covered pretzels, likely brought by the guests.

"How *does* he pay for all this? Seriously."

"Free produce," Lis answered. "Perks of working at the Sustainability crew."

"And we do pay, but we make it seem like we don't," Evie explained.

"Kale's . . . forgetful," Tate explained, noticing Việt's confusion. "AggieCard, assignments, he loses everything. So, whenever he 'finds' cash lying around, I just tell him it's money he had misplaced. Or he just assumes so. Actually, now that I'm saying all this, the only time he isn't forgetful is when he's cooking."

"Uh. That's . . ."

"Unbelievable, right?" Lis finished. "Yeah, but once, I stole his cozy, fuzzy blanket from his bed, and he didn't realize it until two weeks later."

"That was you?"

While Lis made excuses to Kale, who joined right then, Evie laughed. "Just hand over as much as you want. Tate will plant it somewhere soon."

Việt's five dollars seemed inadequate, given the amount of food, but he didn't want to protest more. Kale encouraged him to eat up. He eyed Việt as he piled up on food, until discomfort creeped over him. The older boy only stopped after Tate elbowed him and said, "Leave the kid alone."

"Just try the appetizers!" Kale insisted.

"He wants to know how the food tastes," Evie explained. "We're his guinea pigs."

Việt understood. When he worked at Bảo's family restaurant, Bảo's mother had some servers taste-test batches of entrees, even though she never took their meek critique seriously. Stubborn and proud, that woman. Because Việt was no longer terrified of her, knowing that she was soft underneath all those thorns, he felt comfortable offering his feedback. And she listened to Việt's suggestions, to a certain point, accepting them with a "Maybe I will do that next time." And then she would never do it.

Well, at least she asked for his opinion.

Sensing the upperclassman's watchful eye again, Việt tested the appetizers, and was grateful that there were only two: the sweet potatoes and carrots. Separately they were perfectly sweet, but two sugary appetizers overpowered his taste buds.

"That's why I think the appetizers were a nine out of ten," Việt concluded after a few minutes.

"Interesting." A smile slowly formed on Kale's face. "I like this kid. He's honest," he proclaimed to the others at the table.

With some astonishment and a speck of lingering fear—because Kale was now determined to get his opinion on the main courses, until thankfully, Tate shooed him away—Việt sat through dinner, until he was absorbed into the many random, slurred conversations around him. Lis appeared relieved that he enjoyed Wednesday's club meeting. Evie asked about his first few weeks of classes, nodding because she'd taken similar courses.

At one point, Tate asked Evie where Jake was, and she only sighed, said he wasn't free tonight. The older boy nodded at her response and there was no follow-up, though Việt thought Tate had sent Lis a look. Did that mean the boyfriend was always busy? Or just busy whenever they had their Saturday Sins dinner? Besides the brief sigh, Evie didn't seem bothered by Jake's absence.

One conversation made him think of Wren and their talk.

Someone had brought up identities and maintaining them in different groups—school, work, and home—whether that was a good thing or a bad thing. Banished by Tate to the other end of the table, Kale argued it was neither, but just an inevitable thing.

"We're all different someones, depending on who we are with. It's impossible to be consistent, and anyone who thinks they are is in denial. Me, for example—I'm much louder here than I am at home, with my family, *especially* my extended family, I'm not as open. It's because I'm the baby, the wild card to some." Kale rolled his eyes. "I don't even get to touch the kitchen because apparently, my aunt is the queen of the kitchen, when really"—he stage-whispered—"she could use a little more of something called salt in her meals."

"It's hard to hold too many someones in your body, though," Kale's friend, Amina, said softly.

"I don't think I have too many someones in this body," Việt said honestly. He'd had some wine, which was offered to him "in moderation," Tate joked. "I'm too busy trying to figure out *one* someone." Maybe it didn't make sense, but other people nodded like they understood him. Evie was one of them.

"When I'm with my family, I'm much surer of myself. I have a role." Evie paused. "I had a role, I guess."

"What's the role that you want now?" Tate asked.

"Good question!" Evie pointed at Việt as if he'd just said the most enlightening fact. "Be my own person. I need to figure out how."

"It's the people around you," Kale said, bursting into their personal space as if he were summoned. He plopped down right beside Tate, letting his hand brush along his boyfriend's shoulders. His face was fully red—same as Evie, he realized. A quick selfie check—Việt too. Damn you, ALDH2.

Though his answer was nonsensical, Việt could feel the older boy was making a point, and maybe the true meaning would dawn on him later, once he slept away the wine. The table had already split into separate conversations. He overheard a rumor about a bed with chains in one of Hutchinson's bathrooms. . . .

Kale continued, projecting, "People will bring out all the different sides of you. Sometimes in the worst ways. But mostly in the best, and freeing, and fulfilling, way, ever."

There was a brief solemn silence. Even the din of forks and spoons halted. And then:

"What the *hell* are you talking about?" asked Amina, and the whole room laughed.

Ali: [sends a picture of her campus newspaper]

Ali: front page baby!

Linh: I'm sure you broke some new record for freshmen writers getting the front page

Bảo: seniors are quaking in their allbirds

Ali: 😈

CHAPTER 10

EVIE

She pressed send, finally done with the clinic application. Now it was out of her hands. Setting aside her tablet, she stretched out on her living room couch. Time for some lazy time—she deserved it after this week. Her General Virology professor assigned a nauseating amount of reading, and she also had a lab report due in three days.

Jake hadn't texted her since last night, when he'd turned in his application. It wasn't an issue; he went offline whenever he needed to focus on homework. At least they were able to study together a couple of days ago at Jake's place. In contrast, her Saturday Sins group chat in just a few hours was an endless exchange of memes, everyone despairing about their heavy workload. Kale was quick with his thumbs and dominated the chat while Việt, who was added recently, lagged behind. His latest meme: a fainting Elmo.

Evie didn't think much about friend groups until after they were made. It just happened. Often by sheer proximity. Without their rooming situation, she and Lis would have never met. Without Lis's involvement in the forensic science club, she could say the same thing about her friendship with Kale and Tate.

Unlike kindergarten, where any playmate became your friend—even for only a few hours—friendships at her age were a magical web of trust, feelings, and understanding that started with a shared interest or experience. Connections made during a coffee run, a lunch date, a movie night, until it didn't matter where they would meet. Evie and her friends shared a telepathic connection after so many years together, their words often perfectly capturing her thoughts, but conversely, they knew when words were unnecessary.

There was friendship between her and Jake the night they confessed; if words were assigned to the sparks floating in the air, it'd be *excitement, fear, hope*, and perhaps a thousand more words. And it was present that very first morning her friends formed the idea for Saturday Sins. She, Kale, Tate, and Lis gathered in the dorms, still drunk. Kale had stood up, and randomly declared himself the breakfast king, and then they all laughed because they must have looked ridiculous with their bedheads, baggy eyes, and pounding headaches. It was magnetic. It was natural.

It was fated.

Over the years, they kept their group to only the four of them. They all had friends outside of this, but Evie would bet everyone would say they were closest to the people inside the group. This wasn't on purpose. Those friends lingering outside their group had other groups they perfectly belonged to.

Evie sensed Việt hadn't found his group yet; maybe they would become his. She didn't know too much about him, but he wasn't socially awkward or unlikable. He might be a drifter, a chameleon. Considering how easily he blended in at their dinner, full of third-year strangers, he could fit in in a lot of places.

Friendship took time, and Evie figured she would help him as much as possible. Not out of pity. Not out of curiosity. Was it too drastic to say out of need?

During their runs, Việt felt solid next to her; an extension of her, almost. If the two of them ran hard enough, and together, they would get to their destination quicker. It wasn't logical, but that was the thought that'd popped up. Their running routine had started after crossing paths again on their respective runs. It surprised Evie since the campus was huge. So she and Việt decided to run together, three times a week, starting at seven because it worked with their class schedule. As they cooled off on the lawn, which had become another custom of theirs, a memory of home would occur to her and she'd share it, and Việt would immediately catch on. Reminiscing together was always fun.

At Davis, she wasn't close to anyone from Westminster, and some topics she couldn't mention, not without having to explain herself. Evie liked the pull of knowing someone from home, some-one connected to her by infinite threads that stemmed from places like school, temples, grocery stores.

For example, there was a cranky cashier at Sage Street Market, a café for students. Each time, without fail, the fifty-something-year-old woman would ring Evie up and call her by different names. To her credit, they all started with *E*: Emily, Emilia, Emerald. Close enough. Evie saw no harm in letting it continue. She was actually amused by it because there was a gym teacher at La Quinta who also forgot everyone's name, and it became a running joke among the high school students.

The other day, Evie was with Việt, who made the same connection, and they laughed together. Việt had been early for their run, not just on time, and as he approached, he used his hand to shade his eyes from the sun. A handheld water bottle was in his other hand. Neon green, which, despite Evie's limited personal knowledge, seemed too bright for his personality; Việt's groundedness and his everyday clothing suggested neutral colors. He then explained that the color was meant to be eye-catching in case something happened to him. Depending on the perp's—"Perp?" she laughed—movements and planning, the police could possibly find the water bottle and extract DNA or fibers from it.

"Your mind's pretty dark."

"Yeah, but my water bottle isn't." Việt shook it for emphasis.

Well. He wasn't wrong.

Evie smiled at the first-year's meme and replied with her own carefully selected meme: a reality TV personality, a notorious mother hen, praising her child with her camera in hand. A wish for herself and the Saturday Sins group.

CHAPTER 11

VIỆT

The phone calls to his parents always disoriented him. The switch from English to only Vietnamese threw him off. Back home, he was never away from his family for too long, and so he code-switched frequently at his house and at Bảo's family restaurant. His languages coexisted harmoniously, ready to be used when the situation called for it. His Vietnamese was decent; he could answer his elders respectfully, but put him in front of an academic or an expert and he would freeze.

As he spoke with his mother now, the words stumbled through his mouth, dodging his tongue. A small part of him worried that soon enough, he would forget the language. He didn't really speak Vietnamese with Evie. Couldn't even imagine it. She knew the language, but . . . calling her "chị"? It was like calling Bảo "anh," and no way was he ever going to acknowledge that Bảo was older. It didn't feel right.

If his mother noticed, though, she didn't say anything.

"How are you?" he asked, only half listening. He was supposed to go to another Saturday dinner and ran through the belongings he couldn't leave without: wallet, key, AggieCard . . .

Gazing into the wall mirror near the door, he listened to her steady breathing, picturing where she was right now: alone, in the kitchen, resting after work, arms and legs sore from her delivery runs. Maybe waiting for the rice cooker to finish.

"Mẹ's okay." Her fatigue reached him through the phone, and underneath was sorrow. He guessed what likely happened.

"What did you two fight about?"

No answer.

Việt's stomach felt heavy. It must have been really bad this time; she'd at least rant to him, telling him about his father's wrongdoing, even if it was trivial. Once she complained he bought a more expensive bag of sweet potatoes, the wrong Vietnamese herb, and forgot two or three more ingredients she asked him to get from the supermarket.

"You want me to call him? Ask when he's going to get back." Another thing, the only thing, he could do to help his mom. Even if Ba didn't pick up, he'd at least reply with a text. The most he could do being six hours away from home.

"Con không cần lo," she said, which was her usual way of evading his question when he'd comfort her in the past.

"I'll call him right now," he offered again.

"No, just stay on the line. It will all be fine."

. . .

Việt skipped Saturday Sins dinner.

His mother's sadness became his. He was her only child; he was always by her side after the fights, and all her turmoil turned radioactive. Now coupled with his mountain of schoolwork, the thought that he'd never catch up, a familiar darkness took root in him overnight, and became the reason he couldn't muster the strength to get up from bed Sunday morning.

In high school, when he felt sideways—when the outside became dull, when his attention drifted, and voices turned monotone, and smiles felt invasive—he knew to recognize the signs of his depression and how to cope. Every bad feeling he had—it took a quick run and fresh air to lessen its heaviness. Or Bảo would somehow know to text him to hang out. He went most of the time, only because he didn't want his parents to see him like this at home.

He went to a school counselor, once. Only once. It was after three weeks of feeling down, listless, miserable, so he knocked on the counselor's office, its windows covered in happy-go-lucky students with bright pearly smiles. He went in thinking there would be a way forward, but when he sat down across the counselor, he realized it wouldn't be that easy. The counselor was his running coach's cousin. What if, somehow, their conversation reached his coach's ears? Then wouldn't his parents need to be told?

So Việt chickened out, and instead asked the counselor if he could get his college application fees waived, which he incidentally needed.

He had found some distractions on campus this year: his runs with Evie and the forensics club, which he attended three more times since the first meeting. Việt had also gone to the past three Saturday Sins dinners, and as expected, the numbers dwindled each time. The last one, it was only the five of them and Beth, the sleepy vegan who flicked Kale off that first morning. The two of them were actually good friends; they shared the same humor and loved banter with a bit of bite but no true hate. Beth and Kale met in a culinary class, and on the days Kale didn't feel like cooking, Beth treated him to her vegan meals. "He acts like he hates vegan cuisine, but he could really eat anything," Tate had said with a fond smile.

The couple's energies couldn't be more different. Kale acted first; with cooking, he forged ahead without a recipe and instead let his imagination lead. Which meant he left chaos in his wake: dirty pans, food discard on the floor, opened cabinets. Conversely, Tate was rational and pragmatic, cleaning up Kale's messes and convincing him to cook less because they would have too many leftovers.

The invisible wall had faded between him and Wren, and they also tried to have weekly hangouts watching videos of animals and other random YouTube clips. They didn't grow their friendship beyond that, but he didn't mind it much. They each had their group of friends outside their dorm. He'd once seen Wren sweeping their floor, using the straw broom his mother had bought from ABC Supermarket, deeming it a part of a first-year's essentials. The boy marveled at its effectiveness. Việt let him appreciate his culture.

But after hearing his mom over the phone, Việt saw himself as a car running out of gas as it edged toward its destination. Always a Toyota Camry, for some inexplicable reason. This seemed to be college: a cruise at one point, then an excruciating push through assignments, projects, and exams that promised an exit to something better. He knew his life wasn't impossible to bear—not in the slightest. His mind and body just chose to think it was.

Việt didn't desire death, but he wouldn't deny it. He thought of it in terms of a game of *What if*. What if he went on a run and just kept running until his heart stopped? What if he lay in bed long enough—would he disappear from this world?

He ended up sleeping all of Sunday. Invisible chains kept him in bed. His phone was on silent. If Kale or the others were looking for him, he didn't know. If Wren had come in and out during his sleep, he wasn't aware.

He skipped his Monday classes, then his Tuesday classes. Ordered delivery. Slept. Rinse and repeat.

Wednesday was when he started to smell, so he twisted free from his blankets and sat up. Wren had left early in the morning, after asking if Việt was feeling sick, and after Việt answered "Yes."

Right away, he noticed a banana nut muffin waiting for him on his desk. His roommate had left it; Việt felt a pang of guilt. He didn't want anyone to see his dark moods, to notice how he couldn't even take care of his basic needs. Việt had put everything that was meant to be on the floor on his desk—and everything on his desk on the floor. His chair held a pile of old and fresh clothes. Hiding away was unavoidable when you had a roommate, when you lived so close that you couldn't fake your own happiness.

When he unsilenced his phone, he saw a tsunami of Saturday Sins' group texts.

He groaned. The most recent ones were memes, so he had to scroll back to figure out the original message—a picnic, at the top of the Hutchinson Parking Garage, at around five tonight. A midweek pick-me-up, a sunset meal. It was one in the afternoon now.

He was about to reply and tell them he was busy, but then a new wave of texts landed—all of them containing his names, all caps, followed by explanation points. Kale won with the most. It turned out that they were looking for him before, and because he was dead asleep, their texts piled on.

He rubbed his face.

> Việt: I'll think about it. thinking of napping soon!

> Lis: first-years aren't ALLOWED to nap!!!

> Kale: these first-years are SPOILED

He heard their playful and indignant voices inside his head. If he went to the picnic, he'd probably bring the mood down.

Against his mother's wishes, after their phone call, he did send a text to Ba before getting to bed, who only texted that he was back home again and that everything was fine. Thumbs-up emoji. Việt knew better; there'd be a few weeks of icy silence, melting into polite interactions. Followed by some peace, only for another issue to push his parents apart.

His phone buzzed again. It was Evie, who had texted him separately.

> Evie: didn't you say that yesterday? and the day before? We missed seeing you at Saturday's dinner!

> Evie: come outside for a run with me!!! Weather's nice and cool. it'll wake you up.

> Việt: idk maybe.

> Evie: pretty please?

It took another half hour for him to kick off his sheets and slide down from his bed. He wolfed down the banana nut muffin, silently thanking his roommate, then left for a long shower. Admittedly, he felt somewhat better with all the physical grime down the drain, though the self-hatred came back when he looked in the mirror. Why did he look sleep-deprived, even though he'd slept for so long? There was barely any facial hair, which he guessed was a good thing since that was one less thing he needed to tame before feeling human. He spritzed himself with some Nautica Voyage—a gift from this past Christmas.

Once his shoes were on, his feet carried him the rest of the way. Spotting Evie at their meeting spot, seeing her warm smile, another wave of guilt hit him. How could she be so nice to him, when he was the one avoiding her and the others?

Why did Wren give him food? Why did Kale, Lis, and Tate try so hard to befriend him, when he was the one who wanted to waste away in bed?

The third-year met him halfway. "Long time no see!"

Việt inhaled. He didn't deserve her concern. "Sorry for ghosting everyone. . . . I wasn't feeling well."

She nodded, peering at him.

"Are you really okay?"

"I'm fine."

"You sure?"

"I said I'm fine, didn't I?"

A painful silence followed his words, their harshness lingering in his ears. His gaze went to the grass. This was why he stayed away. When the darkness hit him, his words became slippery down his throat. Ironically, he knew that he might feel less burdened if he talked about this black cloud. His parents probably wouldn't get it, or not understand how he, who didn't have much to complain about, could be depressed. What was even the Vietnamese word for depression? He'd never heard it come out of his parents' mouths. And Evie . . . she'd probably just pity him.

"Sorry, that was harsh," Việt started. "It's—"

"Let's just run." Her voice was cheery. He gazed up at her and saw a kind look. No judgment. She then smiled. "You'll feel better, I promise."

The sun was blinding, the sky blue, the breeze light—everything outside was obscenely, stupidly perfect and beautiful—then here he was: a mess. Oblivious to his tangled feelings, to his leaden body, nature was there to receive him with open arms. And Evie ran straight into their embrace, picking up speed. She sprinted ahead of him. Farther and farther away, and suddenly Việt was desperate. He needed to catch up. He *wanted to*. But his legs, his mind, his heart—

He felt it happening before it happened: eyes burning, chest tightening.

He stopped right there, stumbling toward a row of grass and collapsing on his back underneath a large tree. "Damnit," he said, voice trembling. He threw his right arm over his eyes. As if that would stop the tears now.

Evie had come back for him; he heard her fast breathing and the scrape of her sneakers on the ground.

"I didn't want to cry," Việt mumbled.

"Don't give me shit like 'Boys aren't supposed to cry,'" Evie warned him.

"No, I'm just worried my mascara's going to run," he attempted to joke. This *was* embarrassing. He hadn't cried for years. He always stopped himself. Why the hell did it have to be now? He was pathetic. Still, he remained where he was, letting the tears come. His arm was wet, the tears tracked down to his ear.

"Runners can't really control their bodily functions after running, right?" Evie sounded much closer. He guessed she was lying down next to him, her mouth by his ear. Soon enough, there was nothing left but the rapid rise of his chest. He slowed his breathing.

"Yeah, that happens to marathoners and long-distance runners for the most part."

"So that means they can accidentally pee or . . . the other thing. When you think about it, tears aren't that bad, compared to those two."

A gurgling noise escaped his lips, a sound close to a laugh. He finally let his arm drop to his side. "I guess that's a good point."

"Look," Evie said softly, "you probably don't want to talk about what's bothering you right now, and that's totally fine. But if you ever, *ever* need extra ears, I'm here. If you just need to cry, fine, I'll stay here and say nothing." Her words were slow, hesitant. "And Kale, Lis, Tate would say the same if they were here. They like you, you know; they were worried when they didn't hear from you."

"Sorry."

Evie waved away his apology, then kept her hand up to block the sun from her eyes.

"I'm sure Lis and Tate are fine. And if Kale is ever offended, he'd tell you right away. Actually, I think he'd take revenge first." She cracked a smile. "And so far that hasn't happened, so I think you'll be forgiven."

"Sometimes I wonder why they even like me." They were happy and strong. He was not.

"Well, why do you like *them*?"

"They're fun to be around. They don't care that I'm a first-year and have been kind to me. I like Kale's cooking. Lis and I both like forensics. Tate's a bit quieter, like me."

"That's why I love them too," Evie said. "Being around them is easy. See, Lis and Kale are so chaotic, and Tate can be that or chill, depending on things. I always felt like the calm one in our group, but then when I'm with them, I feel more alive than ever. I'm laughing more. I forget my worries." Việt heard a smile in her voice; she was no doubt remembering moments the four of them shared. "I can't speak for them, but I think you complete our group. Kale was always frustrated that we told him his food was delicious—but you give him actual notes that are both complimentary and helpful. Lis has tried hard to recruit more people to the FSC, and she was so happy that you joined. And Tate—he told me he was glad that you and I were normal."

He shook his head. "I'm a mess."

"Who isn't?"

And that was all, she didn't try to pry. For that, he was grateful he left the dorms, and that she was the first person he saw outside.

"Come to the picnic, but only if you want to. We don't mind, really, and we never want to force you." She was offering him an out.

A picnic . . . Hours earlier, he would have just lain in bed. But Wren had come by and dropped off a muffin. His friends had sent through random pictures to share what they were up to.

The weather was unabashedly perfect. And his run with Evie had turned out better than he expected.

"Thanks. I'll go to the picnic."

Her eyebrows jumped before a smile bloomed. "Everyone's gonna be glad you're coming." She got up, offered her hand, and pulled Việt up when he accepted. She brushed away grass from her shirt. "And I'm glad there's another sensible one who will be there. Inside at night, they are okay, but under the sunset, they get rowdy. It's a strange phenomenon."

"Sounds fun to me." And he really meant it.

CHAPTER 12

EVIE

On the top of the Hutchinson Parking Garage, their picnic underway, Evie noticed Lis speaking to Việt, and felt a wave of gratitude toward her roommate, who didn't speculate when she asked if their younger classmate seemed distant lately. Lis merely decided, "I'm going to have a word with him. He'll be fine. Make sure he comes to the picnic."

Kale, of course, prepared some sandwiches: ham and brie, tomato and mozzarella, and tuna salad. Everyone else lugged over soft drinks. The sun was just starting to set, blue, purple, pink, orange, and yellow gracing the skies, accentuating the mountains. The intramural field below the garage was packed with other students who had the same idea to leave their workload behind for a few hours.

Jake rested his head in her lap. Truthfully, she didn't think her boyfriend would make it because of his schoolwork; she even said so to her friends, apologizing. They didn't seem to care. Imagine her surprise when Jake came to the picnic spot.

Her boyfriend didn't clamor to spend time with them, even in the previous years. It was the same for the other three. She didn't want to push them together; she just wished it had happened organically. One time, her parents had had a holiday party at the restaurant and invited the employees, friends outside of the business, fellow business owners, and a handful of distant relatives. She remembered feeling secondhand embarrassment as she watched her parents awkwardly fail to have their friends mingle. It was almost like they had several parties going on at once. She wished there was a way to bring together her friend groups.

Lost in her thoughts, she didn't realize she had stopped touching Jake's hair.

Jake noticed, and tilted his head back. "Something the matter?"

She put on a smile. "Nothing. I'm just glad you're here. We've all been so busy."

"Truth. This year's been packed." He sighed. "Interview requests for the clinic go out tomorrow. What should we do to celebrate?"

Had it already been a month since she submitted her application?

She tugged his ear. "You're getting *way* ahead of yourself. Let's wait until we get the emails, and then we can make plans."

"Got to be prepared."

"But what if . . . what if we don't get through the program together? Or one of us is rejected?"

"I don't see that happening."

Evie was envious of his confidence, then. Even if it might be arrogant, at least he believed in the two of them.

She felt eyes on her and turned slightly. Việt faced her way, a tiny smile on his face. What was going through his mind? Questions were on the tip of her tongue today during their quick run, but when his tears flowed, she didn't want to press him. Comforting him was her goal, and it seemed to work. She waved her free hand.

Việt jolted; it was obvious he had zoned out, and she laughed at his wide eyes, his smile now sheepish. He gestured behind her.

The sunset. Gazing at this sight, bolstered by the happiness around her, she felt eager for the events of tomorrow.

The next day, Evie kept refreshing her emails, even in class, underneath the desk and out of view of the lecturer. She didn't see any email—neither an invite nor a rejection—so she held on to hope. She used her phone so often throughout the day that she ran out of battery, and had to race back to the apartment to plug it in.

Evie switched over to her tablet, fingernails tapping against the screen as she waited for it to turn on. When she opened up her browser and mail account, she saw there was one new message.

From the clinic.

Dear Evelyn Mai—

She walked normally to the café, but inside, she felt like skipping. She got in!

Jake had a study group here and told her to come by after she texted wanting to meet. There he was, toward the far end of the café, books and papers out with three other students. Beaming, she waved at Jake who waved back. He mouthed that he'd come to her in a few minutes. Not wanting to interrupt, she sat at a table closer to the entrance, and scrolled through her phone. The Sins group chat showed their rabid congratulations.

"You look happy," Jake said ten minutes later. They kissed, before he sat down across from her. He looked ragged—probably another all-nighter.

Guilt picked at her, wondering if it was all right to share the news when he might not have checked his email yet.

"I heard from the clinic. I got in."

He nodded. "That's cool. Congrats, babe."

Her stomach knotted. "Did you . . . hear back yet?"

"Yeah, I didn't get in."

Evie took his hand. "Oh no. I can't believe it." A part of her thought he was going to make it through, with or without his dad's help.

"S'right." He sighed. "I've got plenty of other things going on." Evie had to smile at that—he didn't sit with his disappointments; he always focused on the next step.

"Want to go out this weekend?"

"Hmm. Might be tough for me. I got some plans with the guys the next two weekends. Maybe end of the month?"

Evie looked down. "I just . . . thought it'd be nice to celebrate this with you this weekend. Or at least take another break . . ."

Jake raised a hand at his friends when they called out for him. He didn't seem to hear Evie. "I'll see what I can move around, promise. Okay, got to get back with the study group. Text you later." He dropped a quick kiss on her lips, then ambled back to his own corner.

A few minutes later, they left the café, likely searching for some place less crowded. Evie forced herself not to watch them leave. That creeping feeling—it made her heart sting. Sure, getting the interview request wasn't like winning a Nobel Prize or anything like that, and Jake was probably busy with all his schoolwork. He was always under pressure.

Another part of Evie wondered if her good news mattered to him at all.

Sitting there, her mind racing from her internal debate, she didn't hear anyone approaching. From behind, Lis threw her arms around her, nearly yanking the chair onto its back legs. Kale, Tate, and Việt, holding a coffee cup, came into her view. Evie laughed. "Lis, you're choking me."

"Friends are allowed to choke each other when good news happens!"

"Makes no sense," Tate said.

"My turn to choke her!" Kale, ignoring his boyfriend, hugged her from the front after Lis backed away. Then he mumbled about a celebratory dinner for the next Saturday Sins. "Anything you want—I'll make it for you."

Turning red—from both embarrassment and a lack of air source, probably—Evie met eyes with Việt who smiled on. She saw only unbridled excitement, so she gave him her own wide grin. He looked much better than yesterday—clouds clearing after a long rainstorm.

"It's no big deal," Evie said. "And remember, I need to interview first before anything can happen!"

"That's *still* a big deal, though," Việt said. "But no one's surprised because we all knew you would get through. Really—congrats, Evie." He set down the coffee cup. "A small treat for you. Mocha latte with two pumps of syrup instead of three. Lis told me."

"You didn't have to, Việt," she said, but she accepted it. Their fingers touched for a millisecond. "But thank you. And Lis, I guess." Her roommate sent her a proud look.

She allowed herself a few seconds in Kale's embrace and basked in their smiles. They all seemed to know exactly what she needed.

CHAPTER 13

VIỆT

The morning after the picnic started like his previous days—"his dark days," he decided to call them. He stayed under his blankets, listening to Wren quietly get ready. Heard him stub his toe and his cut-off swear. Which made Việt smile—not because he wanted his roommate to get hurt but because Wren was trying his best not to disturb him. Then guilt flashed through Việt. Wren had put up with his moods. Yesterday Evie had to coax him to step outside. He hadn't cried like that since he was a child, and of course it had to be in front of his friend. But Evie granted him silence.

His friends were worried, but he didn't want them to, not anymore. He would try to be better. Maybe that meant going to the mental health center, which felt daunting. But maybe it could start with getting out of bed.

So he gave himself fifteen more minutes, hoping his brain

would send the right signals; then he pushed down his covers, sat up, and met Wren's eyes. The other boy was checking himself out in the mirror by the entrance. A laugh escaped Việt's lips before he realized it. Still felt strange to laugh. Something to do with his roommate's wide eyes—at being caught at an awkward moment, or at the sight of Việt getting up on his own accord.

His roommate unfroze. "You don't look much better," Wren threw at him, all bark, no bite. He followed through with a smile. "And get your own food today. What am I, your butler?"

If Kale were to open his own restaurant, Việt imagined it would take off. True to his celebratory promise to Evie, the chef had served up Hawaiian BBQ chicken and veggie skewers, salmon teriyaki rice bowls, and haupia at the following Saturday dinner. Việt, feeling better than the week before, ended up having three servings of the latter, which was from Kale's family recipe. If a true restaurant critic were there, they'd give the sweet pudding no less than five stars.

Việt found himself at The Green a few days later, as a taste-tester. One of his lectures had gotten canceled, and his homework assignment that night wasn't complicated, so he agreed to help Kale with another food experiment.

Today's menu item was a dupe of the Rebel Within muffin from Craftsman and Wolves, an eatery in San Francisco. Kale's cousin had brought him there the summer it debuted, and there was a two-block-long line of people waiting for the sausage, chives, and cheese monstrosity that had a perfectly boiled soft egg inside—a gourmet on-the-go breakfast. People were supposed to eat it with a sprinkle of Tabasco salt, but not being able to find it, Kale had used some Frankie's seasoning powder. The first batch was delicious but needed a bit more salt. The second was delicious. And the third—

He wondered how food tasters and cup bearers in old royal courts endured their tasks, knowing they could potentially ingest poison. He wondered if someone could die from being overfed.

"No more, please. Hand it over to Tate." Việt pushed away a half-eaten muffin, still steaming from the oven. He wasn't sure there was someone with as voracious of an appetite as Kale's runner boyfriend.

Kale scowled. "He's not critiquing; he's just eating."

"You hate leftovers. I'm helping with that," Tate answered with a shrug, finishing off the muffin that Việt could not. "But maybe you should just stop baking today."

"If I don't keep busy with my hands, I'll text Evie, and it'll distract her." Her interview with the clinic was scheduled for today. "I want to support her but not overwhelm her."

At one point, when Kale was too focused on baking to talk—and Tate had eaten more than his portion, then disappeared into his bedroom to study—Việt sank into the living room sofa. Bảo and Linh were FaceTiming him. Maybe Bảo had a sixth sense for reaching out to Việt during the times he needed human contact the most. The couple were on Linh's campus, finally spending a weekend together, and were hanging out on her dormitory bed. Việt mentioned off the cuff that he was at a friend's apartment.

"You have friends?" Bảo asked, and Việt considered pressing the end button.

When he showed their video call to Kale, the older boy exclaimed: "Is that a baby Evie?! That's her boyfriend, right? So adorable."

Which probably froze Bảo's brain because he was never used to impromptu compliments and probably froze Linh's brain because she didn't expect Việt to hang with anyone in her sister's group. It didn't help that Việt had yet to update the two of them about Saturday Sins. Their texts were mostly about silly things and random complaints.

Oops.

He tried explaining to Linh, "We ran into each other one time, and—"

"She hasn't told me anything!" the girl exclaimed.

"Ah, well. She's been busy. I didn't have a chance either—"

They caught up that way, interrupted by Tate, who emerged once hearing all the chattering. He wandered over to the sink to wash dishes but was shooed out by a territorial Kale, and then soon enough, Việt had to end the call to prevent his friends from glimpsing bloodshed, and immediately three texts came through.

Bảo: send me them muffins!

Linh: Việt, i have more QUESTIONS

Ali: huh what did I miss?

Right, he did have a lot to answer for. Before he could begin typing a response, a chorus of phone dings echoed throughout the room. Evie had sent through one emoji in their group chat—😬.

Their phones went off again: another 😀.

Followed by three crying emojis.

"She's the picture of calm," deadpanned Tate.

"Maybe I should go see her. Calm her down. But—" Kale glanced, annoyed, at the batter-splattered bowls and broken egg-shells he'd ignored during the baking process. The Tabasco seasoning had also tipped over at some point, dotting the counter like a fire ant infestation.

"I'll go." Việt climbed down the stool. "Maybe she just needs someone to talk to, get things off her mind before the interview."

"That should be Jake's job." Tate sighed, shaking his head.

"You go ahead, Việt," Kale replied. "Bring along a muffin too. She probably didn't eat yet."

There. That tone. It sounded too . . . knowing.

The coffee cup, their fingers touching. Did Kale sense his feelings, then?

Or did he notice what had happened at the picnic?

The picnic was the second time meeting Jake—and he wasn't a fan. He was tall, composed, and as the third-year walked over to their spot, he was constantly stopped by other classmates, and delayed getting to Evie, who seemed familiar with his popularity.

Jake was seldom brought up by Evie, and he figured the others didn't like him that much. Tate's earlier words suggested as much.

Their group exchanged brief hellos, and he remembered the guy's blank expression when Evie re-introduced him. Jake stuck close to Evie and didn't really talk to the others. Had that distance always been there? Was that why he wasn't a part of the Saturday Sins group? Did it bother Evie?

Jake later lounged with his head in Evie's lap. Việt caught her mindlessly running her hand through the guy's hair. It was intimate. It proved that Evie was one-half of a couple; he'd never considered that she might be a different Evie with Jake. Was she more serious? Was she calmer? Did she run with him on the days she didn't run with Việt? From what Việt saw, they were clearly content together.

And he'd never felt lonelier.

He must have stared for too long because Evie, waving at him, snapped him awake, and he needed to seem composed. He couldn't reveal it was her who caught his attention, not the sunset behind her.

Kale now told him to wait; he was wrapping up the muffin in tinfoil, happy that he could hand off his food to yet another guinea pig.

There was nothing to worry about. A friend was allowed to do this.

When they heard Evie had gotten an interview request, Việt had bought her a congratulatory coffee to mask his guilt, which swarmed his thoughts since then, and were now at a low simmer. Guilt that he wanted to be close to her when she saw him as nothing more than a good friend. Guilt that, just maybe, he confused his gratitude for her act of kindness—their talk and their run—with affection. His heart clenched.

He couldn't have this crush, whatever it was called. Because they could never be together.

CHAPTER 14

EVIE

Nervousness over her upcoming interview with the Paul Hom committee prevented her from thinking too deeply about Jake's reaction—or lack of reaction—after the results were announced. She was still hurt, and that was why she only messaged him a couple of times since then: inane good mornings and good nights. Jake responded like usual. Like their conversation at the café had never happened. She hadn't even told him that her interview was today.

Should she call him now? She had an hour or so until her interview, and maybe they would talk, clear things up.

Her grip tightened on her phone. Evie shifted in her chair, flinching as its plastic leather squeaked. She sat on the second floor, near the windows, and the interview room a few doors down the hall. Outside was a picturesque courtyard filled with flowers and greenery, what would be a calming view in any other situation. Part of her was reluctant to reach out to Jake now because she wasn't sure where the conversation would go. The interview already compromised her emotions; she didn't want to add to that.

Evie turned to her Saturday Sins crew. Lis, Kale, and Tate had already texted their good-luck wishes almost the instant her text had landed. She saw nothing from Việt, but then again, he always lagged behind the others.

Then, surprising her, his message popped up: Downstairs in the lobby. Can I come up?

Within a few minutes of her reply, the first-year emerged from the stairs.

He started smiling, and then his expression changed. "Whoa" came out almost involuntarily, and she guessed what had caught him off guard. She rarely dressed up like this—a black jumpsuit, a white long-sleeve blouse underneath. For the umpteenth time she thought she overdressed. She chose full makeup instead of her typical concealer and blush.

"I look way too serious, don't I?"

"No, it's just—you look—"

"Nervous."

"I got that sense from your earlier texts. But your nervousness isn't showing."

Once he sat down, across from her, Việt opened the front part of his backpack. Evie spotted a pencil—and was that a cow-shaped eraser on top of it? Then her friend handed over a bundle of foil, warm to the touch. "Courtesy of Kale, who said you probably didn't eat anything."

"Our friend is right." She gratefully unwrapped the foil and saw a muffin. Kale raved about it one time but still proclaimed he could make a better version. She broke it apart and admired the steam rising from the middle, the perfectly soft-boiled egg. Việt shook a small baggie, and she realized it was supposed to be the salt. "Oh my god." She tried the combo, and it was just what she needed.

"Better?"

"Mm-hmm." She said another silent thanks to Kale. "Sorry that Kale had to send you all the way here."

The dark circles under Việt's eyes faded with each meeting, and Evie hoped that meant he was on the mend. Her friend was usually stoic, so she never wanted to see him break like that again. Maybe one day he'd find the words to express himself.

"I wanted to come."

Evie quickly devoured the muffin. Her fingertips tingled from the heat of it. "I don't really like in-person interviews. Puts me on a spotlight. Makes me want to barf. I'm always worried of word-vomiting answers or forgetting what the question is in the first place."

"You can practice with me. Pretend I'm the person interviewing you," Việt volunteered. He pushed aside the crumpled foil. "You probably came up with a list of questions, right?"

"You don't have to. I'm sure you have a ton of things to do!" she rushed.

"Yeah, I'm dying to get back to my chemistry assignments."

Giving in, Evie pulled out her questions she imagined the interviewer might ask. She only managed to come up with twenty. Việt cleared his throat at the sight of it, and now she realized she might have gone overboard with her preparations.

"Let's skip over the things you shouldn't be nervous about—like your major, your background . . . Why did you apply to this program?"

Evie exhaled and answered the way she'd practiced last night. Her passion had always been to help others—ever since she was a kid. She even remembered bandaging up her sister Linh's pretend boo-boos, and sometimes her real boo-boos, though she knew this was a bit too silly to mention to her interviewers. Instead she cited her pediatricians who kindly explained everything to her parents, back when their English was still a bit rusty, and how they always made her feel safe. She hoped she could be just as helpful as those doctors.

Việt nodded, and they continued working through the questions. Soon enough her nerves abated, and she let go of her hands, which had been clasped together before.

"Final question—name ten reasons why you'd be the right fit."

Easy. Evie opened her mouth—only to be stopped when she looked at Việt, who was holding back a smile.

"You wrote five reasons; it's kind of funny you were prepared enough to list ten."

"Never hurts to be prepared," she said defensively, though after a few beats, she realized how ridiculous ten answers would have been.

He shuffled the pages, causing her statement of purpose to fall out. She'd printed it out last night when she realized the interviewers might refer to it and she might forget everything she'd ever written. He was reading it now. Evie shifted in her seat and resisted the urge to snatch it away from him.

Those were for her and the clinic's eyes only; if he read her statement, it'd be like he was inside her head, and no one was ever inside her head (except for the voice that sounded like Lis sometimes). She never told her roommate this; she'd be insufferable. Nervous in the prolonged silence, Evie babbled on as he continued reading, telling him that the interview process was competitive, that other people had better grades than her, that her Vietnamese was not good enough, especially when it came to dialects, that—

"They'd be out of their mind if they don't let you into the program," Việt said, stopping her mid-rant. He slid the essay back into place, closed the notepad.

"But what if—"

"Then they shouldn't even be running the program. Because they should know, once you walk in, that you deserve to work at this clinic."

"Thank you," she finally said. Her eyes went to Việt's backpack, still open. She was right: he had a cow-shaped pencil eraser. "Was it a coincidence that I found you near the cows, or are you secretly obsessed with cows? I haven't seen these erasers since I was kid! When the school would sell supplies—eraser heads, Ticonderoga pencils—"

"Ah, the smell of lead," Việt commented dryly.

"Shut up. Some people had the Scholastic Fair; I had that the supply store."

Việt leaned down and removed the eraser before handing it over. "Keep it."

"No, I don't need it!" Evie protested.

He pulled another one from his backpack. "I have another one. See? *Mooooo*," he mimicked loudly. Evie laughed. "Think of it as a good-luck charm."

She made a fist around the eraser, squeezing it as if the small piece of rubber would give her some power.

"I'll leave you alone now." He made to go back downstairs, when Evie stopped him.

"Please stay. I don't mind the company."

So he stayed. Pulling out his books, Việt started on his chemistry assignments; he stayed quiet and left Evie to her thoughts. His pencil scribblings, the flutter of his notebook pages, the occasional hum of his phone vibrations, put her at ease. Her eyes wandered to the outside; the sun shone through even stronger than before. She was glad it was Việt who came. She loved the others, of course, but they were more liable to distract her through conversation.

When someone emerged from the hallway to call her name, Evie managed to smile and felt her nerves melt away. And even when she was only a few feet away from the interview room, she still clung to the eraser.

The eraser was not the only thing he'd given her.

As she folded and tucked her pages in her purse, she glanced down at her pages one last time—only to spot a new addition to the top right of the first page.

Good luck! You can MOOO it!

Below that, Việt had drawn a tiny cow figure.

An hour later, Evie had breezed through the questions, never stumbling, and she could read the interviewers enough to see they were satisfied, maybe even impressed. Several times they nodded at her answers.

"We were struck by your essay, by your equanimity, as you've shown just now," they said at the end. "We have one final question: Name the moment you started your journey in medicine."

Was that in her list of questions? It was not. She mentally went through to confirm.

"We don't want you to deliberate this moment too much or consider what you think we want to hear. Just say what's on your mind—perhaps something we haven't yet heard in your answers today."

A kind woman, reminding her of the bent-back elderly customers who'd shuffle into her parents' restaurant during downtime, must have seen her panic: "Remember, in this room, we are your interviewers. But out there, we're in the field of medicine. We all have our reasons, but there was perhaps one moment that made us never forget why we started."

The image of Linh popped up in her mind.

"Boo-boos?"

Oh no. She had unknowingly said this word to a room full of medical professionals. And her answer had nothing to do with this particular clinic, which mostly served the elderly, and not children. Still, an interviewer chuckled, and Evie pressed on. It couldn't get any worse from here.

"I'm the oldest daughter. It's just me, my parents, and my little sister. When things at the restaurant got busy, and my parents had to work most of the day, we became latchkey kids. It was me taking care of her at home, even though I was only two years older, and yes, that might have been illegal, but in my family, I guess you should say it's necessary to break some rules"— someone chuckled—"so I watched her most of the time. But my sister's feisty and free-spirited.

"One time, she got her hands on a small stepstool and pushed it close to the kitchen counter. She wanted her sippy cup. There was a small knife, right at her elbow, the kind my mom used to cut fruit. I don't remember how it got there—but there it was. My sister grabbed her cup, but on her way down, her elbow brushed up against the knife. It was just a small cut, almost like the size of a paper cut.

"I didn't want anything bad to happen to her." Evie had been only a kid, and that was the most scared she'd ever felt. "In hindsight, like I said, the cut wasn't anything serious, but her cries made it all sound serious. Something in me wanted to hold her and make sure she was all right. To take all the pain away. I eventually ran down the hall to the bathroom and found the first aid kit." Lies—her family wasn't organized enough to keep a kit; their scattered Band-Aids were shoved deep in the back of the kitchen's Everything drawer.

"So that was it. My moment, I guess. Neosporin. And a Band-Aid," Evie finished lamely. "If I could take away someone's pain, for just a moment, like I did with my sister, then I've accomplished something."

Three beats passed before anyone spoke. "You didn't wash your sister's cut, or your hands, first?" someone asked.

"Well, I—" Evie stopped when she realized the person was smiling. Actually, all of them were smiling at her.

It made her feel . . . relieved—and comfortable enough to answer, "That's a lot to ask of a seven-year-old."

Evie: remember that time you cut your elbow from the knife on the counter? i was seven, you were five i think

Linh: yeah, that was funny

Evie: funny?! not for me, you were crying so much. It was TRAUMATIC.

Linh: uh excuse me YOU were the one crying!! the cut was barely anything, but you thought i was dying 🙍

. . .

Evie: I passed the interview for the clinic!

Mẹ: My daughter, Dr. Mai!

Ba: can I be your first patient?

Evie: If you want to drive six hours, sure!

Bảo: [sends a picture of a food review]

Bảo: review of a local Peruvian spot off campus that has fire ceviche

Linh: 👏😍

Ali: don't forget—you would be nothing without me! Don't forget where you started

Việt: congrats man!!!

CHAPTER 15

VIỆT

Later that night, Việt, Evie, and Lis sat on the boys' sunken couch, printouts and note cards fanned out before them. The Spotify playlist was playing Connor Price songs on the living area TV, lowered to a café decibel. Tate was somewhere else in the apartment. They had finished a regular dinner, not a Saturday Sins meal, where they celebrated Evie getting through the interview process and becoming a Paul Hom volunteer. She tried to brush it aside, saying they had already celebrated her a few weeks ago, but Kale eventually screamed at her to "just take the compliment."

Call it premonition, but Việt knew she'd aced the interview process, even though it was notoriously hard, he learned. He knew it the moment he got his hands on her prepared questions and answers and skimmed through her statement, her voice clear in his head. Her answers might have been textbook perfect, but it was her intent that mattered.

Evie had smiled wide when she dropped by Kale and Tate's apartment right after the interview. She'd waved off Kale's cat-calls at the sight of her outfit. Việt hadn't seen Evie with makeup on, or maybe he just couldn't tell. But when he'd met her earlier, before the interview, he'd never seen her hair half up half down, just slightly wavy. It looked so soft that he wanted to reach out to feel it. . . . As soon as the thought had crossed his mind, he'd axed it and tried to focus on why he was there.

If he thought about it more, he'd admit he had a thing for intense girls. They knew what they wanted. They would give you straight answers. They wouldn't string people along for the fun of it. He used to have a high school crush on a girl named Kelly Tran, who ran their Asian Club, but she was *too* intense—a mean intensity. She'd yelled at him and Bảo for skipping some volunteer opportunities and was always snarky after that. He might have had a crush on his friend Ali when they'd first met; she'd kept pestering him to write a column on all the movies and TV shows he watched. But it had become clear that she was already in love—with journalism.

Evie's intensity lured him in, in a good way, and he could imagine—

Wait, wait, wait.

Việt blinked several times.

Boyfriend. She had a boyfriend.

Anything he was feeling now—anything he was *thinking* now—needed to end. Immediately.

At the moment, there were other things to worry about. Beside him, oblivious to his internal storm of thoughts, Lis mumbled under breath as she read a note card. In two weeks, the FSC would hold a qualifying test to determine who'd represent the school at the spring competition. The first portion contained a forensic science knowledge exam, and there was no way to tell what would be on there. The latter portion, the crime scene study, was at least guaranteed context clues. Lis had talked about it since the very beginning, but he didn't realize it was happening so soon.

Which led to the mountain of forensic note cards before them.

"Why didn't either of you tell me it was coming up so soon?" Evie asked.

Lis waved away Evie's concern. "You had more things to worry about. But if you feel so guilty, you can help me study."

"Việt, can you give me a hand here?" Kale asked from the kitchen. As always, he was more preoccupied with food preparation than studying.

"You're cooking something else? We just ate."

"I do what I want." His friend gestured him to come closer with a peeler. "Chop up these carrots. I'm making carrot chips."

"*Carrot chips?*"

"Don't say it like that, or you won't get any when I'm finished. They're really good. Have you had any reason to doubt me yet?"

That shut Việt up. Kale *was* right.

Việt pulled a knife from the wooden block; it was Kale's favorite.

And it got Việt thinking that maybe he should find more friends besides Kale, because who has a favorite knife?

His friend was now observing him—but surely it wasn't to evaluate his knife skills.

"You like her," he whispered.

"What?" Việt whispered back.

"You were just staring at Evie for a good five minutes. Love our friends, but wow, they are oblivious!"

"No—that's not . . . I mean." He had to tread this conversation carefully.

"You, Việt, like her." Kale only tilted his head in her direction, but he may as well have just called out her name. Subtlety was not his forte. Luckily, Evie was testing Lis, flashcards flying through her hands, and didn't even notice he'd left his seat. "I caught you staring at her at the picnic, too. And I sensed you felt more than friendship when you volunteered to go see her before the interview. Then I realized that out of all our texts, you seem to reply to Evie quicker and react the most to anything she says."

Correction: apparently, Kale was more stealthy than subtle.

Việt had two options: continue denying his crush, which would only make Kale more insistent with his probing—or come clean and admit it. Neither appealed to him because it still didn't change the realization that he had feelings for someone he shouldn't. A friend. A really nice friend who already had a boyfriend.

His brain decided for him; it was tired of holding it all in for the past week or so—his sudden revelation, his panic, all contradictory emotions. "Yeah, I think I do."

Maybe he hadn't said it loud enough because Kale didn't even blink in acknowledgment. He'd gone over to turn on the air fryer, and Việt felt it was a good thing that he was distracted. Better for Kale to forget and for himself to remain quiet.

A couple minutes passed by. He felt Kale's eyes on him again.

"Stop staring at me," Việt said, feeling sour.

Kale was now beside him, a small bowl in hand. "I can't help it. This is adorable."

"What's adorable?" asked Tate, who had emerged from his room to grab a Celsius from the fridge.

Việt flung the end of a carrot at Kale, who dodged it immediately. "Nothing. Just teasing our friend here." And that seemed enough to make his boyfriend go away, disappearing back into the depths of their hallway.

"Thanks for not telling him," Việt grudgingly said.

"Don't thank me. He already suspects."

"What?!"

"He's my boyfriend. We talk. We love conspiracy theories. And gossip. He knows." He waved a hand. "But he's not going to tell anyone else. He doesn't have any other friends." Once again, Việt *had* to find new friends. "And I'm definitely not. I wouldn't do that to anyone. I just think it's cute. There's nothing wrong with liking Evie. She's amazing."

"Nothing wrong? She has a boyfriend." Việt's knife went down hard against the cutting board. He couldn't understand why his friend was being so casual about it all. And if he and Tate knew, did that mean he was *that* easy to read? How could they be sure that Lis—or worse, Evie—didn't know either?

"Yeah, she has a boyfriend, but I'm not sure how long that'll last." Kale shrugged. In a small bowl, he had mixed olive oil, black pepper, salt, and garlic powder, and was now plucking each carrot from the cutting board and plopping it into the mix. "Things seem rocky lately. And maybe you've already noticed it, but he's not around a lot."

"Aren't you friends with him, too?"

"I'm her friend first. And yeah, maybe I was his friend too. But he hasn't been a friend to me in ages. Not that I mind. Friend groups can change; that's just how life works." Việt could tell Kale had more to say about it but didn't push. He finished cutting the carrots, Kale moved the coated pieces to the air fryer. "Wasn't it hard hiding all your feelings?"

"I didn't even realize I had them until right this minute," Việt mumbled.

"You *just* realized now?!" Kale laughed. "Oh this is too funny. Poor you." As the carrot chips cooked, he busied himself with chucking the carrot rinds into the compost, while Việt munched on leftover carrots.

"And how about those other feelings?" his friend asked softly. "Everything good there?"

Ah. There it was.

Since his depressive episode, he wondered if the others had become more aware, more watchful. No one remarked on his brief absences from that time, but perhaps they were being polite about it. He wouldn't have minded if Evie said something. He knew the others wouldn't judge him.

The mental health center had been heavily advertised during orientation, but Việt didn't even think about it until after his talk with Evie. Solutions were not easy to see when he was lost in that mindset. He hadn't felt that bad since the phone call; rather, there were flickers of darkness—moments when he woke up and couldn't move his body; when he stared blankly at the wall as he showered; when the food he ate had no flavor; when he sat in class and the professor's voice droned on and on.

One day maybe he'd stop by the center, if only to figure out how to better manage the flickering.

"I'm feeling better now, after talking about it with Evie," Việt answered truthfully.

"I'm glad. You seem to keep a lot to yourself. If you ever want to talk more about it, know I can be there too. I've been to the mental health center and thought it was pretty good," Kale said with a nod. "Carrot chips are in!" he announced, pouring them into the air fryer basket.

In the living room Lis and Evie let out muted cheers. The latter, the very person they'd been talking about before, stood up and stretched, her shirt lifting up to reveal a sliver of skin.

"*Ahem.*"

Việt jumped, guilty. It took every ounce of self-restraint he had to not meet Kale's eyes because he was sure his friend was smirking.

All right. So he liked someone who was already taken. Great. Perfect. *You sure know how to pick 'em, Việt!!!*

He needed to acclimate himself with the poetic pain and joy that came alongside time spent with Evie, in a group or alone. Where was Bảo when he needed him? There had to be a more eloquent term besides *sweet torture*. It was exhausting not to watch her in his periphery. To remind himself that he should not stand next to Evie, when there were also people present. Now that he knew Kale was watching. *Look away for five to seven seconds, Việt. Good. Gooood. Ah damnit, I'm looking at her again.* It was tiring not to feel like he won a medal whenever he made her laugh. To refrain from liking her text messages first, whenever he did remember to respond to the Saturday Sins group. Because Kale might be watching.

He started sitting in the farthest seat from Evie—never across from her anymore, to prevent his tendency to stare. If there was a small space, and self-imposed distance was not an option, he used their friends as buffers. More than once, Kale refused to move.

"There's no harm in sitting close to her, Việt! Calm down," he hissed one time when Lis and Evie had disappeared into the bathroom.

Without discussing it with Evie, Việt reduced their thrice-a-week run to twice-a-week, claiming he was falling behind—which wasn't a complete lie. On their running days, however, he was excessively self-aware, and specifically preoccupied with his limbs: Was his chest out? Were his hands holding invisible potato chips? (The coach who taught him this was probably hungry.) He sucked in his stomach when his breathing got harder; Việt didn't want her to hear him sounding like an asthmatic horse. Not that Evie had any reason to notice him, because he was just her friend.

Really spectacular.

Evie: dinner and a movie tonight? want to see you!!

Jake: Sure, six? My place?

CHAPTER 16

EVIE

Lis and the rest of Saturday Sins refused to stop celebrating her acceptance into the clinic; it was almost embarrassing. So, she didn't *need* Jake's congratulations . . . but she wanted it. She wished for it. Yet, two days passed and he didn't reply to her last message about acing the interview. No phone call, a thumbs-up, a heart.

She couldn't sit with this unease, this uncertainty, a shred of which she felt right after getting her interview request. Had he been mad at her for getting an interview request? Jealous? Evie was the one who brought up the clinic to him because her advisor had mentioned it. His silence might make more sense if he had mentioned it first, applied, then got rejected. If that was the case and Evie was in his shoes, she'd feel jealous and slightly resentful.

She didn't think this was a reason for Jake to get jealous, though.

She'd never seen him jealous—especially of her—because they never fought for the same thing.

Whatever the problem was between her and her boyfriend, Evie couldn't just let it sit there, unaddressed.

Jake's roommate was out, but Evie saw the remnants of him around the apartment: his unwashed dishes, his water bottle, and his back-pack on the kitchen bar. On the other end of the bar was a laptop, which Jake returned to, once letting her in.

She wrinkled her nose at her boyfriend's sour, musty smell; he must have sat down right after coming back from the gym.

"I just need to finish this quickly. Pick a movie, any movie, and I'll be there!"

She quickly chose a detective series people were raving about online, and for the next fifteen minutes Evie passed the time by checking her own emails, and spotted the formal congratulatory email from the clinic selection committee, which brought a smile to her face. The official start date wouldn't be until the next year, but she was asked to schedule an introductory tour to walk through the basics. Contrary to her imagination, they weren't expected to wear white jackets but were offered maroon T-shirts. She ordered hers in medium.

Soon, realizing it was getting close to a half hour, Evie set down her cell. She got to her knees and leaned against the back of the couch. Her boyfriend was typing away on Word now, working on a different assignment entirely, focusing on that and nothing else.

"Want to do this another time?" she offered. Jake finally turned, blinking several times. If Evie was distracting him from an important assignment, she'd feel bad. Then again, why would he accept her dinner and movie invite?

"Ah no! I'm finished now." He hit "save," then closed the laptop. "Hold on, I stink! Can I shower first? Before we start the show?"

"You read my mind. Go on, I'll wait."

His shower took ten minutes, and he re-emerged in a white tee and gray sweats. He slid down the hall in his socks, launching himself at the couch like a kid, and Evie backed into the armrest, pretending to escape his outstretched arms. Dove soap and a minty aftershave reached her nose. This was the Jake she was most used to.

"Sorry to keep you waiting, babe." He brought her in for a tight hug, an arm around her shoulder, and after a millisecond of hesitation, she sank into his embrace.

"You seem busy today," she whispered. "What's going on?"

Ticking down on his fingers, Jake listed his workload and his latest duties as a board member's son. As she listened, like she always did, she chastised herself. He was busy; he couldn't help it.

"But forget all about that," Jake finally said. He leaned over and pressed play. "Let's just watch this. Heard people talking about it in class."

The blue-and-gray-toned first episode unfolded, following a traumatized detective who's pulled into a puzzling case that causes her haunted memories to resurface. Even as the moody soundtrack surrounded them, Evie couldn't quite get into it. Her own thoughts kept her at a distance. She realized Jake didn't even ask her about the interview, which he definitely knew about it. They texted about it.

Evie waited for him to ask her how she was doing, waiting for him to ask whether the interview had gone well.

"You're not gonna ask about how I did?" she ventured quietly.

"With . . . what?"

"The interview for the clinic."

"Oh shit—that totally didn't cross my mind!" On one hand, he was busy with other things. On the other hand, was he that busy that he couldn't even text her back or give her a call? "I mean, I'm assuming it went well." His tone pitched up to turn it into a question.

Evie sighed. "Yes, I got in, actually."

"Evie! I'm so proud of you."

She finally mustered the courage to ask him. "Jake . . . were you mad that I got the interview request?"

Jake froze. "You thought I was mad at you?" She nodded. "Ah, sorry. I guess I was pissed at myself, thinking I'd get in."

"I wish we could have done this together," she admitted. She had to tilt her head to see his face. She moved with his shrug. "I don't know what the clinic is thinking."

"Yeah, me too. That would have been great. But I guess the clinic wants to keep us apart. It's not like I need it on my resume." His comment was meant to be light, but was there also a hint of . . .

She was imagining it; he wasn't suggesting that *Evie* was the one who needed the clinic on her resume.

She mentally shook her head; no, he wouldn't think that. He knew she worked as hard as him, and he had wanted for the two of them to get through together. Just as she did.

Movie night ended without an issue; she and Jake felt close to normal again. The next day, Evie sent a text asking Jake if they could spend some time together, somewhere off campus. Just the two of them. Told him that she was heading to the FSC's qualifiers, but otherwise she'd be free.

His response: "Have fun! And sorry, I have a study group tonight. Maybe sometime this weekend?"

Fighting off her disappointment, she pocketed her phone. She was lagging behind the group as they crossed a lawn to the Forensic Science Center. She jogged to where Việt was trailing Lis and Kale. She secretly loved it when her roommate was like this: deliriously happy, waves of energy coming off her in a way that was almost contagious. Kale had caught some of it because he'd looped his arm through Lis's and squeezed her close.

"Are you nervous?" she asked Việt.

Another person who often disappeared on her over the last two weeks was Việt. He texted her whenever he couldn't make their morning runs. She wasn't offended by his absence. More pressing was the concern that he would retreat into himself—like last time.

Her concern was baseless. Unlike the other two, he was strolling with his hands in his pockets, the vision of calm and cool. Before she really got to know him outside of running—the even rhythm of his breathing, the assured stride of his ASICS, the satisfied smile he'd get as he lay down on the grass next to her during their post-run ritual—Evie initially thought it was because he felt he needed to be that way around them. In truth, he enjoyed listening.

Lis and Kale were obviously amusing him because a soft smile played on his lips.

"I don't think I'm allowed to be nervous," Việt answered. He gestured toward their friends. "I wouldn't want to ruin their fun anyway."

"To be honest, they're in their own bubble now. They could care less about us."

"Việt, *come on*. Evie, stop hogging our teammate!" Apparently not. Lis stood arms akimbo ahead of them. Kale gestured his arms like a marshaller directing a grounded plane.

Evie rolled her eyes. "Never mind." To her roommate, she said, "I can't help it! I haven't seen him in a while."

It was a joke. But not really.

"Sorry," Việt said, looking at his feet, avoiding her eyes. She wished she could read minds.

If only Lis's wanting to win so badly could guarantee that very win. But a few minutes after showing up at the lab, they realized something was off. The fourth team member, Kyle, who said he'd meet them there, was missing. Swearing under her breath, Lis dialed his number and once he picked up, she walked into the hallway, practically hissing through her cell's mouthpiece.

Like all the labs Evie had been in, the room was ten degrees colder than outside, and everyone glowed blue under the overhead lights. There were more people in attendance than she ever expected. She remembered the weak numbers from previous years, when she came out to support Lis.

It was unusually quiet, reminding her of the morning she'd taken her SATs, when she had random mathematical equations and vocabulary spinning dizzyingly in her mind. She somehow felt it in her stomach, too.

Everyone was taking this competition seriously. The other team all donned lab coats borrowed from the graduate program. Việt slipped his on and Evie hid a smile.

The vision of him being in a crime lab, someday in the future, felt just right.

"What?" he asked, noticing her immediately.

"Nothing. You just look like you belong here."

"Oh." Việt looked down, fixed a button that didn't need to be fixed. "Thanks."

Sure, he was usually self-possessed, but even he couldn't fight a blush.

Evie was about to channel Lis and tease him a bit more, when her roommate came back, nearly slamming the door shut. Kale followed close behind, having gone to check on her. She fast-walked over, gestured for them to lean in, and said, "Apparently, Kyle's sick. He can't make it."

Multiple groans erupted.

Kale cursed. "What a traitor. I knew we couldn't trust him."

Việt's head swiveled. "Wait, what do you mean? He's sick—how is he being a traitor?"

"He's friends with my ex," Lis said. "Or at least friendly with him."

Ex was perhaps in exaggeration; they had only dated for a few months, before Lis dumped him. Kale nodded. "And I bet you a five-course meal that he dropped out so the ex's team would automatically win."

Across the room, in his own circle, the ex lifted his head and shot them a smug smirk that made Evie wish she had something heavy to throw. She saw why Lis might have liked him in the first place; on the outside, his style was classic academia, but she bet he was just some spoiled kid who went abroad to some fancy boarding school. She imagined he had everything handed to him—and if not, he had the means to eventually get what he wanted.

At the front of the room, under a poster that said UNCOVER THE TRUTH, a graduate student clapped her hands. She had paired a lilac headscarf with a white long-sleeve shirt and beige pleated pants and held the room's attention better than some professors. A glittery blush on her cheeks made her dark brown skin shimmer. She introduced herself as Ilyasah. "Okay, we're about five minutes away from starting. Pick a spot—each seat has a test and a pencil. You'll have an hour to fill in fifty multiple-choice questions. After that, we'll move on to the staged crime scene, which is in the room next door."

"Excuse me, but I think the other team is short one player," shouted Lis's ex. Of course his voice was also unbearable.

"Jerk," Lis whispered.

The grad student frowned. "If you don't have four players total, then I'm sorry, but you'll have to forfeit your participation. Those are our rules."

Kale stepped forward. "Wait, but it's not *our fault*. It's—"

Lis touched his shoulder, saying quietly, "Save it. It's not worth the explanation. She's right. We don't have enough players. They win this time." Her tone had never been this monotone. Evie didn't like seeing her this way, like some villain had zapped away all her energy. She made a note to buy her roommate all the snacks she wanted after this.

Then the grad student narrowed her eyes in concentration, having noticed Evie standing a few steps away from the group. "Wait, there *are* four people." She stared at Evie. "Aren't you going to participate?"

Of course. Why didn't Evie think of that?

Her roommate sighed. "No, she's just—"

"Oh yes. I'm sorry. I wasn't paying attention just now. I'm the last member." Evie stepped forward and set down her backpack. She ignored a trio of bewildered looks as she grabbed a lab coat.

The judge, whether she knew the truth or not, only smiled, gesturing for them to take a seat. Lis's ex looked at them like an aristocrat regarding a commoner. Meanwhile, his team members seemed to care less . . . which suggested a few things about the group dynamics.

"Evie, what are you doing?" Lis whispered.

"Look, if you lose now, just because you're short a member, that's going to suck. But if there's a chance I can sub in and somehow help you, I'm willing to do it. Then if by some miracle we get through, all you have to do is find someone to replace me."

Lis hugged Evie. "I don't care if we don't make it through. I just hated the thought of forfeiting right away—and now we won't have to!"

Ilyasah, the judge, spouted the rules printed at the top of the test. The scores would be averaged after, meaning if one person bombed it, you basically lowered your team's chances of moving forward. Evie tapped her pencil against the table. One-two. One-two. What if she wasn't as confident as she was five minutes ago? What if she ruined this for Lis and everyone?

She glanced over to her right at Lis, who seemed to sense her hesitation. "Evie, you know this shit; you helped me out so many times over the years. But even if you *do* score low, somehow, it doesn't matter. After this, I'm going to shove as much ice cream as you want down your throat."

"That's a bit violent," murmured Việt who sat behind the two of them.

"No, that's love," Lis retorted. Shooting Evie a smile: "I really owe you one."

Hope sprung within her. She would try her best. For her friends.

"You got this." She turned around as Ilyasah counted down from ten, and saw Việt's encouraging smile.

Evie concentrated on the cool paper under her palms just as Ilyasah told them to begin.

CHAPTER 17

VIỆT

Jittery legs, heavy sighs, mumbled swears.

Việt didn't sense any of the test-taker-suffering signs coming from Evie, who barely let her pencil rest. Maybe she absorbed things through the benefit of being roommates with someone whose quirk was thinking out loud.

Ilyasah, at the front of the room, cleared her throat, and Việt saw her gaze on him. He ducked his head, focusing back on the questions, thinking that they'd gotten this far. They couldn't let the ex win.

At the sound of Ilyasah's voice telling them to stop, all the pencils dropped. Club members groaned to let loose their tight shoulders. The grad students—four including Ilyasah—went around to collect the tests, telling everyone to go outside—"Touch grass or something," Ilyasah said—and come back in fifteen. The crime scene would be staged by then.

The moment the group spilled into the hallway, Lis back-hugged Evie, like a young koala to her indulgent mother. "What kind of ice cream do you want? Mint? Chocolate chip? Plain vanilla?"

Evie shrugged her away with a laugh. "Really, it's no big deal! I just hope I'm not going to make it harder for you guys."

Alex's group stuck to the other end of the hallway, but a pair broke off—Sally, a girl with thick curly hair and red glasses, and Nishant, a boy with shoulders as wide as a swimmer's. They each carried snacks and slowed when they got closer to their group.

"We know what happened. With Kyle," said Sally.

"But we didn't hear about it until five minutes before you showed up," Nishant said earnestly. "Alex didn't tell us what he was planning, we swear."

"Thanks," Lis replied after a beat. But she still had her arms crossed.

"Back when we were freshmen, the group was so small that the members *had* to go and rep the school. That's how I ended up in the competition, but I think it's time for other people to have a chance."

"Not sure why Alex doesn't see that," Nishant said. He held out a bag of Starburst. "Want any?"

It seemed like a peace treaty, and Lis ended up accepting it.

They were called back in.

In the next room, larger than the one before, the grad students had moved the tables against the wall, opening up space in the middle. The crime scenes were bisected by a black curtain; Alex's group went one way, theirs, the other.

The scene recap was given to them.

On Saturday morning, December 8th, a trio of UC Davis alumni visited the Forensic Science Graduate Program to do mock interviews with six promising graduates nearing the end of their schooling. One worked at the Oakland Police Department, one at the San Francisco Police Department, and the other was an adjunct lecturer at UC Davis's Forensic Program.

The interviewees were the adjunct lecturer's students. The interviews would take place in the building's largest classroom, at one long table. They received two interviewees each and were expected to start at 10 a.m., and end at 1:30 p.m., with a lunch break between noon to 12:30 p.m.

After the panel, two witnesses spotted the Oakland alumnus, the adjunct lecturer, and the U of SF alumnus arguing in the hallway, but thought nothing of it and walked away.

At 3:15 p.m. the adjunct lecturer stepped back into the room, then screamed after making a gruesome discovery: The U of SF alumnus was found dead, sitting in the spot where he conducted his interview, head on the table. His lunch was abandoned in front of him, a peeled clementine lodged in his throat.

When the police arrived, they noted the items found at the crime scene and everyone who had been in the room around the time of discovery. However, they would need forensics to figure out what had happened to the U of SF alumnus, whether his death was accidental or suspicious, and if any of the students and two other alumni had anything to do with his death.

The group of suspects included the alumni and the six students who came in for their interviews, and all but two remained in the building around the time of the lecturer's death. The adjunct lecturer, after the argument, said he'd walked to the cafeteria to get lunch, then came back to discover the body. The other student had forgotten to take his allergy medicine, so he ran back to his dorm for it, but in the time he was gone, the lecturer died.

Everyone else remained in the building, but all claimed that they had no contact with the lecturer during lunch.

The group was given the suspects' bios, from their physical descriptions to friends' testimonials about their daily habits and personality, to their psychology and motivation as students of the forensic science program.

The crime scene was localized to the seat where the victim was found. There was an open can of Coke, a half-eaten tuna sandwich, and the clementine peel. But the evidence that was bagged included note cards in place of the physical items—hair strands, fingerprints, and such.

They would need to consider all of this in order to find the culprit. Việt exhaled loudly; there was a moment of silence as they finished their reading and looked at each other—uncertain and overwhelmed by the information.

And yet Lis stepped forward; Việt noticed that during the time everyone was reading the bios and the scenario, she had scribbled notes. She became a different person, so serious, so intense—not the same person who would goof around with Kale and Tate.

Lis said, "Okay. Theories?"

And that was when Việt knew that they would be okay.

About an hour later, their group spilled out from the building, fresh air replacing the sterile scent of the lab. Việt took in the cool fall air like this would be his last time outside, but really, he was savoring the feel of it. Was the air different? Something just felt *different*. New, almost.

Lis and Kale walked ahead of him again, but now they had Evie trapped between them. The two chanted "One of us, one of us!" They passed a pair of students who eyed them as if they had completely lost it.

Miraculously, and in ways that Việt wouldn't dare to question, their group had won the mock competition, ensuring their spot to represent UC Davis at the Northeastern competition next year. When their results were announced—fifty points more than Alex's team—no one moved. No one could believe it. Then the grad students were clapping, and soon enough, Kelly and Nishant from Alex's group joined in, and suddenly Lis had tugged the team into a group hug. Kale lasted five seconds before threatening Lis to release him: "You're suffocating me!"

Việt had won team sports before. He was a runner, and he always loved it when the final teammate crossed the finish line and a mass of limbs dashed forward to surround that runner, and they'd cheer and laugh and think, *Finally!* Knowing that every excruciating practice had all been worth it.

He felt that now, but it was somehow so much better than winning a sports competition.

There were two culprits, they discovered. The adjunct lecturer and Suspect #3, though the latter was more directly linked to the crime.

The key was the clementine, which supposedly the victim had choked on. But a clementine must be peeled, yet the victim's fingers were entirely clean. This only meant that someone else had peeled the clementine, and made it look like the victim had eaten it.

The motive came down to jealousy and desperation. The adjunct lecturer envied his former classmate's storied career at the Oakland Police Department while the student had a history of wanting to outsmart authority, including the lecturer, who had initiated their plan. He thought he could get away with it; nothing visible on him could connect him to the crime. He even washed his hands. But after examining each suspect's clothing, traces of pith—the white tissue found on citrus fruits—still clung to his clothing fibers, linking him to the crime scene.

Apparently, the grad students told them, the culprit had confessed. After all, he hated all authority figures, even the one who recruited him in the first place.

Việt was the one who connected the dots. He remembered how his mother loved citrus fruits while his father was sick of them. One time, after peeling an orange, she told his dad to open his mouth and he did, without looking, thinking she just wanted him to taste something. The moment his mother fed him the white string, his father spat and whined about how disgusting and đắng it tasted.

"You really know this stuff, huh?" said Evie, who slowed down to walk beside Việt. She gave him a look, and he felt that she probably finally understood why he liked all of this. Solving something that was right in front of him. "You were brilliant."

"Me? What about you? You basically aced the test for us." She managed to score higher than Việt, and just a few points below Kale and Lis; impressive, considering she'd only been on the peripheral of forensics—at least, not as obsessed as Việt and the others.

"Looks like all that time Lis talked my ear off when we shared a room paid off," Evie said. Which Lis heard, then jokingly pushed her away by the shoulder.

The group quieted for a few beats, taking in the relative silence of the campus as people were out to dinner.

Việt spotted Evie frowning at her phone. He'd noticed that she'd done the same thing on their walk to the qualifiers. "You okay?"

"Of course, I'm fine." A smile quickly appeared. Việt knew better but he didn't want to pressure her.

Kale announced that there was a party at her friends' place at the La Casa de Flores apartments. "Let's celebrate! We deserve it!"

Evie's steps had slowed as she glanced down at her phone again.

"A party sounds like a good idea," Lis said. "After all, we should do something to celebrate Evie!"

She looked up quickly as Lis's and Kale's voices jumbled together in agreement. A small smile appeared on her face, and it was aimed right at him.

Việt's stomach turned.

Friend. He was just her friend.

CHAPTER 18

EVIE

The large sign with neon-green letters announced the La Casa apartments. One apartment glowed blue, and the windowpanes vibrated along with the car-crash noise of a dubstep song. The parking lot was packed, the nearby bike rack full. Someone had stuffed paper bags into the trash can, which were probably used to carry Trader Joe's alcohol from a half a loop away. The air had the right fall crispness that Evie loved.

Unsurprisingly, Kale's presence received applause and screams, and he led them all in. Evie recognized and was friendly with the hosts, but no one could compete with Kale's popularity. Beside her, Tate, who met up with them, glared at someone pushing against him. "An hour tops and I'm leaving. Even if it means leaving that guy here."

Evie knew he was not too fond of crowded parties and deafening music; he preferred smaller venues and mostly liked throwing them with Kale at their apartment. His safety zone. "It's okay if you disappear. Kale will be taken care of. If not by me or Lis, then someone here I'm sure."

Tate smiled back at her. "Thanks. I'll probably hang with Việt and—" Lis was also gone, having been absorbed by another group. "Never mind, just Việt. Poor guy."

"Why do you say that?"

"I don't think he wants to hang out with *me*."

Evie frowned. "He likes you!"

"Well, I just think he'd much rather be around—"

Crisp white button-down and relaxed jeans. It wasn't an uncommon outfit, Evie convinced herself, when she spotted a Jake lookalike toward the center of the room.

Except, it *was* Jake.

He was coming back from the beverage table, Solo cup in hand, but stopped at the sight of her. Then he blinked and smiled. "Hey." His arms wound around her waist. She smelled his cologne first, then the alcohol on his breath. He must have been here for a while before they arrived.

"I thought . . . I thought you had study plans."

"It started out that way," he smoothly explained, "but then we got the text about this party. Sorry, babe." He dipped his head to kiss her, then offered her his Solo cup, filled with some brownish-green drink. His drinking philosophy was to go all the way, but Evie went more slowly—or else the night would end, quick.

Lis and Kale met up with them, Việt trailing behind. She quietly thanked Kale for the White Claw he slipped into her hand. Then Tate stepped up to make a tight circle. Jake received one-armed hugs from everyone, but stopped at Việt, pointing, then snapping his fingers: "Band-Aid Guy!"

"Jake, you met him at the picnic, too."

"Just kidding. I remember. Nice seeing you again, man." Việt nodded back. There was an awkward pause. Her fingers clenched around her can, and Jake's touch fell away as she shifted.

"Band-Aid Guy—what kind of nickname is that?" Lis protested. "We should come up with new ones!"

"Please, no," Việt remarked. His expression was already so tortured; it was adorable.

"VroomVroomVroom Việt," Kale said. The group groaned. "What? Because he runs!"

"You probably had that tucked away for a while. Keep it there," Lis mumbled.

"Valiant Việt. Or Victor Việt," Evie offered, hoping that would end the conversation. "For cinching the win today." She turned to Jake. "Lis and the Forensic Science Club are going to represent the school at the spring Northeastern forensics competition."

"Congrats. I didn't think it was a *thing*."

Evie didn't need to look over to see the hurt on her roommate's face. "Hey, Jake—"

"We've never won before," Lis cut in. The tips of her fingers were as red as her Solo cup. "It was always seniors who went to rep

Davis. Now it's us—third-years and a first-year. It hasn't happened since the club started up."

"Cheers," Jake said, grandiosely tapping his Solo cup against Lis's cup.

"We've been studying hard for it," Lis continued, her voice much weaker.

Evie felt the sensation of being stuck in the snow as she watched an avalanche begin.

"You worked so hard for it!" she said. "I'm so happy for us." She squeezed her friend's arm.

"We should give *you* a nickname, Evie. Especially since we made it through the first round because you stepped up," Việt said.

Her boyfriend was confused. "Evie played?"

"Yes, and she *played* well." Lis looped her arm through Evie's, squeezing it in either support or excitement from the win. "We had a member drop out last minute, and she totally stepped up."

"You didn't deserve to forfeit all because of Alex. I couldn't let you lose." That was all true.

"I didn't know you liked all that forensics stuff," Jake said.

She thought she saw Lis flinch at "stuff." "Absorbed it from Lis, I guess."

A moment later, the group was pulled apart. Lis wanted to dance; Jake was pulled into a beer pong game. The separation relieved Evie from that awful, impending doom from their conversation. Jake likely didn't know the effect of his words, but she couldn't stand seeing her roommate wilting as Jake all but dismissed the club as unimportant.

There was also the matter that he'd come to the same party as her. Of course he didn't have to report his every action to her—she didn't tell him about the party either—but earlier today, she'd suggested spending time together, and he turned her down. Shock was apparent on his face when he saw her there. Like someone caught in a lie.

What else had he lied to her about?

As the night wore on, she begged Lis to let her go sit for a bit. Her roommate found other friends and drunkenly clung to them. Only one person sat by the couches, and that was Việt clutching his own Solo cup. He didn't look lonely, but he was alone. She felt a twinge in her heart. Since he was part of their friend group, it was easy to forget that he was younger and likely knew no one at this party.

While she was not as extroverted as Lis or Kale, she always lingered somewhere close to the center. It was hot, disorienting, and she was never more aware of her body. As she walked toward Việt, the outskirts felt more freeing, cooler . . . calmer, even, like anyone could pass through her and she wouldn't mind it.

Their eyes now locked, Việt said, "You don't have to check in with me, you know."

"Why do you think I was checking in?"

"The look in your eyes. Determination."

Evie sank down next to Việt. "I just need to rest. Been dancing all night."

"Seems like you were MIA before today. Any reason?" she asked.

"No reason," he answered quietly into his cup.

"Have you been . . . feeling down?"

He laughed. It was unexpected and strange, and Evie felt as if she just missed some crucial information. "Sort of, but not in the way you think. Not like before." He shook his thought, deciding to ignore whatever was floating in his mind. "But it's all good. I'm here now."

"I just hope you can have a good time."

"I am having fun. I'm here, with you." There was a teasing note in Việt's response. He took a sip of his drink, eyes still pinned to her. She spotted the slight curve of his lips—a smile. His time with Kale and Lis might have brought out this side of him. Only when he spilled some of his drink did he break character.

As Evie laughed, Việt grabbed a tissue from a tissue box and dabbed his wet chin. "I always manage to embarrass myself in front of you. Like the first time I tripped and fell—"

"I thought you were somersaulting?"

"Yes, of course. And then when you found me by the cows. You already saw me cry. And now this."

"I'm happy I can see all these different sides of you." She meant it.

They didn't stay alone for long; Evie felt the change in the air on her left side when Jake joined them. Now she sat sandwiched between the two boys.

"What's going on here?" Jake lackadaisically slung his arm

around her shoulder and nudged Việt with his hand. "Girl talk?" His eyes were hooded, and his words were beginning to slur.

Evie shrugged off his arm as casually as possible; it was too heavy. "I just needed a break and was catching up with Việt."

Her boyfriend looked past her and right at Việt. Several long seconds went by before he mumbled a few words, almost to himself. Evie heard "like a lost puppy."

"Jake," Evie said sharply.

"Oh, sorry." He only rolled his eyes. How much did he have to drink? His arm went around her shoulder again, squeezing her closer to him. Evie felt Việt shifting away. "When's the clinic thing starting?"

"After the break," she answered warily. She wondered if his roommate was here, if he could take Jake back to his apartment in one piece.

He was almost pouting. "You'll probably be busy."

"So? I'll still see you."

"I don't like that the program's gonna take you away from me," he continued, head drooping toward the crook of Evie's neck. "Everyone thinks it's great, but it's just a stupid volunteer thing. There are other clinics out there that are better, and you don't even need to apply or interview or any of that shit."

Ouch.

"Wow, Jake." She inhaled. "I don't even know where to begin with that."

Việt intercepted, "Maybe you should get him some water. I'll watch him for now."

Tears building in her eyes, she almost pushed Jake completely over, but she held back and leaned him against Việt who accepted his weight. On her way to get water, she crossed paths with her roommate again, who nodded toward the couches.

"Jake and Việt seem to have gotten close."

In that moment, she recalled Jake's comment to her and the ones he'd made before. Evie hadn't done much to defend Lis. "Jake—he's . . . he's just drunker than usual. That's why he said the things he said before. He really needs to sober up."

Lis laughed weakly. "Not going to lie, I was feeling a bit offended, and you know that's hard to do."

"I know. That was awful." Evie hugged herself. What he said about the clinic was also hurtful. "I don't know what to do with him."

In this corner, she had a good view of the mass of people crowded in the apartment: snapbacks, high ponytails, casual to glam. Kale waved from the center, tilting his head in a silent *You okay?* to which the girls waved back.

"Lately you don't look happy when you're with him, Evie. I can tell." Her roommate paused, considering her next words. "And I know Jake's probably not a bad guy, but he has a lot of insecurities, and he would rather put other people down instead of dealing with his own problems."

Lis was right. Evie would rather not verbally confirm that her words were true, so she merely nodded. She refocused her attention on Jake, just in time to see Việt leaning her boyfriend back on the couch, letting his head tip up. Jake was seemingly asleep now. "Let me grab him some water."

Minutes later, she was back at the couches. "Thanks for looking after him, Việt."

"We had a good girl talk," he deadpanned. She shook with laughter as she brought the cup of water to Jake's lips. He lazily gulped it down.

"I'm fine," he protested then, swatting away her hand.

"Now that everything's under control, I think I'm gonna head out too," Việt said.

Evie felt a pang of disappointment. "Oh. Okay."

She didn't understand her feet were following him until she caught a glimpse of him as he silently slipped through the front door.

She quickened her steps, setting her cup down on a window ledge as she passed. Việt was halfway down the steps when he turned at the sound of his name.

"Yes?" he asked with an undercurrent of amusement.

"Sorry . . . about before."

Việt walked back up a few steps so that her view of him was not as steep. "Why are *you* apologizing?"

"Because he dismissed the competition and sounded like an asshole."

"But what about you? What he said about the clinic, that seemed to hurt you too." Việt shrugged. It looked casual, but she wasn't convinced. "You shouldn't be apologizing. If anything, he should apologize to you."

"I think Jake's just insecure. He applied to be in the program, but he didn't make it through, and he might have felt as if he failed. His parents put a lot of pressure on him to be perfect, and this may have hurt him more than he wants to admit."

"Sure, that's a reason, but why does that have anything to do with undermining what you went through? You got in, but he doesn't seem very happy." He paused. "Don't you want him to be happy for you?

Evie sat down on the top step, Việt next to her. She hugged her knees to her chest. "I do. I want him to share in my happiness. I've tried to say this, but I haven't found a way. And even if I talk to him about it, I don't think he'll . . . understand where I'm coming from. Then our conversation's always over before I realize it, and the moment's passed."

"Sorry," Việt said suddenly, his words rushed. "I don't know him too well, so maybe I'm being overly critical. I just saw your face change when he bashed the clinic. That was hard to miss." It surprised her that he was watching so closely, but she also recoiled from an invisible sting of humiliation—that her boyfriend said such inebriated, callous words, which she couldn't even respond to because she was so taken aback. There was no defending Jake because he made a similar remark when he was sober.

They shared the same view of the lawn. Groups of friends wandered afar, heading to and from other campus parties. Public safety was curiously out of sight.

She let her feet fall to the next step and sat taller. "You're not leaving because of Jake, are you?"

"No, honestly. Being in crowds . . . it drains me."

Evie nodded, understanding. He was like Tate—fully present, until his social battery ran low, and then he'd retreat. Their friend would probably sneak away soon.

"Do you want some company on the walk back?"

She didn't know why she said that. It wasn't like—

"Are you asking just because . . . or are you offering to come along? Because if it's the latter . . ."

She was almost swayed to go home. If she left now, she could be back in her apartment, in a ratty tee and soft pajama pants, face mask on, or drifting off to sleep with lo-fi music blanketing her body. . . . She wasn't missing the party's suffocating room, the grating loud music that shook the windows.

She embraced the comfortable silence between them on their way back, the kind that always snuck in whenever they cooled off after a tough run. No words were needed. It was enough to know he was breathing next to her.

A longing surged through her body, and its force nearly knocked her over.

Lis was still at the party, along with Kale and Tate. And Evie's boyfriend, who was likely still asleep on the couch. She needed to make sure that someone watched out for him.

"Việt . . ." Evie paused. *What was this feeling?*

"It's okay," Việt said softly. "Go back to the party, Evie. Jake's gonna probably wake up and wonder where you are." He stood first, then offered her a hand. "And hopefully he'll realize he was wrong for saying all those things before."

Maybe it was the drinks she had, but she felt that if she got up by herself, her legs wouldn't hold her up. So she allowed herself to be pulled to standing. Her hand lingered in his; she couldn't be the only one who noticed it. He let go first. "I'll see you tomorrow or some other day."

Back inside, Evie paused before her friend's apartment door, her hand on the knob. It was shaking.

When Việt asked if she'd come with him, then trailed off, she was glad that they left it at that. She wouldn't be comfortable giving him her honest answer.

Neither would Jake.

CHAPTER 19

VIỆT

He liked to think he wasn't imagining things. Adding significance to an otherwise normal thing. But when he asked Evie if she wanted to leave the party together, he was certain her eyes showed some hesitation. Certain her body wavered in his direction as he helped her up from the steps. Certain that she had whispered his name, and it sounded like wonder.

She had thought about it. Thought about his words. Sure, her reason probably had little to do with Việt and more to do with the tiring rush of today's events, and the deadweight of her boyfriend's careless words.

Still, she never said no.

If she had said a straight no, then Việt wouldn't be picturing their walk across campus, to feel the heat of her hand, so close yet still out of reach.

Earlier at the party, the discomfort from the picnic returned, in full force, when he spotted Jake approaching Evie. It happened in slow motion—the guy's cheeky smile, Evie's small jump when his arms circled her waist. Stayed around her.

Just let go already, he'd wanted to say.

But of course her boyfriend would find it hard to let her go. Evie was glowing tonight. Crop top and jeans, Converse, nothing fancy. Just her. While they all got ready at their respective places, she'd put on makeup and curled her hair a little, and the corners of her eyes were dabbed with glitter, accentuating the happy twinkle in her gaze. Likely because she finally met up with her boyfriend. Good thing it was dim because if Việt was able to see all of her, he'd be staring the whole night.

Then Jake had to say something completely unnecessary. Việt's immediate confusion allowed him to skip over being angry; he thought he misheard Jake, thought the other guy was joking in his own asshole-y way. Việt couldn't remember all his emotions; he just wanted to exit the conversation completely.

But what hurt him, what killed him, was seeing Jake's arm around Evie, yet again, when they sat at the couches. Bursting Việt and Evie's bubble.

"Hey, wait up." Tate jogged up to him outside. "I'm heading back. You too?"

Việt nodded. "Kale coming?"

"No, he wanted to catch up with some friends. But if I stayed and drank more, I'd probably not make it back to The Green. Cool if I join?"

Wordlessly they started walking south toward EC Garden. Tate was much calmer than his boyfriend; he was probably even quieter than Việt. But his silence wasn't a wall; it was an invitation.

"I felt like I was suffocating in there," Việt admitted.

"Even after three years, I still can't get used to parties. Not my thing back in high school either. I never go alone—only if Kale or Lis or Evie are going." Tate looked at him in the dark. "I could tell you felt the same."

"Yeah?"

"You were tucked away in a corner." Tate shrugged. "I was tucked away in the other. Meanwhile, Kale—"

"Was at the center." Việt grinned. Kale had no problem mingling with other people; it was always impressive to watch.

The older boy nodded. "It might shock you, but Kale's not a natural extrovert; he says he needs three to five business days to recover after any social event," Tate said affectionately. "But he tells me he never wants anyone to feel lonely, and that's why he goes out of his way to meet people. That's why he never closes our apartment door when we're there. He might act like he hates company, but really, he's the one who encourages it."

They were two opposing energies, but when they were together, they canceled each other out.

"He's cool. I don't think—" Việt said, unsure of how honest he should be right now. If he could stop himself from voicing everything on his mind. "I wouldn't enjoy life here as much if it weren't for him—and the whole Saturday Sins group."

"Well, we're glad to have you." Tate peered over at him. "Look, what Jake said back there—"

"All good. He's drunk," Việt said.

"Doesn't excuse shitty behavior. I don't know why Evie's still with him. I think you feel the same."

Việt was struck by the boy's observation; like Kale, he knew more about Việt than he let himself reveal. Even his feelings about Evie.

"I know I'm not supposed to like her."

Tate scoffed. "'Supposed to.' As if our sentiments could be controlled and put under lock and key.

"Unrequited feelings suck. It's happened to me a few times in middle school and high school. It's bad because you're inside your head too much of the time."

"What do you mean?" Việt said.

"I had a crush on a girl for the longest time—my very first girl crush when all my others were for boys. We were good friends since elementary school, so it made sense that I'd feel more for her. But then she got a boyfriend.

"I liked her so much that I started building up an imaginary idea of her. Eventually we got together, after her breakup, but I'd spent so much time feeling jealous of her ex, of imagining what it'd *be* like with her, that the real thing was almost a letdown. Is that the right word? Not sure, but something like that. I'd forgotten the most important thing—my friend, who she is, how she made me feel." Tate shrugged. "It sucked. The relationship didn't last long. And I think our friendship pretty much died after that."

"You're saying I shouldn't like Evie, then."

"No."

Việt tried again. "That I shouldn't think about Evie and Jake so much?"

"Oh god. I'm tipsier than I thought!" As if on cue, Tate veered a bit to the side, then righted himself. "I guess I'm saying, just be there for Evie now, as a friend. Be what she needs—even if she doesn't voice it. Be *with* her. Present. Maybe your feelings will go away, and that's fine. But if they're still there—and there's nothing wrong with that because how can you *not* feel something like that. . . . Now, what was I saying?" Tate stopped and looked ahead at the darkened path. They were a few feet away from the Garden, which Việt realized was the midway point between The Green and his dorm. This was where they'd split apart, and he bet this was the last time they'd have this type of conversation.

"I basically told her Jake shouldn't treat her that way," he blurted out. He tried to recall the exact words, but it was like even his mind agreed that he shouldn't remember how he completely embarrassed himself in front of Evie.

"You . . . what?"

"I don't know—it just came out." Việt tipped back his head to stare at the sky. The stars were hiding. "Oh shit, that was bad, wasn't it?"

Tate burst out laughing; it started low, and then it got higher, and breathier. Việt had never seen his friend laugh like that, but maybe the others, especially Kale, had.

"Kale said I'm not supposed to say this because it might embarrass you too much, but we're all *really* glad you're in our group now. You're the missing piece."

Suddenly Tate stopped and tilted his head. From afar, someone yelled out, "Hellooooo!"

"Speak of the devil," the boy muttered.

Kale jogged toward them. "Didn't you hear me call out before?"

"What are you doing here?" Traces of laughter laced Tate's voice. "Thought you didn't want to leave yet."

"I missed you." He was either in love or drunk, and honestly, was there a substantial difference? Kale stopped and bent over to catch his breath. "Oh god. I can't do this. I'm not made to run."

"Tough." Tate shot Việt a mischievous look. "We were about to go on a night run, one-way, from here to the Aquatic Center. We got a lot of energy to spare."

Việt caught on. "Yeah, want to run with us?"

Kale eyed the two of them. "I'm not running. I *hate* running."

"Just think of the meal you'll have when we get back home," Tate said.

"That's not going to help."

"Shin ramen. Piping hot, savory broth."

"Ugh."

"With melted cheese on top. I'll even add a soft-boiled egg."

"Stop seducing me! Also, you don't know how to make soft-boiled anything! I'll do it myself." Kale started jogging without further questions, and soon enough, the three of them were heading down Orchard Park Drive, past wired fences, parked Ford trucks and white vans belonging to university employees, green pastures, more lawns, the normally beige upkeep buildings lighting up, one by one, by motion-sensor lights. Three students, dressed in . . . not exercise clothes . . . running in the dead of night.

Việt never predicted he'd be in this situation—not only running without a care across campus but talking openly about the growing feelings he had for their mutual friend.

His mom called at three a.m. Việt had only been asleep for three hours. His legs burned as he hopped down from his bed. Kale had collapsed halfway, demanding a piggyback ride, which—of course—Tate gave him, and they went their separate ways at the end of Orchard.

Việt pawed at his nightstand in the dark, swearing when the ringing stopped. From his bed, Wren murmured something, and Việt threw out a quiet apology that went unheard. He found his phone, and fumbled with it, thinking he left an old alarm on. He saw text messages from Kale and Tate, then Evie and Lis—all got home okay.

Fear spiked inside him at the caller ID.

He couldn't imagine any good news if his mom was calling at this hour. He left the room barefoot and answered in a hurried whisper when his mother picked up.

"Hi, con." He didn't hear any panic in her voice.

"Hi, Mẹ. It's three. What's happening? Is everything all right?"

"Con đang ở đâu? Ở trong dorm hay ở ngoài?"

Việt pointed out the time again.

"Ah yes."

"What's going on?"

"Mẹ called to hear con's voice."

The silence was long. His mom was still there, breathing. It felt heavy. She and his dad must have had an argument.

"Mẹ?" Việt prodded her. "It's late."

"Yes, Mẹ biết rồi. Can con come home a little early? Ba can drive you tomorrow."

He planned on going home the day after tomorrow, but he supposed he could go a day earlier. "Yeah, I can. Is there something wro—"

"Good. Mẹ will see con."

She hung up. The hallway's lights were still blindingly bright at this hour. Việt remained frozen in the hallway and stared at his phone.

What he was feeling wasn't fear, but it was in the same family.

CHAPTER 20

EVIE

The clinic was in a former accounting firm, which explained the gray filing cabinets, various ergonomic chairs, and outdated computers. Other furniture was brought in by student volunteers throughout the year: a hodgepodge of white plastic stacking chairs, folding tables, floor lamps, and a water cooler that was all dried up. Alessandra, the clinic coordinator, tried to cover up the latter during her walkthrough with Evie, reassuring her that it'd be replaced once the new semester started. She added that their medical equipment was only two years old, so there was no need to worry.

Evie waved away the older woman's explanation; the clinic was student-run, which meant there'd be little money coming in, and some clutter was to be expected. Plus, given her own parents' hoarding habits and the disorganization at their restaurant back home, she was used to dealing with a mess.

As the coordinator gathered up her purse at the end of the tour, Evie stood in the middle of the room and ran through what Alessandra had told her. Clinic hours opened at seven thirty on Saturday mornings. This place should be packed with patients, undergrad volunteers, med students, and medical supervisors from Davis and SacState. The elderly patients would already be there before the volunteers and wait in red seats to be called in. They might browse pamphlets about various medical issues in different languages—Korean, Chinese, Vietnamese. They would get their consultations from a team of med students and undergrads who'd often speak the patient's language. In between consultations, patient advocates like Evie would take vitals and assist with lab work, and outside the clinic would be expected to join committees centered on specific topics like women's health, diabetes, neurology, and more.

Her body tingled as she imagined the future. When she first thought of applying, it was because her advisor told her she should; it was expected. When she heard Jake would do the same, she thought it would be a good way for the two of them to spend more time together. But Evie forgot the most important thing: herself. This was her chance to help better someone's life, one patient at a time.

Alessandra returned with her purse. "Did I scare you away with my tour?"

"No, I'm both excited and nervous for the new year," Evie said, walking with her to the door. "Is it . . . weird for me to say that I didn't really understand what the clinic meant until today?"

"No, I get it. It's a new experience." Alessandra stepped out after Evie, then turned and locked the door. "Think of the ocean. You don't know how cold the ocean is until you dip your feet into the water. It's a slight shock . . . but doesn't it feel good?"

"True," Evie replied. She liked that analogy. "I really can't wait."

"I'm not supposed to say this, but so many people applied for this program," she said. "Only a select few got the interview request. We had people with fantastic grades, great recommendations, and some impressive volunteer and job experience. But it's the interview that really narrows down the pool. It's easy to be impressed by something on a piece of paper, but more impressive if that person shows up and blows us away.

"I still remember your answer to the question, 'What was the moment that made you pick this life path?' Your answer about your sister, about the boo-boo—yes, don't be embarrassed—showed us who you were. Are. Who you will be to the people you'll help in the near future."

"Thanks," Evie said, her voice dry.

"Continue being yourself, Evie. Humble. Trust me: there are some kids out there who need to be reminded of that." She laughed suddenly as a memory came to her. "I shouldn't say this, but there was this one kid whose application was textbook-perfect, if bland. Even before we decided on the interviewees, I got an email from a colleague who got *another* email from the kid bragging that his father was an important member of the Aggie community. That was a major turnoff. Legacy doesn't matter at the clinic. It shouldn't."

Evie struggled to keep her expression straight. Her boyfriend had always bemoaned the favors his parents asked him to do, how he had to act perfectly in their stead. But clearly Jake used his father's status to his advantage, despite promising that he wouldn't. The program saw through him—and he hid all of this from Evie.

"If he hadn't mentioned his father, would he have gotten the interview?" Evie asked.

"Perhaps."

Memories washed over her. Jake's lukewarm response when learning she got through the interview and into the program. When he lied about studying, when he said no to all their Saturday Sins dinners, when he openly mocked not only the clinic but also the forensics team. There were so many signs that her relationship had gone sour.

They needed to talk. Soon.

Alessandra and Evie went to their separate cars. Right before sliding into the driver's seat, her phone vibrated. Her sister, Linh, had sent her a photo. She was with her boyfriend in what looked like a studio. Had to be at her school, then. There was a picture of their finished canvases side by side. Linh's was expert-level, of course, but her non-artistic boyfriend had only drawn a confusing glob of colors, and Evie laughed at the stark difference.

Her smile faded.

Even though Linh and Bảo lived miles away from each other, they always made it a point to spend time together. They were united. Unlike her and Jake.

. . .

Once back on campus, she texted the group chat that her walk-through had gone well, receiving hearts and likes fifteen minutes later. They were all busy, but she was glad her friends and family had never stopped being there for her, for one another.

> Evie: going to the Arb to clear my mind. In case anyone wants to join!

> Lis: can't grl. But I'll be home later. Wanna hear about your day!

> Việt: 🤚 will meet you there!

Evie had resisted flowers for a good chunk of her life. Flowers meant being dragged by her mom to stand next to them for a photo opportunity. See a bush of lilies, roses, hydrangea outside a neighbor's outside garden? *Take a picture of me*, Mom would demand. *And quickly, before they can catch us*. Eight-year-old Evie definitely felt the pressure then. Don't even get her started about hoa mai, its yellow colors reminding her parents of the Lunar New Year back home. They always went crazy over that, as if they didn't see the same thing every year.

But, Evie, ultimately, was her mother's daughter, and as a

second-year, she found herself going to the Gardens, sometimes with Lisbel, but mostly alone, whenever she felt stress creeping up on her. Today was her first time visiting since the school year had started. She'd found other means to relieve her stress, like her runs with Việt and her Saturday Sins visits.

Evie roamed for fifteen minutes. Then she heard her name.

"Việt?"

"Evie?"

"I'm right here!"

They were playing Marco and Polo. She heard the laughter in his voice too, and the sound came closer and closer. Over a tall, pruned bush, her friend's head popped up. "Hey!"

"You found it."

"Almost got lost."

"Glad you *didn't* get lost." Pain shot through her feet; Evie was hurting from standing on her toes to talk to him. "You want to come around here?"

"Oh! Yeah, let me just—" Putting his running skills to use, he dashed all the way down to the end, found a natural opening, and leaped over it. Now he was just a few feet away. "Like I said, this place is a maze, and I almost—oh, and there's a gate. Fantastic."

Evie turned; he was right—he didn't have to wind around the entire way; he could have conveniently gone right through the gate.

She tried not to laugh. "Not your fault, the gate's pretty hidden."

They started walking without a word. Her thoughts were on what she'd say the next time she and Jake met up. Wanting it to happen right now but also dreading it. Her friend let her stew in silence for a few minutes, and Evie figured she should admit she wasn't very good company right now, apologize for wasting his time, tell him she just needed to figure some stuff out—

Việt stopped. His hand went to Evie's elbow, turning her to face him. His honest concern shone so clearly it made her forget to breathe. Because when he looked at her, he really looked. "Evie . . . is something wrong?"

It was rare to comfortably sit in silence. Hidden in a secret pocket, under a willow tree, all to themselves. It reminded her of the first time they were truly alone—surrounded by cows, just lying in the grass. In the last few months, Việt had become so vital to her everyday life. Being around him was uncomplicated. Natural.

She felt this rightness the first time she and Jake kissed. And with Lis, it was their nightly catch-up at their apartment. When Kale and Tate had first started Saturday Sins, coming to the realization that she had become a part of *something*. She belonged with her friends, but she no longer fit next to Jake.

"Jake is my first real boyfriend, you know," Evie said aloud. She felt Việt turn to her, but she remained staring at the canopy. "And I've spent two years with him. That first year, was everything I could have hoped for. The second year he started feeling more pressure from his family and threw himself into his studies. This year, he's been busy all the time, and when I try to talk to him, it's like he doesn't have a moment to spare.

"I mean, I know everyone's busy. And I know he isn't lying. I don't *need* to see him all the time. But sometimes I just want to talk to him, face-to-face. I thought we could do the clinic together. Then I got in. He didn't—and he didn't care that I got in. He was bitter about it—I mean, you were there."

Việt didn't interrupt; she figured he was probably remembering that same night, at the party, when things turned awkward.

"It's like our relationship's become nothing. We don't . . . fit together anymore," she finished. "Maybe it's been like that for a while, but I only realized it recently."

The branches of the willow tree swayed, their sounds a soothing *shhhh*. How many watershed conversations had this tree heard in its many years of existence?

"My parents were so busy with their business when I was younger, I don't think they had the time to fight," Việt said. "But I noticed last year, and this year . . . it was happening more often. Over the most random things. Complete overreactions." His legs were outstretched in front of him, and he dug his heels into the soil. "I'm sure they loved each other at some point . . . but they seem to have grown . . . tired. I don't know how they have managed to stay together all these years.

"And now I'm going home early because my mom wants me back for something. I'm wondering if it has anything to do with her and Ba. Another fight for me to clean up, even though I don't know how."

His expression shifted. "I'm sorry. I'm not suggesting that

what's happening with my parents has anything to do with you and Jake. . . . I guess I wanted to share something personal too," he said, and gave her a small smile.

She wondered if his family had caused his distress earlier this year. It's hard to shoulder burden when it stems from the people you love. "Thanks for telling me. I'm sure this hasn't been easy on you. And I get it," Evie said, smiling back. "You're not trying to compare my two-year relationship to your parents' two decades of marriage."

"Just to make it clear."

Their laughter quieted.

"How are *you*?" he said.

"Me?"

Việt shrugged. "Yeah, you have a lot of thoughts. Lots of concerns. But how are you feeling?"

Evie sat with that question.

"I feel . . . tired, maybe? But I don't trust myself sometimes. With feelings. I can be perfectly logical, but feelings are just wild. I don't go with the flow, not like my sister and her art and her outward emotions. I *never* go with the flow."

"It's dread," he said.

Evie looked up at Việt. "What do you mean by that?"

"I've been sitting with this feeling, ever since school started. It's just this consistent feeling, but I haven't given a name to it, until now, I guess. Not shock, not fear, but dread." He paused. "It's in the same family."

"Yes." Her breath shook as she exhaled. He read her mind.

"Watch out for the spray!"

A few steps away, the Arb employees were working their magic on the plants. Two women stopped to examine a dying bush, completely oblivious to the two of them.

"Darn. Looks like this one won't last. I've tried everything to feed it," one woman said.

"Some flowers aren't meant to last forever, Daphne." Her coworker sighed. "Sometimes they have lived out their life."

Daphne gazed forlornly at the plant before moving on.

Evie glanced over at Việt. He held her gaze, like he always did.

"It looks like you've made a decision," he whispered.

CHAPTER 21

VIỆT

On the 5, their car cruised over a flat expanse of sand and dirt and trees that somehow agreed to stop growing at the same height. The sky was a smoggy gray, but no rain. It still felt just as miserable. They had left the rural sameness of Davis, for more farmland, wild mostly, and the highway stretched on and on. His dad initially peppered the silence with questions—none of the answers required more than two sentences. That was how he always answered other people's curiosity, so to receive the same length made sense to him. Only to him, it seemed.

"Why did Mẹ want me to come home a day early?"

"Can't your mother miss you?" Ba said, his tone light.

Việt let out a weak laugh. "Sure, I guess."

"How's school?"

"It's been good. I made friends. Joined some clubs." *And I like someone, but she's in a complicated relationship with someone else*, he added.

"Good. Good."

Việt made a comment about his music choice—some folk music channel—and in turn, his dad made a comment about the driving habits of the car in front of them. That was it. He didn't have it in him to get creative with additional questions.

His mother stayed home this time. Her voice at three a.m. still lingered with him. It was sad. It was hushed. Maybe she'd been hoping to rant about her father, then decided against it. He glanced over at his father, wondering what they could have possibly fought about this time. The business? Money? Laziness. Possibly. That was always her mother's accusation against Ba, and Việt secretly thought her idea of laziness was not what most people thought. It was just any effort less than hers.

Ba let Việt sleep. When they hit the 405, they pulled into a rest area to fill up the gas. As they left, the rain, hidden for most of the trip, finally caught up to them. He stared through the blurry front window, at smeary red, blue, and black watercolors. There were so many cars honking, another nap would be impossible.

Soon highway trees grew more spread out. Việt couldn't understand why, but the landmark that always told him he was close to home was the Seal Beach Tennis & Pickleball Center. The owners didn't even try to get creative with the name. Next were the places of his childhood memories: the Map Sports facility, where he had physical therapy after twisting his ankle from running; Costco, where Việt once fooled around on the keyboards, attracting not the admiration but the ire of busy shoppers; his parents' loading dock, where he'd pretended he was in a cave and yelled into the back of empty semis to hear his voice when he was bored. Bolsa Ave was packed with restaurants and storefronts, and yet its four-lane, five-lane width sometimes made Việt feel like there was nothing around.

They hit the sleek, slippery asphalt and arch of the Today Plaza, and Việt knew he was just about home.

Outside their house, Ba parked but left the engine on. After Việt gathered his luggage from the trunk, he noticed his dad still hadn't moved, so he knocked on the passenger window. It slid down and he poked his head through. "What are you doing?" The windshield wipers hit a wobbly rhythm against the rain. The drops falling against his nape.

"I'm not staying."

"Where are you going?"

"Not far. But I won't be here tonight, con."

Việt glanced back at the house, noticing only the kitchen light was on. His mother was home. "I don't get it. Ba Mẹ cãi nhau or something?"

"No fight. Nói chuyện với Mẹ đi. Ba sẽ gặp con another time." Ba's face changed then. All of it started to twist, like he was going to cry. Before Việt could say anything else, his dad shifted gears and drove off.

It wasn't unusual for his dad to go on a drive after an argument. And for Việt to check on his mom before she brushed away her angry tears. But his dad would come back, and things would be normal. That was the way it always had been. He'd come back.

So what was this poisonous sensation, sitting in Việt's stomach?

Việt had never been away from home for this long. Maybe the longest was two weeks—when they visited family members in Texas. But entering his home now was the same as before—his house had its own smell: a mélange of lit joss sticks, garlic from last night's sautéed dish, mustiness seeping up from the basement. He took off his shoes. His parents had cleaned up the shoe rack, which, for the longest time, was a true hazard zone. He let the house's scent lead him through, like an owner trailing behind their leashed dog. The soft straw broom with its striped red-and-green handle still leaned against the hallway table for easy access. His high school diploma now hung underneath a portrait of the big belly Buddha and above some market-bought watercolor of a rice paddy field.

His footsteps were light, as if he'd woken up in the middle of the night and was trying not to disturb anyone. His muscle memory returned. The doorway to the kitchen had a raised trim, requiring anyone to take a bigger step so as not to trip. He swerved to the left to avoid the potted fig tree partially blocking the doorway. Why had they never thought to move it?

Still, everything just felt wrong. Off.

In the kitchen, at their round glass table, his mom sat alone, haloed by the ceiling light. A steaming cup of what he imagined to be jasmine tea was before her. She was in her bathrobe—it was older than Việt, she always liked to brag—and her wet hair was held together in a bun by a clip.

His growing list of questions could wait for a minute. Before his mother could turn her head, he went behind and bent over to embrace her. She hugged tight, tighter than the last hug she gave him when she'd dropped him off.

When they broke apart, Mẹ held him by the cheeks and she smiled. "Trời ơi, con ai đẹp trai vậy?" Việt pretended to bat away her hands. He wasn't any handsomer, but he let his mom dote on him. It chased away his worries for the time being. She then asked, "Con ăn chưa?"

He couldn't hear any oddness in her tone. It was as if she never spoke to him last night. "Still full. Grabbed some things from the rest area."

"Okay, good. Well, con muốn ăn gì thì nói Mẹ."

"Don't worry; I'm not hungry." He noticed his mother glancing over his shoulder.

"Did your father leave?" she asked.

"Yeah, but he didn't say where." He sat down so he could be at eye level with her. "Did you guys have another argument?"

"No, not this time." Her hands wrapped around her mug. "He is staying somewhere else."

There was a hazy memory from his childhood, when it was storming worse than today, leading his father to book a motel room. He had dragged his feet into the kitchen the next morning, disheveled in his clothes from the day before, and Việt's mother took one look at him, shook her head, then told him to sit down and eat breakfast. The reason for his father's brief departure was forgotten, but he always remembered the relief on his father's face when he was told to join the meal.

So, Việt thought, his father just needed a night away. At least, he expected his mother to say something to that effect. Not—

"He found an apartment and has started moving in."

An apartment? "Was the fight really that bad, Mẹ?" he asked.

"It wasn't a fight this time. It was a decision."

"Ba and Mẹ đã chia tay?" A more serious word for divorce existed, but Việt could only think of this one—a separation of hands.

His mother nodded. "Ba Mẹ . . . we didn't want to fight any-more."

"How did—when did you two decide on this? Why didn't you tell me this was happening?"

"Ba and Mẹ didn't want to distract con from school. You're too young—"

"If I was five, I'd be too young. I know you had to hide stuff from me then. But I'm almost nineteen now," he said in a raised voice. "You should have told me! I didn't know things were this bad. That it'd get to this point."

"What could con do?" she asked. Now her voice hardened, as if to remind him that she was the oldest in the room. "Ba Mẹ made up our minds; there was no stopping our decision. Even if you came home the day we signed the papers, that would have changed little."

Việt had no response for that.

"We sat in this empty house"—she gestured around her—"and realized we could not share the space anymore. There was no more happiness because we took each other's happiness." She shook her head. "Remember when con would comfort me, and would ask what happened after a fight. Trong lòng Mẹ buồn, nhưng Mẹ không muốn con buồn theo." She thumped her heart with her fist. "Children shouldn't know how much their parent suffers. It is not right."

Too late. Emotions weren't that easy to safeguard; he'd always felt his mother's, she must have known that, but without words, without Mẹ sharing her pain with him, there was nothing he could do. Maybe if she had said something, put a name to their issues, maybe he could have been there for her now, unlike the way he floundered in his past. Instead of asking *What happened?* he should have just said *I'm here. Let me help. In any way.*

Just as he kept them together, his departure split them apart. His irrational side criticized himself. Told him he should have stayed at home, gone to a nearby college, because maybe then his parents would still be married. Except he would have hated it, being stuck inside their arguments, forced to pick sides, finding no way to help them since he was just the child and they were supposed to be the adults. Did that mean they spent all these years, together, just because of him? Was all their misery because they thought he couldn't handle a divorce?

More questions—no, they were demands—were racing through his mind; they were shouting, and he couldn't tell them apart. He couldn't say them aloud. Because as his mind raced, his heart twitched in pain. His mother was like him—bottling up all that sadness. The only difference was that Evie and his friends noticed before he did, while he was far too late seeing the depths of his mother's pain.

Spewing more angry words wouldn't get them anywhere. His mother, her anguish—her mask from when she happily greeted him was gone; he called to mind his last look at Evie. Her resigned acceptance, the empty look in her eyes when she was seeing all the flaws in her relationship with Jake.

He rose from his seat. "Can I go to bed? I . . . I'm tired and need some sleep."

"Okay, con." His mother's hands went back to her mug for warmth. "There's work in the morning, but let's talk at dinner."

> Bảo: hey man i heard smtg from my mom about your parents?

> Bảo: call me if you want

Việt didn't end up calling Bảo. So Bảo rang him. Three ignored calls later, Việt figured he might as well silence his phone, but his best friend seemed to give up after that. Maybe he had gotten the hint.

He wanted to be alone; he couldn't manage his own thoughts, let alone someone's words of condolences. Was that the right word for this type of situation? Condolences came with death, and in a way, his parents' marriage did die. But whether it died unexpectedly, or it was terminal . . . ironically, if Bảo was here, he would know how to phrase it.

He had the house to himself; his mother woke up before the crack of dawn and headed to work. She left him some cash on the counter to order whatever he wanted, which had never happened before. Did she feel bad? Did she think Việt would be mad the next day? Was the money her way of making amends?

Spite surged through him as he ignored the money, and dug into a cabinet for stale, off-brand cereal. The fridge had soy milk, and it wasn't his favorite combo, but it would do for now. The doorbell interrupted his glamorous brunch.

Correction: his best friend interrupted his glamorous brunch.

"Hey, man." Was Bảo always this tall? Kid must have grown an inch or two at school. "I just wanted to check in on you. See if you're all right."

"My parents are getting a divorce, Bảo. Of course I'm not okay."

That voice—laced with anger—it couldn't have possibly come from him. The subsequent silence proved him wrong.

"Yeah, of course," his friend answered quietly. "Of course you're not okay. That was—I'm sorry. I don't know what to say. Words aren't coming easily today." He smiled weakly. "And I'm supposed to be the English major."

Việt looked away. He gripped the screen door's edge, leaned his back against it to keep it open.

"I kind of want to be alone right now. No offense."

"Yeah, sure. No problem." And yet Bảo didn't move. "Linh says hi too. She knew I was coming to see you."

"Does she know too?"

Bảo's eyes widened. "Well, yeah, but—"

Việt clenched his jaw. *"And what did you tell her?"*

Việt imagined his mom out working alone, the judgmental eyes on her. People speculating why they divorced now—throwing darts at targets just to feel the rush of victory. Bà Nhi, the most malicious gossiper out there, was no doubt sitting in her usual booth at Bảo's family restaurant, doling out rumors to her listeners—the very people Việt's mom regarded as clients.

"I . . . I told her I was gonna see you."

"What, so that you can confirm if the rumors are true or not—"

"No," he quickly said. He stepped forward. "Honestly, I was just worried. You weren't texting back or answering, so"—he exhaled, as if the strength to speak had left him—"I really wanted to know how you were holding up. Sometimes I can't tell what you're thinking. I got worried."

Việt was disgusted, not with Bảo but himself. Some inaccessible part of his brain knew Bảo hated gossip as much as him, and that *of course* he was here as a friend. And of course Linh found out from someone; it wasn't like she sought out rumors either. Did that mean Evie also knew? She was probably going home now. Or was already home.

His disgust morphed into anger, and it caught fire, and he didn't have anyone else to target but the best friend in front of him.

"You should go. I don't need anyone to talk to. I don't feel like talking, okay?" He walked forward with bare feet while Bảo walked backward, nearly stumbling on the porch steps before he caught himself. All the while he looked confused and there was hurt in his eyes too.

No anger, though, which Việt would have preferred, because that would mean they were on equal footing. Hating himself even more, he shut the door before his friend could protest. He heard him shifting his weight, his sigh, and his receding footsteps. Việt didn't move until his friend's car roared to life and pulled away from the curb.

One day, maybe, Việt would have the courage to apologize. But not now, not today. He abandoned his faux Honey Bunches of Oats cereal and trudged upstairs. In bed he buried his head in his pillow, squeezed his eyes shut, and wished he could be anywhere but there.

CHAPTER 22

EVIE

Evie made her decision. She didn't need to say it to Lis, who, for once, was up before her that morning. Lis was leaving campus a day earlier than her and probably had some packing to do, and that had never been Lis's strong suit. When Evie finished showering, there was a toasted bagel waiting for her on the counter.

They both ate breakfast without chatting. On any given day, she would chock Lis's silence to being a late riser. Today was different, though. Before Evie could fully step out of their apartment, she felt Lis's arms around her, heard her gently wishing her a good break and—

"There will be ice cream in the freezer. Just so you know."

A wave of gratitude swept through her, and Evie was reluctant to leave her best friend's embrace.

• • •

They planned to meet at the Coffee House in Memorial Union. Once Evie arrived and spotted Jake waving her over, she paused. It was crowded, but the noise wasn't yet deafening. It would be soon, once the rest of the student body woke up from last night's partying. She wanted to turn around and leave. She never wanted to be *that couple*—the couple whose whispered fights in public became everyone's entertainment. They were often painfully unaware they had an audience, or that strangers were actively choosing sides as their arguments ramped up.

She made it to the table. Jake rose to kiss her, but she flinched and took a step back. After a second's pause, Jake sat back down.

"Can we take a walk outside?" she asked quietly, holding his gaze.

For the first time, Evie felt as if he was really looking at her. It was silly, but it was true. It'd been ages since they were alone together, without obstacles like exams and assignments and friends. He was studying Evie like it was the first time he'd ever laid eyes on her.

With furrowed eyebrows, he nodded.

Evie led the way to a bench facing a small pond. Boulders bookended the bench, and she often saw birds basking in the sunlight. She sat down, tightly clutching the coffee that Jake had purchased for her, while he remained standing.

It was a beautiful morning, she realized with a stab of pain.

Jake folded his arms. "Is something happening?"

"You feel what's coming too. I know you do."

He laughed, but he ran his hand through his hair. A nervous

SOLVING FOR THE UNKNOWN

habit. "Can you just spit it out, Evie. Because I'm thinking of something that's not good. But it *can't* be what I'm thinking—"

"I want to break up." The words left her in a rush. Her heart pounded in her ears. Early this morning, she'd thought of all the breakup phrases she heard throughout her life, from films and shows and books. *Let's part ways.* Formal, businesslike. *Let's end this.* The word *end* felt so solemn. Sometimes people said *Let's see other people*, but she didn't want to say that. No, it wasn't like she wanted another relationship with anyone else—

Are you offering to come along or asking just because?

Why did Việt pop up in her mind? She shook her head.

"I've been thinking about it for a while. I realized we barely see each other, and when we do, it's like we can't sync up. Like our minds are stuck on other things." She inhaled deeply. "I'm saying all of this now because I don't want to drag things out over the break. And I thought the time apart might make all of this hurt less."

"Are you actually hurt? Because you don't look hurt." Jake's voice was loud, the opposite of hers; he didn't care who heard them. "Meanwhile, here I am, feeling like I've been stabbed multiple times." His confusion faded only to be replaced by annoyance. Anger. At her.

"I woke up thinking we were just getting coffee, and now you're sitting here telling me you don't want to be with me anymore? Evie, what the hell?" Jake grabbed her by the shoulders. "Are you still thinking about what I said the other night to Lis and that first-year? I didn't mean anything by it. It was dumb of me, but I'm only human."

Evie shifted away from his tight hold. "A lot of things happened the other night."

Jake blinked in realization. "You found out where I was during that forensics event, didn't you?" He laughed bitterly. "I saw you talking to Kerem. Knew he'd spill it. Yes, me and him were hungover and we went out for breakfast instead of going to your little competition."

Evie paused. "Wait, what?" She looked up at Jake, confused. She did talk to Jake's roommate, but he didn't reveal any of that. His anger faded into brief embarrassment, having realized that he was the one who just now gave them away. "Wow. You could have just told me you couldn't make it, but instead—" She closed her eyes. "You lied."

"I showed up later, though! And we celebrated! It was a good night."

"Only because the party was in your plans anyway. One you never even told me about."

Jake pressed his lips together. "I don't see why you're making such a big deal out of this."

Evie studied her hands, which were wrapped tight around her coffee. No one could read minds, so she should have said more about what she wanted. She saw Jake's point. But as her boyfriend, shouldn't he be naturally interested? Shouldn't he ask about her day anyway? Shouldn't he see how many times he'd brushed her off just because he had his own plans to take care of?

"It was something that mattered to me," Evie said softly. She forced more strength into her voice. "The clinic, especially the clinic. I was happy that I got accepted. You were the first person I told. But when I did—" She swallowed hard. "I wanted to show you how happy I was."

"So all of this happens and you wait until now to tell me this. What were you doing before—building a case against me? Making me seem like the bad person?"

She shouldn't have let all this fester for so long, because from the outside, maybe she was the one being overly harsh—

Then, out of nowhere, Việt's concerned look entered her mind, his words telling her she should put herself first.

"Evie, you don't *get* it," Jake said. "You don't understand how busy it is for me. How there's so much on my mind. I'm sorry that you feel that I wasn't paying enough attention to you." He'd adopted a sickeningly sweet tone. "*Oh, you were annoyed* because I didn't go all-out congratulating you? That I didn't drop everything on my schedule for you?" He switched back to his normal voice. "You know I'm busy. You know I got shit to do. My parents are up my ass every day. So maybe I don't have time to constantly make you feel good about yourself."

Throughout their relationship, and in his interactions with her friends, she somehow missed the signs of its deterioration. It was in the way he never wanted to eat at her favorite restaurants and always ended up going to his. But there were so many other signs. They were in the way he'd complain about his family to her, wanting her to echo his thoughts, wanting to be comforted by her. It was in the way he almost resented Lis, Kale, and Tate's closeness and their antics—"They're something, all right." He'd said that when they had the picnic together.

It wasn't worth pointing out how he tried to use his father's name to get through the program. Even if she could say it, their conversation didn't need another bomb.

She wasn't blind to his mistakes, was silent about his callousness. Jake had listened to her, but he never seemed to take her words seriously. As if he knew she would let things go his way. Those were all signs she should have seen.

"You played a main role, while I had a supporting role, and I let myself get used to it, and I don't like that I didn't see it until this year. I can't see that changing even if we were to put everything behind us and keep on dating."

"When did you become so needy?" That tone. She heard it at the party a couple nights ago—so full of judgment. "Are you seriously going to break up with me just because I didn't pay attention to you a couple of times?"

"Stop it," she said with as much strength as possible. "You're making it seem like I wanted the world of you. But all I wanted was some . . . recognition. That something I did is great, that you're proud. That I was worth celebrating."

Jake didn't say another word, but he remained there, so he'd at least heard her. He picked up a small rock, jabbed it at the boulder, made angry white etches. Evie welcomed the silence, the reprieve from being looked at as if she'd committed the worst of crimes. Her tears started leaking out; every time she wiped them away, more came back.

She'd ended things with her first serious boyfriend. It had to be done, but still. She wished the clarity she felt this morning—after skirting around reality—could return now.

Jake finally left his boulder but kept his back to her. He smoothed out his hair. Recalibrating. Putting on his appearance— the one that everyone saw, and Evie usually saw through. Now he was just closed off.

"So, we're *done*? Like *done, done*?" His voice was hard again.

Evie squeezed her coffee cup. All she had wanted was for him to see her, to listen to her. But he wasn't going to change or admit his faults.

"Yes," she said.

"Okay, then. It was nice knowing you. And I hope I never see you again."

She flinched at his brisk tone, his quick dismissal. He walked away while she stared after him, her words stuck in her throat.

Evie longed for relief. To breathe easily again. To ignore how horrible Jake made her feel during their last conversation.

She hoped things would get better.

CHAPTER 23

EVIE

"So what's your deal?"

Evie's little sister, also back from break, dived onto her bed, making herself perfectly comfortable. Evie pretended to ignore Linh as she scrolled through her social media. She thought about all the times she'd seen high school classmates date and break up, then delete every sight of their time as a couple. But she never thought that would apply to her. Just an hour ago, her thumb had hovered over the delete button: the latest photo was of her and Jake, at the Saturday Sins picnic. They looked happy, but there were no other "couple" photos in the weeks after. She wondered if newly single people archived or deleted their photos? Archived meant that Evie believed Jake and her would get back together. But the idea of deleting digital traces of him and her seemed dramatic.

She changed her mind and decided to archive, but she shifted on her bed at the wrong moment, and her thumb hit the delete button. Once that happened, she couldn't stop and kept on going. She was in the middle of her sixth deletion when Linh burst into their shared room and belly-flopped onto the bed.

Evie would have gone on pretending she didn't exist—if only her little sister didn't throw a pillow at her.

"Hey!"

"Oh, she speaks!"

"What do you mean? I was talking during dinner."

"Yeah, but only when Mẹ or Ba asked you questions. They might not notice how you're acting, but I do."

"You do?"

"Normally you don't shut up." She launched the pillow back at Linh, but her sister ducked. The pillow fell to the floor with a soft thump.

"You deleted some photos from your socials?"

Evie winced. "I didn't think anyone would see it so soon."

Linh regarded her, kicking her legs like she was swimming free-style. Then she rolled over onto her back and tilted her head to look at Evie upside down. "So you and Jake are done? Like done *done*?"

She rested her phone on the nightstand. "Happened right before break. Truthfully, it was just a matter of time."

"Did you break up with him or did he break up with you?"

"Does it matter?"

"I'd feel more comfortable knowing your answer before saying the next thing."

"Fine, I broke up with him," Evie said.

"Good. He wasn't good for you." Linh didn't know that much about Jake, and yet she had already picked a side. They were definitely sisters.

"And if he broke up with me?"

"Impossible." Linh smiled. She wore a pimple patch on her forehead, and it shined under the overhead lights.

Evie slid her back down the headboard until she was lying right next to her sister.

"Did it happen for any particular reason?" Linh asked.

She had explained it to Jake, as best as she could, but given his reaction, she wasn't certain if she even made sense. Honestly, their conversation was a blurry mess in her mind; all she could recall was his stinging accusation:

When did you get so needy?

Growing up, she had no opportunity to be needy. Needy meant clingy. Needy meant she was an attention seeker, even though her whole life she did anything she could to avoid attention. She accepted all the hand-me-down clothes from cousins instead of asking for new clothes. When she was sick, she begged the elementary school nurse not to call her parents because they couldn't leave while the restaurant was open. When her parents were at work and they had no babysitter, she turned down birthday party invites and hangouts to care for Linh.

Jake was wrong. If anything, *needy* was a word that described *him*.

"We just grew apart," she finally answered, wanting to keep it simple.

"At least you're not crying. Which means you're probably not too upset."

"Or maybe I'm just numb. Is it wrong of me to feel numb?"

"Are you required to cry after a breakup?" Linh wondered out loud. Absentmindedly she went to pick at her pimple patch, but Evie batted away her hand. "Not all breakups are bad," Linh added. "When an object breaks, you can create something new with the pieces. In Japan, people take broken pottery pieces and bind them back together with lacquer and gold coloring. It's an actual art form."

Trust her sister to use an artistic metaphor. Evie shook her head. Linh must have thought she didn't understand, so she added, "Or think of a piggy bank. It's filled with coins, but then you break it open one day and there you have it: extra cash."

"I don't think five dollars and ten cents will do anything to help me right now," Evie said with a tired smile. "But thanks."

Linh reached over to slip her hand into hers. Gave her three squeezes.

The two sisters breathed together, nice and slow.

"Tell me about you and Bảo. And where you're getting all that money to go back and forth between campuses. All because of Mẹ, right?"

Linh grinned annoyingly. "I probably softened her up."

"I softened her up first," Evie replied.

In a way, they might as well have been arguing about the chicken and the egg. They were both telling the truth. Evie paved the way so that Linh might have an easier time, and Linh was brave enough to tell their parents the truth. They wanted the best for Evie, too, she knew that.

"You and Bảo—are adorable. Ridiculously cute."

"You think?" She smiled to herself. No doubt thinking of Bảo.

"You complement each other. Different, but the same. For a while, I thought that was what me and Jake were—complements. But the balance wasn't there."

"I was trying to imagine Jake in our house, but I can't see it," Linh said.

"I had to teach him how to do his laundry," Evie remembered. "He bleached his first load, and it was colors."

"The idea of his parents meeting yours."

"His mom—the definition of the tiger mom—would've probably thought Mẹ would be a good target."

"Little did she know, though," Linh added.

Their mom blended in when she wanted to; food was her space and she was fine with it. But she sharpened up at immediate danger.

"Should I take over?" Linh gestured at Evie's phone, where the rest of her photos waited to be deleted.

Winter breaks were always the same: her family shared meals together, and they would visit some relatives and close friends, but otherwise, she and her sister just lazed around. They occasionally shared a funny meme or updates about a former high school classmate. Linh had practically maxed out her storage with pictures and snapshots of her and Bảo visiting or FaceTiming with each other.

They were hanging in their bedroom when suddenly Linh shot up into a sitting position, her eyes fixed to her phone.

"What's up?"

Her little sister stood up and hurriedly grabbed a jacket from the closet. "Have to head out for a little. Friend needs me. But if I'm out too late and Mẹ and Ba want me home soon—"

Only someone with siblings could read between the lines: Evie needed to cover for her in case she was late.

"Is something wrong with Bảo? Ali?"

"Việt. The minute he got home, he learned his parents were getting a divorce." Linh's face scrunched up. "Ugh, I wasn't supposed to say that. The other day, Bảo and him—"

But Evie tuned out her sister's words. The Saturday Sins group chat was relatively quiet, and even quieter without him. Why didn't he say anything? He mentioned his parents' struggles the last time they were together, but Evie didn't know it was this serious.

"People are starting to talk. So that's the reason Bảo went to see him, but he shut him out. In our group chat, Việt's not the best responder, but I know he reads our messages. He's been silent, so we're going to check on him somehow."

"How are you going to get him to talk?" Evie's mind flashed back to when Việt struggled with a depressive episode. She was lucky; she reached out before he'd gone anywhere too dark. But learning about the divorce . . . knowing how much he lived inside himself . . .

Linh's phone pinged again, and her face relaxed after reading the message. She whispered, "Thank you, Ali."

"Ali?"

"She's driving over to him now. Her parents had divorced too, remember? He might feel comforted talking to her."

Evie did remember. Ali took it hard. The younger girl's usual self was a storm, ready to knock down anything that stood in the way of her goals. But when her parents split, she became a hurricane, even lashing out at Linh and Evie. She stayed away from the restaurant for a while.

But soon, with time and conversations with her mother, Ali finally calmed down. Their afternoon homework—and snack—sessions started again.

The knot in her chest that appeared at Linh's exclamation had loosened, but she still felt it. She followed her sister to the hallway, watched as she bent over to tie her shoelaces. In her rush to get dressed, the left collar of her jacket was flipped inside out. Evie fixed it without thinking.

Linh was Việt's friend, and that was why she was going to see him—Evie knew that. But wasn't *she* also his friend? If anything, they were closer, rarely going a day without seeing each other on campus.

Evie cursed. And right before all of this, she was complaining about a relationship that should have ended ages ago. It was trivial compared to a divorce.

She wanted to see him. She needed to see him.

"I'm worried." Her admission slipped out before she could stop herself.

"Evie?"

But was it right to go along with Linh? He didn't tell Evie about the divorce—would showing up with Linh be . . . too much? Her sister stared in confusion. Evie suspected Linh, even being friends with him, didn't know where his mind could go. How far away he could feel . . . how much he needed someone there to pull him up from a sinking hole—

"Hey, can I drive you there?"

Linh: everyone clear with the plan?

Bảo: 👍

Ali: Yep! I have rope!

Linh: ???

Bảo: ???????

CHAPTER 24

VIỆT

Not for the first time since winter break started, Việt woke up feeling like he had barely slept. He was sure his mother had come in to check on him, remembered her gently touching his hair.

Normally she wouldn't be opposed to opening his door without knocking, telling him to get up, that it was already noon—even when the time could have been ten a.m. But she hadn't tried to wake him; it was as though she just needed to confirm he was there, still in the same house as her. Even if he wanted to leave the house, like his father, he wouldn't know where to go. He had pushed away Bảo, who didn't text him again, didn't have close relatives nearby. Anyone he knew with a house was just his parents' friends.

Did their friends have to choose sides now? Who was the better friend: his mom or his dad? It was the last thing they probably needed to figure out, but soon enough would have to confront. At least Việt didn't need to make any choices. As a kid, he knew class-mates with divorced parents—none of them Vietnamese, strangely. His classmates seemed to have their favorite parent, and he could tell by their moods which parent they were staying with over the weekend. It was the worst when he saw a classmate stop visiting one parent completely—and sometimes it wasn't their choice.

He turned on his side, digging his nose into his Downy-scented sheets. He used a generic pod at Davis and almost never added softeners. He spotted his beanbag nestled in the corner of his bed-room. The burgeoning light illuminated the dust on its surface. Việt hadn't brought his game system with him, and so it had met the same fate as his beanbag. If he didn't leave his bed, maybe the dust would get to him, too.

Gossip spread quickly around here. Việt should have known that. He'd seen its damages. He didn't think his parents would publicly air the news of their divorce, but then again, it only took one sly and hawk-eyed auntie to sniff out the truth. Worse, and inevitably to come: the aunties who didn't care about the truth, only the sordid stories they could obsess over while cooking with friends or shopping at the Asian Garden Mall.

With Bảo's mother being a notorious gossiper, of course Bảo would find out. Otherwise, Việt didn't know when—no, *how*, to bring it up.

There was an uneasiness in the unknown. It was a liminal space. Việt almost felt like he was a superhero in a film, one who finally defeated the final boss, saving the world, but then they'd take in the wreckage around them. Sure, the past was defeated, but the present was awful, and the future was just a concept.

A piercing, prolonged honk pulled him out of his bubble. Someone was laying it on their steering wheel. Who the hell would do that? Việt left his bedroom to investigate. There was a car, a white Nissan, parked in his driveway. The horn continued to blast. The front windshield was slightly tinted, so he couldn't make out the driver.

Việt opened the front door and stepped out. He didn't need to go any farther, when the driver rolled down their window, and a head poked through.

"Get in, loser! We're going shopping."

Wait.

Hazel hair in a Tomb Raider braid. Sunglasses. And that almost feral smile. It appeared whenever she concocted a brilliant article idea or when her feature earned the front-page spot on their high school newspaper.

"Ali?"

Linh's best friend, who once made Bảo quiver in fear as she ruled their newsroom, was at his house.

He had to be dreaming. She didn't know where he lived. They never saw each other's houses.

She honked three times in response. Yup. It was her. "Come on. Get dressed and get in."

"I—"

She went back to town on the horn, and Việt envisioned cranky

Asian grandmas and grandpas emerging from their houses. No way did he want to deal with that, today of all days.

"Okay! Just hang on!"

"Hello," she said, way too perky. Việt stared incredulously at her from the passenger seat.

Two mugs of coffee sat in the cup holder, one of them half-full, the other empty, which explained the jittery glint in her eyes. Việt turned and examined the back seat where newspapers were piled up. From their group chats, he knew she'd gotten involved with the campus newspaper; maybe these hadn't been delivered before the break. Then Việt noticed the newspaper bore another campus newspaper's name—the closest campus to hers, if he remembered correctly.

"Did you steal those newspapers?"

"You saw nothing."

"You're probably breaking some sort of law."

"I am researching the market."

Ali swerved out of the driveway so hard that Việt's shoulder bumped against the door. He took that as a sign to stop asking about the newspapers.

"I just came back home today. Then my phone gets bombarded with texts from Romeo and Juliet, and they're seriously worried about you." She gave him a long look. "Even though you said, in a *not* nice way, that they shouldn't be in your business."

Việt slumped down in his seat. She wasn't wrong. "I'll give them a call later."

"I know you will. But I didn't come here to make you do that. I know you have a conscience and that you would know if you were being pretty fucking rude. Instead I am here to . . . comfort you." Without taking her eyes off the road, she leaned over and popped open the glove compartment. "I have tissues if you want to cry." Việt held back a laugh. Ali. Comforting him? She had the opposite effect most of the time.

He sighed and closed the compartment. "I'm fine."

"I promise you Romeo and Juliet didn't send me. I came on my own accord. I figured I have some relevant experience in this situation."

"What type of experience?"

"My parents are divorced too."

They were at a stoplight now.

Việt hadn't known. In their friend group, he was closer to Bảo and Linh than to Ali, maybe because they shared a similar upbringing. They were Vietnamese, he knew Bảo first, and then when Linh became his partner, he got to know a good deal about her as well. He'd met Ali after that. Ali used to pressure him to write film reviews for the entertainment section. He always declined, which Bảo later told him was a ballsy move because no one said no to Ali.

Looking back, he never thought to ask about Ali's homelife; he figured she would have told him, being the up-front person she was, if she even felt it important to mention.

"When did it happen?"

"When I was twelve," Ali said. She probably had a weekend bag ready to go, Việt thought. "I'm not going to compare what our parents went through, especially since your divorce is happening right now and mine had happened when I was way younger. And things are pretty settled and my parents don't talk but they are, shall we say, civil. But I wanted to volunteer myself."

"What do you mean?"

"Meaning: I . . . want to be here for you. If you need me." The traffic light finally turned green, and contrary to before, Ali eased her foot onto the gas pedal. "You know when I first met you, I thought you didn't like me. You never said much to me. But then I thought: *Impossible, everyone likes me!* So your behavior had to be because of something else." Việt bit back a grin, and judging by the way Ali was side-eyeing him, that was exactly the reaction she had wanted.

"I figured you were a quiet guy who had a lot of thoughts but never knew when to voice them."

Việt glanced out the window. "I don't really have anything to say," he lied. "About the divorce."

Where would he even begin? There wasn't a clear beginning; his parents' fights had always been there. At first they were merely background noise. He'd watched himself in home videos blowing out birthday candles with them in the back, out of focus, whispering through gritted teeth. Then their fights happened more frequently. And less hushed.

Should he let stories about his parents' petty fights spill out? Those nights when their voices pierced through his thin walls and his cheap headphones were ineffective, so he just curled up in bed, focusing on the notes to his favorite running song. When his dad would leave for a day or two—crashing on a sympathetic drinking buddy's couch—and his mother would be at home, ranting about all of Ba's weak qualities while furiously chopping vegetables.

He never knew what to say to his parents; he was just a kid. He remembered the nights when Ba would drive him home from a late running practice and he wished, as the lights passed over his father's grim face, that he could read his dad's mind, hear if he was as frustrated as his mother after each argument they had.

Then there were good weeks—months, even—when those fights stayed at a distance, felt more like a glitch, and his parents operated as a team, at work and at home. It took almost nothing for an argument to start up. Việt imagined an invisible scale: his mother on one end, his father on the other, and it was impossible to predict where the weight would fall. Việt tried to stay at the center. He really tried.

"Sometimes you're just too inside your head," Ali said. "You might think people can't understand you. And I'm not going to say that I do. There's a whole lot going on up there that I will never hear, and that's fine. Boundaries and all that. But I can at least say that I sort of know what you feel."

"Then tell me: How am I feeling?" In his mind the words sounded aggressive, but the tone of his voice was weak.

"Sometimes it feels like you're holding your breath, wanting it to happen. Then you realize, oh shit—it is. And you can't think of the next step," Ali remarked. "A part of you wanted it to happen. A part of you didn't."

"Because I'm guessing you feel like shit. And guilty for being so angry." She threw Việt a pointed look. "And you don't want to make people feel sorry for you. And maybe you blame yourself. Or your parents, and then you think, can I really blame anyone for being happy? Am I being fucking *selfish*? Or maybe a part of you is secretly happy—that you wished this would happen so that all the fights would stop. And now you're guilty for seemingly making a prediction turn into the truth. And you just don't know where to start. Something like that?"

Việt blinked. He leaned back in his seat. Yes, it was something like that.

"So what happened?" he asked, wanting to shift her attention away from him.

"I gave my stepmother the cold shoulder, until she gifted me an outdated *AP Stylebook* for my birthday." Việt gave Ali a look, and she merely shrugged. "Yes, I was dramatic. It's tiring to be angry all the time. And she genuinely cared about me. It just took time for me to see that. Now I see that having two families isn't such a bad thing.

"I think you're the type of guy who has a whole world inside you, and you've had these walls up to protect it. I might have forced my way inside today—and you'll probably not want to talk to me anymore—but I'm here for you. I want to help."

There are people who enter your life quietly. No sparks. Or

explosion. Like the last gulp of crisp air right before your toe crossed the finish line. That was Bảo. But Ali was like the shock of cold water on your face after a good, long cry.

"No, I needed this. Thanks."

Ali looked shy all of a sudden, and this was yet another emotion Việt never expected from his friend. "Now, if you'll indulge me a little more, we have to stop by somewhere."

"Where are we going?"

"I'm hungry. I know a place. And I think you know it too."

"My man!"

The minute Việt walked into Chơi Ơi, following the hostess, Chef Brian Lê's voice reached him. The chef and owner lifted him up and swung him around. He'd only met the bear of a guy once—Linh was hired to paint a mural on his columns, which he dedicated to his late mother, and there was a jovial grand opening, which Việt attended. It felt like the chef had known everyone in California.

Finally, when his shoes touched the floor again, Việt righted himself and stuttered out a hello. Today had been strangely emotional and he wasn't sure how to handle the chef's overzealous welcome.

Chef Lê's wife, Saffron, whose posture was still as ramrod straight as he remembered, greeted him too, with less strength but an equally warm kiss on both cheeks. It was the French in her. Her perfume faintly smelled floral and her box braids tickled his neck as she released him. They fell loose behind her.

"The others are in the back." *Others*? Then the chef finger-gunned Ali. "Little lady, you've done it again!"

Việt stared in confusion while she merely mock-bowed.

"Ali's been taking on some copywriting gigs for the restaurant," the chef explained as he led them into the depths of the dining room. As he walked, Việt noticed Bảo and Linh were waiting for him. He pushed back the wave of guilt.

"We've seen an uptick in high school customers ever since— targeting a demographic we needed help reaching. Plus, she's been doing some of the copywriting for our restaurant's website."

"On top of college work? Do you have a clone or something?" Việt asked.

Ali didn't hear; she had already made it to Bảo and Linh and was whispering to them: "I didn't need the rope after all—"

Việt probably misheard, though.

Chef Lê sat them at a table with an L-shaped booth, coinciden-tally close to the column that Linh had painted over. "So, what's the special occasion? Bảo calls me out of the blue and asks for a table—of course you have one, you don't even need to call!—so I figured you were here to celebrate."

Linh sat in the corner of the booth, and Việt slid in on the other side while her boyfriend was to her left. Bảo only scratched his nose out of embarrassment at the chef's comment. Since his visit to Việt's house, he'd tamed his hair so it wasn't as windswept, and he wasn't dressed in his usual red-and-black plaid long-sleeve, but an olive-green button-up. He looked more adult than Việt remembered, and the observation intensified his guilt at his childish outburst.

"Uh yeah, I didn't really mention it to the chef. Since . . . you know," he said quietly, glancing over at Việt.

Việt sighed and said to Chef Lê: "My parents are getting divorced."

"Oh damn." He was at a loss for words. Then he added meekly: "Con . . . grats?"

"We're not celebrating, Chef," Linh chimed in, showing him mercy. "It's something that happened, but we wanted to have everyone together in one room anyway. Just to see each other. We're all back from winter break."

"And I'm hungry," Ali piped in. She sat on the outside of the table. The chef gave them a nod and headed toward the back.

"How was the drive over?" Linh asked.

"Great," Ali said. "We sobbed." She read through the menu. "Bonded over the trauma of being kids of divorced parents—or soon-to-be divorced parents."

Linh only frowned at her friend's bluntness.

Việt suspected Ali was actually more embarrassed than anything. He looked up at Bảo, his oldest friend whose eyes were boring into him. The guy couldn't be less discreet if he tried, he thought fondly. He inhaled deeply, making sure his words wouldn't be misconstrued. "I'm going to be okay. Ali and I talked a lot about a lot of things. First, Bảo, you didn't do anything wrong the other day. Coming by and talking to me. You were being a good friend.

And I wasn't mad that you told Linh. Of course you would talk to your girlfriend. And my friend too." At his words, Linh gave a small smile. "I just didn't know how to handle the divorce. I mean, when I got back the other night and my mom told me the news, I didn't know what to do with it. So I'm sorry. I was being shitty."

A grin formed on Bảo's face, letting him know that things would be all right. "I can be shitty too."

"Yes, but I was the shittier one this time."

"Okay, you were," Bảo teased. "But no one blames you. I'm your friend. Your best friend. So if you ever need me—" He waved a hand, indicating he'd be there for Việt no matter what.

"Aw, so cute. Glad you two can kiss and make up," Linh said. Her eyes looked suspiciously wet, though.

"Same to you, Linh. Again, I'm sorry."

She leaned over to kiss Việt on the right cheek, hugging him quickly. "Forgive and forget. I'm just happy to see you again. Me and Bảo . . . we're here for you."

Việt pointed to his un-kissed cheek and said to Bảo, "Yours, if you want."

"No way!"

"What, your masculinity's too fragile?"

"No, I'm worried we might like it too much. Then how are we going to break the news to my girlfriend?" he stage-whispered.

"That'd make me sad," Linh said. "But more than that, I'd be vengeful."

Chef Lê's chuckle broke through the act as he came back to

their table and pulled up a chair beside Ali. He really must have enjoyed seeing them all together again. He leaned back in his chair. Saffron had disappeared into another room, going to check on her son, Philippe, who was in his playpen. "Seems like you two are still going strong, huh. Long-distance things working out?"

"Yes, unfortunately," Ali answered for them. "They're still disgustingly into each other."

Bảo and Linh exchanged looks and secretive smiles, their hands just naturally reached for each other.

"*Ew,*" Ali said.

"Tell us how you're *really* feeling." Saffron was back now, and she sat down beside Chef Lê. Philippe, who was probably at the age where he could walk steadily, still preferred the comfort of her lap. He stayed perfectly still, his rapt attention on the table's conversation, like he was all here for gossip.

"What about you, little man," Chef Lê asked. "You seeing anyone at school?"

The table quieted and Việt suddenly had a dozen curious eyes on him. Fourteen, if you counted the baby.

"Uh, sorry, nothing to report."

"C'mon, really?" Chef Lê teased. "A handsome guy like you?"

Việt remembered Evie's hurt as she talked about her issues with Jake. "There is someone. But she's definitely not interested in me that way. She's going through a rough patch with her boyfriend and—" He heard Linh say, "Oh," but ignored it.

"Heartbreak is hard to get over," Saffron said, and nodded sagely, avoiding Philippe's hand going to grab her hair. "But perhaps she'll heal quicker than you think, and you can tell her your feelings then."

"I don't know. Maybe."

"My love life is an absolute train wreck." Whether Ali announced this as a distraction, Việt couldn't be sure. Still, he silently thanked her. "I was chasing after someone." Việt imagined it—her literally chasing someone, and it brought a smile to his face. "But my other friends told me to stop chasing. Said I was being overly aggressive."

"Wow, that's shocking," Việt deadpanned. "You being aggressive? Can't see it."

"So, did you stop?" Bảo asked, his voice equally flat. Linh, meanwhile, just grinned, as she undoubtedly knew the whole story.

"Decided to switch to more hidden tactics. I might have lied to spend more time with them. Had them look over one of my articles that had a bunch of grammatical errors I planted."

"Since this person was critiquing your work . . . does that mean they're older than you?" Việt asked.

"Yup. Senior."

Both husband and wife let out a long whistle. Leave it to Ali to go for broke.

"Can't help it." Ali sighed dramatically. "I just like them. They're the ultimate grumpy in a grumpy-sunshine romance. And that's my favorite trope."

"The what?" Bảo and Chef Lê asked at the same time, while Linh said, "Wait, so *you're* sunshine?"

Saffron, who had the baby wiggling around in her arms, just

shook her head. "Hate to break it to you, Ali, but I don't think you're really sunshine—"

"Only if sunshine meant 'sunburn-inducing rays'—" Linh said.

"—Then maybe you are," Bảo finished.

That was freaky, Việt thought.

"You've progressed to finishing each other's thoughts. Lovely." Ali leaned back. "Anyways. More to come on my love life. It'll all work out. I'm confident."

"You're kind of scary," Chef Lê said but in admiration.

"Listen, in all seriousness, anytime you need to get away and grab a good meal, there's always a table for you."

They were all getting ready to leave. Dinner finished a while ago.

Việt laughed at the chef's offer. "My college is six hours away."

"I'll see if my Uber team can give you a discount," the chef said with a wink. Việt's "Thanks" was quickly lost in Chef Lê's wide chest.

Việt thought his night was finished, that they'd all go their separate ways after leaving the restaurant.

The sight of Evie emerging from her car proved him wrong.

"Evie, you should have come in," Linh said as she ran up to her.

"I didn't want to barge in on the reunion." She shrugged. "It's fine, I didn't mind waiting." She leaned to the right, looking past her sister. "Hi, Việt."

"Hi." He blinked to make sure he wasn't hallucinating. "You were out here the whole time . . . because of me?"

She was wearing a hoodie and jeans and didn't appear any

different from how she dressed on campus. But under the moonlight, she managed to look ethereal. He wished he could say that. Or maybe he needed some sleep.

"I had to see you. See how you were doing." She glanced at the others—her sister, Bảo, and Ali—and relayed some message so that they gave them some space. "I just hope . . . did the ride over help at least? Linh told me Ali and you had a chat."

"Yeah, it helped." Suddenly Việt remembered his bold friend's haphazard driving. "Though her driving almost killed me."

Evie was shocked at first—maybe the fact that he was making a joke. And it was—a joke. Maybe it was because he wanted to see something besides worry on her face.

"I didn't mean to make you worry about me."

"Of course. You're my friend, Việt." *Damn.* "One of my closest, I think. So when Linh got the text, I just—even if you might not have wanted many people—I just thought—" She paused, glanced down at her feet. "You probably didn't need to see me."

Then he hugged her. He felt a strange gravitational pull the moment he saw her, and he couldn't resist anymore.

It went on longer than it should have and Việt knew it. His brain had the right intentions, touch and go. But once he held her, they were magnets stuck together. Her chin fitting into the crook of his neck. Her arms around his waist. He imagined tree roots locked around a rock, somewhere on the edge of a cliff—both determined to stay intact and grounded, through all seasons.

It took all of him to let go. Evie stared at him long and good and then inhaled. He heard the catch in her voice as she asked, "What was that for?"

"It's a thank-you. For coming here tonight."

This time Evie was the one who embraced him, holding him even tighter than he had. Unfortunately, it didn't last as long, but Việt missed her warmth and weight as soon as she released him.

"What was that for?" he repeated her question to him. He was dazed.

"I think I needed a hug too."

Memories of their last conversation on campus nudged him. "Did you and Jake . . ."

"Yes. But I'll tell you about it another time."

After Evie's car rounded the corner and disappeared, Việt expected to go back to Ali's car. But the driver had different ideas. Ali had other plans and decided to leave first, so she practically dragged him over to Bảo's car and shoved him into the back seat. His arm kind of hurt.

Linh twisted around in her passenger seat, and Bảo did the same on the driver's side.

"Yes, Mom and Dad?" Việt asked. Then he remembered: they must have seen him and Evie hug. Not once. *Twice.*

They wanted answers.

"That was weird," Bảo blurted out. "I feel weird."

"Out of the two of us," Linh said, "*I* should be feeling weird. Him. My sister. *Hugging?*"

"More like I'm disturbed that Việt initiated a hug. I've never seen him hug anyone voluntarily. It was disturbing, period. More disturbing than the eyebrow thing he does sometimes." To demonstrate, he wiggled his eyebrows.

Did Việt *really* look like that?

Việt groaned. "Just drive," he said as he buckled his seat belt.

CHAPTER 25

EVIE

When Evie got home, she found her mother on her tablet, watching YouTube. A colander of just-washed cotton candy grapes was in front of her, and her mother was popping them into her mouth like popcorn.

Evie sat down in her usual seat. "Hi, Mẹ."

At her nod, Mẹ reached to grab a bunch and peeled one before handing over the skinless grape. Only her mother knew she liked it that way. As a kid, Evie piled all the green globs into one pile so that she could enjoy them in succession at the very end, instead of waiting for the next peel. Her father had noticed, and said she was a cunning girl. Khôn.

Watching her mother now, she felt like a kid again, a baby swaddled in her favorite blanket.

Evie ate in silence while her mother continued watching

YouTube, now a video about a Japan-based Vietnamese family whose content consisted of adventures from rural areas through cityscapes and cooking meals that fused both cultures. It was like ASMR to Mẹ. The mother in the video had just finished scrubbing a pile of razor clams clean, and was carefully prying them open, instructing viewers how to clean and discard the inedible parts. Her mother knew all of this, Evie figured, but she was still mesmerized, periodically telling her, "Look at the size of that clam!" Or "I wouldn't do it that way, but I suppose her way still works."

"Bạn trai Linh," she started, offering her a peeled grape. "Is he treating her well?"

Oh, she wanted gossip about Bảo. Evie smiled. "I only know what she tells me, and all I got to say is that they really like each other." Not that Linh had told her anything worth gossiping about, but even if she had, Evie would probably not tell their mother. They were sisters, and sisters had secrets.

Her mother sighed dramatically. "Facebook doesn't tell Mẹ anything."

"Maybe she blocked you."

Evie dodged a piece of grape skin flying through the air, laughing all the while.

"Anh thằng đó . . . It seems like she likes him a lot," her mother said.

"Yeah, I like him too."

"He is good for her. Always believed it."

That comment yanked Evie out of the nameless mood she was

swimming in. "Really? Always?" Her mother said this as if the family rivalry, over their restaurant and their shared past back in Vietnam, hadn't happened last year.

"Yes. Always." Her mother chose to ignore the obvious. "And con? How is school? How is Lis? And Kyle and what is the other boy's name? The one who looks like a . . . what's that animal—con sóc? With his different-colored hair."

"Lis, *Kale*, and *Tate* are doing just fine," answered Evie. She tried not to laugh; Vietnamese parents never seemed to remember names. Instead they latched onto a physical characteristic or one detail like where they lived, what they were majoring in, what their parents did for work.

"We see each other every weekend—sometimes even during the week," she finished. "I love them."

Mẹ nodded, satisfied, and moved more peeled grapes to her paper towel.

"And school is just fine," Evie continued. "Hard, but nothing I can't handle."

"Con phải giữ gìn sức khoẻ. Sometimes Mẹ lo."

Take care of yourself, her mother was saying. Evie thought she had done that, thought that her life was going well. But this semester had changed her outlook, and maybe she had lost herself for some time. She'd made Jake the priority.

"At the restaurant, cô An—con có nhớ cô An không?"

"Yeah, I think I remember who you're talking about. Cô An's the one with a sophomore, right?"

"Yes, she came by and said that her daughter was having a hard time at school. Came home crying because her roommate was not nice. Cô An was shocked; she liked the roommate, and her daughter didn't ever mention having problems."

"Thankfully, Lis and I don't have any issues. We're so used to living together."

"So con's happy at school?"

Evie fiddled with her paper towel. She didn't want to talk about Jake because she'd have to explain the fact that they'd been in a relationship for two years. Sure, her mom was fine with Linh and Bảo, but how'd she react if she discovered what had happened with Jake? First she'd feel betrayed that Evie had never told her she had a boyfriend.

Well, it didn't really matter now.

"Yes, I'm happy."

The words lingered in the gap between them. Her answer was the closest thing to the truth; she knew that once speaking aloud. The breakup made her sad, but only faintly and not enough to distract her.

"Good. Con has always been so strong. Có ý chí mạnh mẽ." Her mother cupped her cheek and she leaned into it. Then, reminiscent of their Sunday mornings when she was young enough to sneak into her parents' bed, her mother pinched her cheek and pressed her nose against it. Breathed her in. One, two, three times. A nose kiss.

It tickled. "Mẹ!" Evie said, laughing and leaning away.

"What?" her mother answered. "Mẹ là Mẹ." And she just

shrugged, wordlessly declaring her right as a mother to unabashedly show her affection.

The front door opened, and Linh called out. A few seconds later she bounded into the kitchen.

"I need some warmth!" Linh embraced her from behind, and Evie shivered from the slight chill, protesting. "Stay still, Evie."

"Go to Mom," she muttered, even as she leaned into her sister's arms.

"I'll stay here." Linh hummed, then whispered into her ear: "I'll need to hear your side of things. About Việt."

"What about him?" Evie also whispered, now tilting her head back.

Her sister only smiled cryptically—devilishly—but didn't say much more.

"Gì?" interrupted Mẹ. "What is this whispering about?"

"Nothing," the sisters chirped.

And their mother just tsked. "Đi ngủ đi," Mẹ finally said. "It's so late."

On cue, Ba's loud, piglike snore from down the hall reached the kitchen.

The sisters grinned, and Mẹ just rolled her eyes.

CHAPTER 26

VIỆT

The humid air clung to Việt as he unlocked the front door and slipped through. It was a change from the last time when his body felt heavy with the foreboding news. Now there were different sensations: his cheeks were sore after constantly smiling throughout dinner, his fullness from all that delicious food. The warmth of Evie when he'd hugged her.

He quietly entered his house, unsure if his mother was asleep. Then he saw her. Sitting at their kitchen table. He'd always been so close to his mom. And wondered if that sadness she carried, the one he carried as well and was now getting better at confronting and overcoming, with the help of his friends, if that sadness inside them was what connected them. Staring at her now, he imagined that in between the silence of their phone calls, this is what she must have looked like. Guilt compounded—for not trying to fill that silence, that he'd let her sit like this, until it had gotten to this point.

She'd taken all that sadness and knew it was getting her nowhere. So she did something about it. Despite divorce being a Vietnamese social taboo, despite what she was probably brought up to think, despite the gossip that would ensue, she made a decision. For that, he could only see her as brave.

"Hi, Mẹ."

His words brought her away from her phone. Shocked that he was suddenly there. Or that he'd spoken to her. Not so sure. "Hi, con. Ăn gì—"

"Yeah, I just ate."

A pause before she gave him a small smile. "How'd you know?"

"Because it's you. When *haven't* you asked if I ate yet?" He lowered himself in the chair. Accepted his mother's silent offering of a triangle of pineapple, one tip dusted with muối ớt. The fruit's prickly peelings littered a newspaper before her. The chef hadn't offered dessert, but maybe he hadn't because, somehow in that disorganized brain of his, he knew this was what Việt would be coming home to.

"Who were you texting?"

A deep sigh. "Your father. He is talking about some paperwork."

"And he asked for your help?"

"No, he didn't ask. But he'll need help. He's very useless."

A laugh escaped him. It seemed ridiculous—that they were texting, as if all their yearlong fights never happened, that she seemed almost . . . nonchalant that this was the way things would be going forward. No matter what, he'd never understand their relationship.

She peered at him over her glasses. "Mẹ không ghét Ba."

"I know you don't." That was the truth. He never thought his parents hated each other. It was too strong of a word. Frustrated, annoyed, tired—these words felt more fitting.

"As long as you understand. We wouldn't have been together this long if all I ever did was hate him," she added.

Việt forced out the words, "How did you—I mean, when did you decide you were going to do it?" They both were so close to touching that word, the elephant in the room. He might as well close the distance now. "I never thought it would happen."

"The solution only became clear after you left," she said in Vietnamese. "A month after you left for school, I came home after work. My bones were aching. My head, throbbing from a headache. But my heart felt so heavy because the whole day your father and I were arguing. It wouldn't stop. I realized we both needed to stop all the hurt. That's why."

"What if I hadn't gone to school? Do you think you'd still be together?"

She shook her head. "I remember thinking that I was glad you weren't home, to see us like this. Then I realized you probably saw it all before. So many years of it—all the yelling and fighting," his mother added, her tone tinged with wonder. Her hand went over his. "And maybe that is why you are such a quiet boy. So much noise in this house, there is no room for you to speak up."

Even in the middle of her own pain, she was thinking of him.

He never expected her to acknowledge what it was like to live with the two of them—what it cost him. Her words didn't give him any satisfaction because, in all the times he listened to their arguments, he only wished for them to stop.

"I saw Bảo," he said, flipping his hand so that he was holding hers now. "He knows. Heard it from people talking at the restaurant. Like, Bà Nhi."

His mother scoffed at the mention of the women in their enclave. "Đồ ngu. She and her followers are the same. They feed on other people's struggles. They think they are strong, so they call others weak. They talk bad about others because they can't talk bad about themselves," his mother said.

"Imagine their shock when I announced it," she added.

His hand froze mid-reach for his mug. "You did?" His mother was never this bold in public.

"Yes, I did. So what? What can they do? Rather than them talking about the divorce, why can't I say the truth, what *I* am feeling?"

"I wish I could have seen their faces," Việt said. "After all the bullshit they pull." Even though she scolded him for cursing, she looked a tiny bit pleased.

A tremble started in his hands. Việt felt his heart beat louder and louder. "I wish . . . I was more like you. Just say things like that, say how I really feel," he said.

"You are every bit like me," she said matter-of-factly.

"No, I'm not," he answered immediately. "Honestly . . . I'm not like you. I'm no good. I can't say it like that. What I feel."

"What do you feel?" she asked him.

"I'm not fine."

"Because of Ba Mẹ?"

At first, that may have been the lighter to his down spiral. Definitely a part of it. But it was other things too. These last few weeks, stewing in his head, being alone, not being able to say what he felt. It was inevitable. If not divorce, maybe something else at school. Another Big Life moment.

"I guess it was a shock. Half of me thought about it all the time when I was a kid—what it'd be like for you to divorce." He glanced guiltily at his mother, but her expression remained unchanged. "So when it happened, I didn't really know what to think." He thought of his discussion with Ali. "I didn't know how to act. But there were other times, when I felt sad."

"What do you mean?" She looked more alarmed than anything. "Sad?"

"You tell me all the time. Don't be sad. Don't be buồn. But I am—buồn. Seems like all the time." He was rushing his words, but he couldn't help it. They needed to get out. "I mean at school, I get into these . . . moods. Comes and goes, and I manage to get out of it, sometimes more quickly than others. But I know I shouldn't be this way. I know you tell me not to be buồn, but sometimes I can't help it."

Whatever bolstered his need to explain himself receded just as quickly. He tapped his fingers along the mug's rim.

"*Don't be* buồn." She clicked her tongue. "Sad is bad, a sentence from an English lesson. Mẹ còn nhớ because it rhymed. But saying that is not true. Nothing bad about feeling sad. But I am afraid to be sad, and I think that is why I told you not to be. Mẹ đâu muốn thấy con buồn.

"It's okay to be sad. How you eventually get past that matters the most." His mother's eyes roamed every inch of his face. "Tonight, you seem a bit better."

"Yeah, tonight was what I needed."

"Sông có khúc, người có lúc," she whispered, almost to herself.

In his mind's eye, he pictured the words as note cards and flipped to the English side: *river, piece, people, time*. But perhaps tired as he was, he was unable to put it all together so that it'd make sense.

"A river is never straight. It turns here and there." She showed the motion with her hands, like how she'd mime a swimming fish when he was just learning his words. "Same as our lives. It's never a straight line."

Việt decided that he liked that imagery.

"Con . . . is every bit of me," Mẹ repeated purposefully. "In the best way possible. And today we will be sad. But ngày mai—" *Tomorrow . . .*

". . . we'll be happy?"

She straightened her back. "Yes, eventually. But tomorrow we'll be strong." She reached out, cupped his cheek. "Okay, con?"

He smiled, his cheeks widening to meet the warmth of her palm. "Okay."

Evie: want to run but i ALSO want a burger

Việt: why not both?

Evie: are you back

Việt: see you at the usual spot

CHAPTER 27

EVIE

Winter break flew by: Christmas turned into a mini-reunion for everyone who was family in all but blood. Toward the end, Bảo came by, and Linh and her parents gifted him what every Vietnamese young man needed in their wardrobe: another nice red-and-black checkered long-sleeve. At some point he pulled Linh away to exchange gifts, and they both returned with secret smiles. And a shiny bracelet around her little sister's wrist. It was too cute.

Evie stretched and put in her earbuds, resigning to a solo run this morning. Until she heard her name.

Việt came.

He appeared as a speck, then as a person, dressed in weather-appropriate neutral colors, with the exception being his neon-yellow running shoes. "You beat me here."

"I'll do anything for burgers."

Odd—she thought maybe she would ask about his break and his parents. Việt would then ask about her break, and so on. They might even mention their time in the parking lot. But she held back from the small talk upon seeing his blooming smile. His eyes were barely open as he grinned at her.

His satisfied smile, his presence—that was enough for Evie.

She needed this run. She didn't run all break, deciding on the much more fun alternative: gorging on her mother's home-made meals and watching Christmas movies with Linh, and her parents—her father snoring away not even a half hour after they started. These memories peacefully enveloped her as her feet pounded against the pavement.

She peered at Việt and got an idea. She picked up speed, pumping her arms, stretching her strides. He caught on and, with a short laugh, did the same—and she remembered, after a few seconds, that he'd run as a sport, while running was just a hobby to her. She was left in the dust.

She yelled, but he ignored her, charging on.

They collapsed on a patch of grass, simultaneously straining for air and wasting it away with laughter. They became a still puddle of nothing, and if there were other students around them, Evie imagined they'd come over to check on their well-being. Prod them with a stick or something.

"Oh god, my body!" she moaned.

"You started it!" Việt replied. "I mean, what the hell! We *just* came back from break."

Evie laughed. "Sorry."

"S'okay." Việt looked up at the sky, his hands folded on top of his stomach. Like always, the silence between was comfortable. Their breathing slowed. "I'm just glad I beat you."

"I'm so happy you're doing okay."

His smile dropped as his wide eyes met hers. Her words sounded far more intense than necessary. But she needed to say them all the same.

And then it happened. She felt a burning sensation in her eyes, the telltale sign that she'd cry. But she shouldn't because she was the epitome of ugly crying. Even when the emotion's passed, when she felt fine, her biology betrayed her, and the tears would surge through.

Embarrassed, she hurriedly wiped her eyes as tears fell.

"Oh shit," Việt whispered. It was either the panic in his look or in his voice that made Evie genuinely laugh, even as she cried. "Did something happen during the run? Did I do something? Are you—" She sat up and reached up her hand to wipe away more tears, but he touched her wrist to stop her. Gone was his laughter; he appeared genuinely worried.

"No," she laughed. She sucked in air. "No, it's just me. Everything's just . . . catching up to me."

"Are you crying because of me?"

"No. Maybe. I don't know."

"You thought about me?"

"Of course I did! I couldn't stop thinking about you. I was worried."

He let go of her wrist and fell back to the ground. "But I didn't go dark on you." *Not like before.* She heard his unsaid words. "We texted."

"I know, I know. We chatted through the group chat. Still—I wanted to know if *you* were all right. Right before winter break, you listened to me complain about Jake. Meanwhile, you learned that your parents were getting a divorce—which is *infinitely* more life-changing—and you never mentioned anything about it."

"For what it's worth, I didn't know about it until the moment I got home."

"Still." Evie wasn't sure what she wanted to get at. "I realized that I haven't asked a lot about you and what you were going through. But you're always there for me. Always. I'm sorry for not being a good friend to you."

Việt busied himself by plucking the grass underneath him. "You might have guessed that things at home were rocky. I thought I could get away from it at school. It was good for a while; then I got a phone call that made it impossible for me to feel good. Maybe it's because my mom and I are close, and I don't like seeing her sad. Or because I just I knew, deep down, that my parents were broken beyond repair." He let out a short, self-deprecating laugh. "Then I *really* knew it was over when I came home. So I retreated. Lashed out at people who cared about me, but they were kind enough to forgive me. They pulled me out of a cocoon, and I'm glad they did."

Grass cascaded down as he opened his fist. "I'm slowly learning how to navigate these moods. I'm not perfect, and I won't always know when I'll feel down. What will cause it. I'm probably not going to find a solution immediately," he said simply. "Should I see someone? Maybe? Do I want to? Maybe, but you know I'm not a huge talker. But one thing's for sure, is until I take the next step, I have a lot of people around me who care."

The sad tears subsided, and now happy tears were incoming. Evie rubbed her eyes. "I want you to promise that you'll come to me if you ever think things feel like they're too much."

"I promise."

"Good."

"I promise you—I promised Bảo, Linh, and Ali—if I needed to talk, I'd know who to turn to." He paused. "I won't ever forget..." His voice was low, as warm as the heat between them. "When I saw you in the parking lot. I didn't ask for you to be there, but you were. And I thought, why didn't I *just tell her*? Why did I get mad at Bảo when he only wanted to see how I was holding up? And at your sister, too." He paused. "Seeing you that night was more than I could ever ask for."

He smiled. He faced the sky again, with his eyes closed.

Throughout the break she had thought about Jake every once in a while, but once she heard about Việt's family, thoughts of the past waned. Instead she focused on the future: how Việt would be once going back to school; how Linh and her boyfriend's relationship would bloom throughout college, and how Evie hoped it wouldn't turn out like hers; how she just wanted to feel the warmth of their next Saturday Sins group again.

Evie felt an urge. She thought of certain moments, like when she looked at the fire alarm in an empty hallway begging to be pulled. She imagined doing exactly that, then running away, bursting through the doors—always toward sunlight—and no one would chase her. She never listened to that urge.

She wondered if she could now. In startling clarity, scenes played out in her mind: her ears pounding, she'd scoot a bit closer; they'd hold each other's gazes; someone would lean in slowly, so slowly; his hand would go to her cheek, hers to his hip. Their lips slotting together.

She snapped out of it, then scrambled to her feet. "Well, I have a lot to do, so I'm going to—" Why was she so breathless? "I'm going to go now."

"Burgers another time, then?"

Seeing you that night was more than I could ever ask for.

"Yes, sorry. I just remembered I need to do something."

CHAPTER 28

VIỆT

After his run with Evie, where he said some cringe-worthy things that made him groan even days later, Việt eased back into the rhythm of school more quickly than expected. His mother had said she would drive him back to campus, but she was always spooked by highways, so he opted for a cheap bus ride. He only had a large suitcase, after all, and the idea of having his father at the front seat, even though he offered by text, didn't sit right. Ba was absent throughout his break; and even during Christmas it was just him and his mom. Initially Việt was more worried than sad.

He guessed he was like his father, who took long drives after an argument, eager to hide any anger or sadness from people who knew him. Vietnamese gossip kept his mother up-to-date about his father: Sometimes he went barhopping with neighborhood buddies and drunkenly sang sad ballads at karaoke. He ate out at friends' restaurants since his cooking skill was nearly at zero. His new apartment wasn't too far from Little Saigon and was in a decent area, which his mother relayed to Việt, her words said in relief. Like she'd said, she didn't hate his father.

On Christmas Eve his dad left Việt's present on the porch: a new pair of Pegasus running shoes. Việt didn't think Ba even knew the brand; he imagined his father Googling *what to get college son who runs.* Still, he texted his thanks and received a thumbs-up in response.

Kale brought back from Hawai'i a sunburnt Tate. The group spent a good five minutes teasing their friend who had the least melanin in their group. As they indulged in the treats he brought back— red coconut balls and Li Hing Mui powder on top of some freshly cut pineapples—they talked about their winter breaks. Việt didn't want to purposefully hide the news about his parents' divorce, but he also didn't want to bring down the mood. Saying it might cause him to slip into a mindset that brought a shadow over everything else in his life.

But his friends, perhaps after speaking with Evie, found out and consoled him in their own private ways. Lis hugged him and Kale and Tate reminded him about their open door policy. He imagined they said the same to Evie after learning about her breakup with Jake.

Now seated at the Coffee House at the square tables, they

waited for their coffee order to be done. The boyfriends took one side while Evie, Việt, and Lis took the other three.

"You never sit next to me," Kale whined to Việt.

"I'm worried I'd make Tate jealous," he threw back at Kale.

"Tate doesn't mind."

"Please, take him," the person in question chimed in, scrolling through his phone. He leaned over to show Lis a picture.

"Children, behave," Evie said absent-mindedly. Her attention was on the counter, and she rose when their names were called. "I'll grab a tray for the coffees."

"I'll help." Việt fell into step beside her. He had an ulterior motive; other than their run two days ago, they hadn't had any time to spend alone together. They dodged bodies to get to the serving bar. When Evie stepped forward, a male voice said, "You just cut me."

"Oh, I didn't know." She shifted a little.

"But I actually don't really mind," the voice, now flirty, added. Việt angled for a look. The guy had olive skin, a bright white smile that was used to put people at ease. Do people pick up others while they're waiting for coffee? He thought that only happened on-screen.

"Um." She paused as she reached for two of their drinks while Việt picked up the others with a tray.

"I'm Felix. What's your name? I don't think I've seen you around before. I would have definitely remembered."

Okay. So he was flirting with her. A knot formed in Việt's belly.

Was Evie going to flirt back? Did she want to? Felix had a confident ease that resembled Jake's. And she was single now. She could do whatever she wanted.

Evie's eyes slid over to Việt who nearly looked away, cursing himself for blatantly staring. "Great, you got the rest of the drinks. Thanks, babe."

Việt's eyebrows shot straight up. Meanwhile, the stranger frowned. "Well, nice chatting with you."

When Felix was a good distance away, Việt whispered, his throat tight, "Babe?"

She turned and hissed back, "He was hitting on me. I panicked. Is he looking over here?" She was about to crane her neck around, so he moved to block her sight.

"Wait."

"What?"

"He's looking over." He wasn't; the failed suitor had left already. "Pretend you're telling me something."

She listened. His eyes touched her hair (why does it look so soft?), zigzagged between her eyes and cheeks (why were they glowing? Was it makeup?), and he guiltily lingered on her lips before his eyes flew back up. He was acting unreasonable. "Okay, all clear."

"Wait."

Việt asked, "What? Do you need to look at me now?" He cracked a smile. "There's not much to look at, to be honest."

"Not true. You always look comfy." He held his breath. "You have nice hair; I much prefer it without any products. You have a great smile. I don't know why you haven't dated anyone. You can have anyone. . . ." She listed all these things without pause, without any embarrassment, without knowing that he was burning up inside, torn between wanting her to stop and wanting to hear more. "Oh, sorry, did that make you uncomfortable? I didn't—"

"I don't mind. It's just—are you flirting with me?"

"I'm only kidding. I was just teasing you," she said with a smile. "Thank you, for pretending before."

"Were you surprised? To get hit on."

"Yes, but I think I also panicked at the smallest hint of romance, especially after what Jake—" She stopped. She never told him what exactly happened or what was said during their breakup. "Never mind. Come on, everyone's waiting." She smoothly pivoted toward their friends. If Việt were a balloon, he would have been deflated by now.

They made it back to the tables. Kale was making grabby hands at his, so Evie distributed the drinks. Somehow his elbow knocked over his own gingerbread latte. Liquid cascaded over the edge and dripped to the floor.

There was no limit to the humiliation coming his way today.

CHAPTER 29

EVIE

When Evie was last at the clinic, she was in a still life. Now she was in a movie. As warned, the elderly patients were there upon opening hours, and they were swiftly paired with a patient advocate and a med student. A group of preceptors—professionals who would step in, if needed—were in the corner, chatting and pointing down at their clipboards.

Evie breathed in, unsure if she was ready for the chaos. But no one seemed to care—their priorities on the patients and not on the PA's comfort level.

"Don't worry. You'll get the hang of it soon enough. Just familiarize yourself with the basics," said Ryan Bui, the Vietnamese medical student she'd assist today. He wore a white coat while she had on the volunteers' maroon T-shirt.

He reminded her that most patients were elderly and some were mistrustful of modern medicine. She nodded, knowing people like that back home. Eagle Balm was the solution for all types of injuries, it seemed.

Their first patient was an eighty-year-old man with a sun hat who came in for a shot. He did his annual exam at the clinic, finding it much more comfortable than other offices. He said hello to the preceptors, shook their hands, and winked at the students. He even called Evie a doctor, and though it was a joke, she appreciated his words.

Their next patient looked like the grandmother that Evie never got a chance to meet—there was a quiet dignity to her as she pressed her back against the chair. Not a spot of hair fell from her tight gray bun. But she gripped her purse and would startle at the chaos and movement around her.

In the exam room, Evie found out why after discussing her patient information. "Needles—don't like!" Her eyes closed, her mouth in a thin line, her forehead tightened.

"I'm sorry," Evie whispered after she crossed and tucked the tourniquet a few inches above the woman's elbow, where her vein was most visible. Ryan would draw the blood. She tried to move the collection tube and needle out of sight, until the last minute, but it didn't matter. The grandmother was already tearing up, no longer the dignified woman. Just afraid. She peered at Ryan who made sympathetic noises, but he was focused on the task and prepared the needle. When Evie interned at a pediatrics hospital, it took a few silly faces to distract the youngest patients. That wouldn't work here.

So Evie held on to the patient's free hand, squeezing it, reminding her she was there. Telling her that the needle was only for a moment and everything would be fine after this.

"Nếu bà muốn bóp tay con thì bóp đi ạ," she whispered, eyes fixed on the grandmother. It was what her own mother had said the first time she got her ears pierced at five years old. Evie had listened, squeezing her mother's hand as tight as possible, but her mother didn't even wince. And now Evie was in her mother's shoes. The woman's hardest squeeze was nothing; she was too frail.

The wrinkles on her forehead ironed out, and she blinked away the tears. The woman was now fascinated, staring as the tube filled up with her blood, and she only loosely held on to Evie's fingers now. Ryan shot Evie a smile.

A few minutes later, the woman's daughter arrived, her hair piled on top in a messy bun. She was apologizing as she rushed in, then called for her mother, "Má!" Once spotting Evie, she switched to English, with just a bit of accent. "I'm so sorry! I was stuck in traffic and couldn't get here in time. Was she okay? She's always fussy about needles."

"Yeah, she's all done." Evie pointed to the tubes that were being collected.

"And she didn't cry?"

The grandmother tsked, putting on a facade. "Little things like this don't make me cry," she said, and shuffled away toward the entrance.

"She's just pretending to be brave," the daughter explained to Evie and Ryan. "She cries like a baby when she's near needles. She usually wants to slap the doctor," the daughter muttered now that her mother was out of earshot. Then, worried for a moment: "She didn't this time, right?"

"This time?" Evie asked, eyebrows raised.

She only grinned—not really clarifying if she was joking, and Evie, relieved that she was, returned it. "Thank you so much," she said.

"It's nothing, I was just here," Evie answered.

"Sometimes that's all that matters. You're great at this. It's so nice to see that someone cares. Thank you again." The woman squeezed her hand, then left to tend to her strong-willed mother, who was trying to sneak mints from the front counter into her purse.

Evie felt her warmth long after the younger woman was gone.

"Two down, a dozen more to go," Ryan said with a sigh.

"I'm ready."

At her apartment building, Evie eased into a parking space that faced the sunset. Her feet hurt from standing up all day; she was bone-tired, but it came with a thrill. For two quarters, this was what her Saturdays would look like. She and Ryan worked through a list of patients, and everything went smoothly after the grandmother. No tears. Nothing but happy patients leaving their examining room.

Evie cracked a smile when she came across pics from this past week's Saturday Sins gathering. Instead of dinner, they each worked on their homework assignments. But time passed, it grew late, and delirium set in, so they decided to pretend to make awkward prom poses instead of focusing on their work. She nearly choked on her coffee at the sight of Tate and Lis facing each other, touching each other's hips at a literal arm's length. That wasn't all: Kale was in between their connected arms, holding their wrists closest to the camera—*their wrists*. Their too-wide smiles added the finishing touches.

Other pictures paired up Kale and Tate, Lis and Evie, and then she took one with Việt. They'd sabotaged their own portrait with their incessant laughter. They eventually posed like normal people. Việt remained in his chair while Evie stood behind, arms over his shoulders and around his upper chest.

Her heart skipped when she noticed how his hand touched hers. Just the lightest touch, from the tips of his fingers. The two of them . . . they looked like they were a couple.

At this thought, she pocketed her phone. In the moment, she didn't put any thought into what she was doing; she just did what was natural to her. That time at the Coffee House—was that really already three weeks ago?—was a fluke; no one had tried picking her up since then. Not that she was in any situation where that was expected. She was glad because she wouldn't know what to say if someone hit on her. Even when Việt was pretending to be her boyfriend, her heart pounded because she was out of practice being so close to another person. Or maybe it was because Evie realized she had felt this way around Việt for a while now—ever since their first run after the winter break. That it wasn't because someone was flirting, but because *he* was flirting with her.

But she couldn't help but remember Jake's words about her

neediness. The logical part of her knew he said it out of spite, that she shouldn't believe him. And yet—and yet—

Evie exited her car and lost her grip on her Stanley cup, which rolled and rolled away, until someone's foot brought it to a stop.

"Thank you—"

Evie stopped. It was Jake.

"Hey." She tightened her grip on her keys and reached for the cup in his hand. Jake was the one who said he didn't want to see her again. Why was he the one to say hello? Why was he here? But she realized the answer soon enough; they both frequently used the parking lot, so of course his car would be here. "Did you just come back from the clinic?"

"Yeah."

She hadn't seen him for two months. She readied herself for heartache or a surge of pity. But she only felt minor annoyance creeping in. And it only grew as Jake remained in front of her.

"Um, is there anything you wanted to say?"

"My parents are visiting the campus in a couple of weeks. Henry and his girlfriend, now his fiancée, are coming too and they all want to get dinner."

Eldest. She recalled from one of his phone calls that Jake's future sister-in-law seemed to be the exact opposite of what the family wanted: someone who chose a creative career—pottery work—and was considered a gold digger. Evie mentally shook her head; all these facts that she knew about her ex-boyfriend—when would they disappear from her brain?

"Your parents must be excited to see you. And congrats."

"Hmm," he answered, not divulging much more on that.

He wasn't just here to inform her about a family visit, right? They had nothing to do with her, unless . . . A guess took form in her mind, but it was too ridiculous for her to consider. "So, you're telling me all this because . . . ?"

"I didn't want to show up alone. Everyone still thinks I still have a girlfriend." *Oh no. No way.* "So I said you'd be coming."

"Jake, please tell me you're lying."

"Look, I'm sorry. It just came out!"

Evie pushed past him and walked ahead. "This is ridiculous. I can't believe you'd lie like that. What's wrong with showing up alone?"

"The words just came out," Jake said. He raised his hands in defense. He glanced around, lowered his voice. Some passerby looked, but lost interest quickly. "It was too late before I could stop myself."

"Why are you here?"

Her ex-boyfriend blinked, almost as if he didn't believe he'd get this far into the conversation. Everything urged Evie to get back up and leave him, but she couldn't understand why he'd lie to his own family like that. He always did what his parents said; he never wanted to fail their academic standards, or worse, continue to be compared with Henry and his other brothers. But did this weird family dynamic also dictate her ex-boyfriend's own personal life? How seriously messed up.

She then took stock of the boy's appearance: dark circles under his eyes, ruffled hair, wrinkled jeans, and white tee, as if he had just rolled out of bed and grabbed whatever was lying on the floor.

"Well?" Evie prompted, suppressing her volume. "What do you want from me?"

Jake took a deep breath. "Can you go with me to the dinner? Just dinner, and that's all. After that, we don't need to see each other again. I need you, Evie, and I promise I won't ask anything else of you again."

She bit back the emotions roiling in her. Of course he *needed* her. It seemed that he *always* needed her, to be there to comfort him, reassure him. "Now who's being needy?"

"Yeah, I know." He swallowed. "I was just angry. It wasn't needy to ask things of me. I am—I was your boyfriend. I should have been better."

Evie didn't hear the word *sorry* but continued to listen.

"Before we dated, we were friends, though. Before . . . every-thing, that's what we were. Even though we can't ever go back, can you do me this favor, just one last time? As a friend?"

First-year Jake came to mind. He'd dropped his mask around her; he wasn't popular Jake or privileged Jake; he'd struggled to live up to his family's expectations. Once upon a time, he'd allowed himself to be vulnerable with her. Once upon a time, her heart was moved by the dichotomy of how he presented himself to the world and to others. And try as she might, as all these past emo-tions surged through her, she felt herself sway. Not because she still liked him romantically. Evie supposed it was first-year Evie who had found someone outside her family who unquestionably relied on her; she was used to this role.

"I need to think," she whispered.

Emotions rippled across Jake's face, but the one that won out was relief. He leaned back and smiled meekly. "Yes, sure thing. I promise, after this, you won't have to see me again."

CHAPTER 30

VIỆT

The forensics competition was two months away. Still, Lis wanted to be prepared, so she asked the FSC officers to prepare mock cases to mirror the real event. They staged a murder scene in the lab where meetings were held. The desks were all pushed against the wall, making the scene the center point.

Việt was sweating underneath his white Tyveks because the AC was off. According to the sheet in his hands, this case was a stab-and-run; the perp fatally stabbed the victim, who bled out instead of dying immediately. The perp left a trail of blood to a nearby trash can, where the weapon, gloves, and shoes were dumped. The individual changed clothing, then disappeared before officials could arrive. The group had to analyze the substances found at the scene to determine in which direction the perp had run and later the perp's identity. The blood trail ended at the trash can, and the incident occurred at a four-way intersection. Unfortunately, no functioning CCTV cameras had captured the crime, and since it was nighttime, there were no witnesses.

The club officer who staged the scene took the job seriously. A dummy lay on his back, wearing a white tee and jeans. The stab wound was on their lower back, and instead of using white tape to mark *X*, which would leave room for the detectives to imagine the wound, the officer had provided a realistic rendition. Việt saw through the wound—a moulage using colored powder simulated the edges—and the blood pooling underneath.

Việt blanched as Kale poked through the wound and brought his bloodstained fingertip to his mouth—

"Corn syrup, but with another flavor I can't clock. Interesting."

"Don't eat things from a murder scene," Lis reprimanded. Their friend merely shrugged in response.

Việt glanced over his shoulder at Nathaniel, a second-year who'd recently joined their group. The blond-haired boy stared open-mouthed at the older members' display. From the short time they had together, he appeared studious, preferred clear-cut instructions, and adamantly followed them.

He felt he had to defend his friends to the rule follower. "Don't worry, at the real competition, they'll be total professionals."

Nathaniel meekly laughed. "That's reassuring." He glanced around. "So, how do we figure out where the perp had gone if there's no blood trail?"

"There's always some sort of trail," Việt replied. He crouched back down next to the dummy on its back. The blood had pooled underneath, mostly from the lower back to the end of its legs. But the trail to the trash can started from above the head, suggesting the perp had come from the back. If the perp had stabbed from the front, the trail would start from the dummy's feet.

With that hypothesis in mind, Việt stood back up. He slowly walked over to the trash can and confirmed that the trail had ended there.

"It looks like there's glitter here," said Nathaniel. Việt circled the trash can, followed where his cohort member's finger was pointing.

Ah.

"It's not glitter."

Again, the officer went above and beyond to stage this scene. They used a glitter gel pen to mimic the pinprick size of a blood splatter . . . a trail of which became more apparent and suggested that the perp had turned right after dumping the weapon at the intersection. If anyone were looking quickly, they couldn't see it, but the lab's overhead lights were positioned perfectly.

"There's always a trail," Nathaniel echoed his words from before, sounding awed.

Việt shared the findings after everyone regrouped.

"That's one half of the answer we're looking for," he said. "Next we have to figure out who this person might be."

Lis held up the items from the trash can, which were arranged on an examining table. "Already on it."

Evie: saw jake

Kale: ?

Lis: ??

Việt: !

Of course, upon seeing Evie's text, Việt ran—literally, since he was in the middle of a run when the text landed—to his safe space, which was Kale and Tate's kitchen bar, where the couple was ready to conference. He didn't have the words yet; just imagining Jake back in Evie's life was torturous.

"She said something about Jake—about what he said to her when they broke up. Has she said anything to you?"

"What was the context?"

"I'm not sure. I asked if she wanted someone to hit on her, and she said no," Việt answered slowly, replaying the moment in his mind. "She mentioned Jake, then stopped because we were heading back to the table."

"So whatever Jake said, it sounds like it's affected her idea of romance in a bad way."

"Yeah," Việt agreed. "Like it made her insecure about herself."

Evie was not immune to her nerves; he'd seen an insecure, nervous Evie before. How she fretted over the questions the clinic might ask, how she prepared her answers as much as possible. And since Jake dated her for two years, maybe he saw more of that side than anyone here. What if he used that against Evie?

Breakups seemed cruel.

"Maybe it's time for you to step in," Tate said to Việt.

"As a friend?" Việt asked, remembering their conversation after the party, which seemed like it happened ages ago.

Kale answered for his boyfriend with the shake of his head. "You still have feelings for her. What are you going to do if she starts dating someone else in the future?" Maybe someone like Jake, maybe someone better than Jake—it didn't really matter. It just wouldn't be him. And he'd have to watch, yet again, from the sidelines.

Kale had seen into his mind, into his nightmares.

"Based on your current expression, I know it doesn't sit well with you." Kale let out a long-suffering sigh. "You're going to torture yourself over this, Việt."

"And indirectly torture Kale," interjected Tate, who had slipped in beside Kale. Just back from a shower after running practice, he was dressed in a white tee and gray sweats, and sipped leisurely at his coffee—looking the very opposite of Việt, who was nearing a breakdown, and his boyfriend, who was just at the precipice.

Kale held up a hand to his boyfriend, the universal sign for *Shush, you*. He turned to Việt. "If it means anything, I think you have a chance."

"I do?"

The older boy pulled out his phone, swiped a couple of times, and showed him his camera roll. The pictures were from that silly night where they posed like awkward prom partners. Evie stood behind him, her arms encircling him naturally. They both looked calm and composed, but his heart had beaten fast at her touch.

"What does that picture prove?"

"I sent it to her. She hearted it."

Việt laughed. "A heart? I should confess to her because she hearted some photos?" The other boy looked ready to argue, but Tate, the calmer of the two, interjected with his own thoughts.

"She looked really comfortable with you. I don't think she even knew what she was doing, actually."

"I don't know. . . ."

Kale sighed heavily. "You tell her you like her; she tells you she's not interested. Or you tell her and she accepts. Aren't those scenarios far better than one where you say nothing and she goes on to date someone else in the future?"

He remembered the envy of Jake resting his head in Evie's lap, the ease with which he touched her. But more than that, his body remembered loneliness. He had always been someone on the outside looking in. It might happen again if Việt didn't step up and be honest about his feelings.

"Send me the photo," he finally mumbled to his friends.

CHAPTER 31

EVIE

Stillness brought her surroundings into focus: the hum of the fridge, the wool throw blanket tickling her thighs, the closeness— the *heat*—of his body. Ever since the Coffee House incident— though maybe that word was too serious—she tried to dismiss the idea of Việt being interested in her like that. But sometimes her eyes searched for Việt, and she'd notice him looking right back at her. Which made her wonder.

Jake's bold request of her occupied a smaller spot in her mind; she thought he would realize his ridiculous behavior and just leave it at that. Surely there were other plans to survive an awkward family dinner that didn't involve an ex-girlfriend. Soon, tomorrow, she should just text him and say to leave her out of it.

Lis was curled up at the other end of the sofa, fixated on the *Criminal Minds* episode they were streaming. Evie stole a glance at

Việt's profile. As expected, he was laser-focused on the show. He'd come from his dorm after a shower, so his damp hair glistened under the common room's light. A white T-shirt peeked out underneath his mustard-yellow hoodie—a perfect picture of cozy vibes.

She averted her eyes. Her cheeks warmed. Việt was mysterious in his own way, though he'd begun to open up to her about his worries. He'd cried in front of her. They talked about everything from silly to serious. They even "flirted," but she ended up panicking and denying it. He might have a crush on her, but what if it was just that—a momentary crush?

She jolted when someone touched her hand. The lights were off now. The TV glowed, showing another *Criminal Minds* episode, and from that faint light, Evie noticed that a throw pillow sat where Lis had been, and to her right, still in the same spot, was Việt.

"Sorry. Didn't mean to scare you awake," Việt whispered. "I said your name, but you didn't answer."

"Oh." She laughed nervously. "I didn't think I'd fall asleep so quickly." Her neck was warm; the blanket covering her legs was now up to her chin. Did Việt tuck her in?

"No worries. I was asleep too." He scratched the back of his neck. "When I woke up, Lis was gone. . . ."

"Strange that she didn't wake us up."

He seemed to struggle with his next words: "Part of me thinks she did it on purpose."

Evie froze; her earlier thoughts came flooding in. "What . . . what do you mean?"

"Hold on." He got up to turn on the light and turn off the television. He sat back down and put some more space between them. "Evie, remember when we were getting coffee and I pretended to be your boyfriend? Right after, I asked if you were okay with guys coming up to you, but you said it wasn't going to happen anytime soon. And then you mentioned Jake. Did he . . . say something to you before the break?"

She didn't think he was paying that close attention. Whatever he wanted to say to her, it seemed important that he heard her speak first.

"I told him I felt we were drifting apart. And even when we were together, it was like his mind was on other things. Or he just dismisses me like I'm nothing." She inhaled. "And toward the end of our talk, he said I was being needy."

"Needy."

She hugged a pillow to herself. "It bothered me in the moment, but I guess I locked it away in my mind until recently. The memory of those words has been coming out. All my life, I didn't want to be needy; I didn't want to cause trouble for my parents or for anyone around me. But what if I was being needy without knowing—"

Việt's next words batted away her doubts. "Being needy is selfish. And that's not you, Evie. Everything that you do, you don't do it out of need. You didn't step in during the qualifiers because you needed Lis's gratitude; you did it because you were worried your

LOAN LE

best friend would lose a battle she was meant to win. You didn't volunteer for the clinic because you need to be praised for being a good person. You do it because you care about others' well-being.

"So, no, Evie. You are never needy. If anything, you should be needier. If I were your boyfriend, I'd tell you that every day. And I'd give you anything you truly needed."

All air evaporated from the room. Evie and Việt stilled as the boy's words hovered between them. His eyes were wide, incredulous at his impromptu confession. Her eyes must have looked similar; she didn't expect any of this when they first planned a TV night.

"If you were . . . Việt, do you mean . . . ?"

"Oh god." Regret stole away the color from his face. "I—" Evie sensed his panic immediately; she wanted to calm him, but she also wanted him to speak.

She reached for his hand. "Việt, please tell me what you want to say. I'm here. I'm listening."

"You know I'm not the best with words. It's hard to talk about how I'm feeling." He inhaled. "I like you. I think I've liked you for a while. At first I thought it was because we're from the same place and we know the same people. Then I thought it was because I was glad that you let me be friends with you and the others. And you've also helped me whenever I've felt down. But it's not just being grateful—even though I am that.

"I know I like you because I think about you more often than anyone else in my entire life. I like you because every time you come back, smiling from your time at the clinic, I just want to hug you, and I can't help but feel so goddamn proud of you. I like running with you and just forgetting about everything. I like you because you're strong and you care so much about others. Which makes me want to care for you twice as much so that you never put yourself second."

Tears welled up in her eyes. She felt the weight of Jake's dig being chipped away by each of Việt's unabashedly kind compliments.

"That's why—I mean, what I was getting at is—" He exhaled.

"Việt . . ." He stared down at his hands clasped tightly on his lap, so tightly that his fingers turned white. It took courage to do this—courage that he might not have had before.

"Thank you for telling me," she said, and that's when Việt looked up. "You still told me even though I know it's hard to admit something so personal." She was glad he was letting her speak at her own pace, trying to slot in the right words to answer him. "How long have you had feelings for me? Recently . . . or before . . . when I was still with Jake?"

"Before." He nodded, looking down at his clasped hands. "Sorry if telling you all this makes you uncomfortable."

Her heart twisted. "You didn't, Việt. I'm not uncomfortable." Never uncomfortable. She couldn't think of one moment where being around him led to any discomfort. Even now, she wasn't exactly uneasy. Her heart was racing, and she could barely look at him directly, but what she was feeling wasn't discomfort. No, sitting at the pit of her stomach was fear of the future, like a hand holding the back of her shirt, keeping her in place. He was her friend, her good friend—someone who was always *there*, but her own feelings certainly went beyond that. . . . But what if things went wrong and they grew apart, like what happened with her and Jake? What if they became strangers? Could she manage to live with that? If she said no, Việt wouldn't get mad at her uncertainty—he wasn't like that. He always encouraged her to think about herself. She could say no, and that would be all right.

But her eyes landed on his hands.

They were trembling.

He was laying his heart out, and there was she, busy balancing hypotheticals in her head. Thinking instead of feeling. Her heart already knew Việt had carved a part inside her when she didn't need it. When she didn't even know. That was why she almost said yes when he asked her to leave the party early; why she couldn't wait to check on him over the break; why their runs were her favorite part of her week . . . She would lose so much more if she said no. His kindness, his understated humor, his steady presence. His devotion that asked nothing of her. And now she wanted him to stay—in her world, in her thoughts, in her heart, because it felt right for him to be there.

"I like you too," she whispered. Then, in a louder, stronger voice, she said once again, "I really, *really* like you."

Việt groaned and covered his face with his hands.

"Việt?" Evie shifted closer to him to touch his shoulder.

"Sorry." He removed his hands and smiled. "It's just—you looked very cute just now." He laughed. Embarrassed too, she buried her head into his firm shoulder, and would have stayed there if not for his hand gently tilting her head toward him.

As if he'd done this a dozen times, Việt met her lips with his. She relaxed against him, losing all feeling, except for the tingling that seemed to spread to her limbs. Behind her closed eyes was a dazzling blur of rings and stars; light that was joy. Ecstasy. It chased away her previous thoughts and anxieties, and all she wanted was to keep her hands in his hair and stay there.

CHAPTER 32

VIỆT

They parted after the first kiss with unabashed smiles, foreheads touching. More pecks followed—some long, some short, some kisses where Việt chased, and others he followed. He wondered, deliriously, if he would ever grow tired of her lips.

Countless kisses later, they had still not left the couch. Evie was nestled against him. His left arm was around her shoulders; his fingers were sifting through her fine, soft—*so soft*—hair. He could stay like this for hours. Lis wouldn't mind an additional roommate, right?

"So you've liked me for a while?" Evie asked.

He nodded. "I think Kale was the first to see it. So Tate knew as well. As for Lis . . ."

"She *did* leave us alone, though she's probably sleeping by now." She continued out loud, "We're in for a long discussion, I think."

"I like our friends."

"I do too." She sighed, nuzzling her head as if she could dig any deeper into him, which made his heart soar.

Saturday Sins would be happy for them—Kale more than others. Should they reveal it at the next dinner? It struck him as ridiculous, the imaginary scene of them showing up and "announcing" their next step together.

"What if we play with them a little? Keep this thing a secret just until the next dinner. We can tell them then."

"Oh, that's evil."

"No, it's fun."

Kale: sooooo?

Việt: 😬

Kale: what does that mean?!?

Việt: 😳

Kale: like, that makes more sense?!

. . .

Kale: she turned him down i think

Tate: do you want ice cream?

Kale: READ THE ROOM

Tate: sry maybe i should have asked Việt instead . . .

CHAPTER 33

EVIE

Evie rarely got sick when she was younger, but Linh was the opposite. When Linh had chicken pox, her parents kept Linh and Evie together, figuring it was only a matter of time before Evie got it. Somehow chicken pox skipped Evie. She was still waiting for the day she'd wake up and see red freckles all over her.

But on Thursday, Evie knew some kind of bug had taken over her body. She felt a terrible weight in her bones when she tried to get up for her last class. Evie had heard of "death bed" stories, of people suddenly seeing the light, their worst and best moments speeding past them. Not that she was even close, but she acknowledged how much thinking and reflecting could be done if you could do nothing but stare at the ceiling for hours while you wait for NyQuil to kick in.

· · ·

Later, she awoke from the longest nap, not knowing which day it was. She was surprised that it was still light out, though dimmer than before. She heard a knock on her door.

"I heard you moving around. How are you feeling?" Lis asked, leaning against the doorway.

"Better." Evie felt her forehead. "I think my fever's gone."

Lis approached her as if *she* were the doctor or the nurse examining a patient. She nodded, confirming that she didn't feel as feverish as the previous day. "Good. You slept for six hours."

"Six?!" Evie whipped off the covers in her bed, but Lis firmly pushed her down.

"Don't even go there. You need to rest. Take it. No one is chasing after you. Homework can wait. Rest today and let's see how you are tomorrow."

"I know. I was just . . . a lot of things happened and so quickly at that."

"Like what?"

Her eyes flashed open, remembering the plan to hide their relationship until they least expected an announcement. "Just . . . everything. School, clinic. Actually, maybe I picked up something from there."

Her roommate nodded at her explanation.

Lis closed the door. Evie's gaze went to her backpack . . . only, it wasn't there. Weird . . .

"And if you're looking for your backpack," Lis's muffled voice emanated from the door, "give up; it's out here with me and you're not touching it."

"I hate you," Evie said weakly.

"My Evie translator tells me you're *actually* saying, 'Lis, you're amazing. Never leave me. I don't know what I'd ever do without you,'" her roommate called back. "And you know what, the translator is *so* right. I'm the best.'"

> Việt: me, how do you make chao ga

> Mẹ: Sao con can biet? Con benh?

> Việt: no it's not me who's sick

Hours later, Evie woke from another nap to insistent knocking on the front door. She rubbed her eyes and slid down from her bed, the carpet rough against her bare feet. Lis wasn't home. Outside, pacing, was Việt, who was carrying a white plastic shopping bag in one hand. He was wearing his running clothes.

"Việt, hi." Had it really only been a few days since she saw him? It felt like ages ago. "I'm sorry, but I don't think you should come in. I'm—"

"Sick, I know." Việt lifted his bag. "I thought I'd make you some cháo gà."

"How'd you know—" Oh, Lis. She was scheming, even though she didn't need to anymore.

Rice and chicken porridge sounded good. She stepped aside for him. Their shoulders brushed, and he set the bag down on the nearest kitchen counter. "I mean, you didn't need to." She'd said these words before—memories from the time he came to comfort her before her clinic interview, from when he sat next to her in the garden.

The corner of Việt's lips quirked up. He was remembering the same things because he said, "I didn't need to. But I wanted to." She gestured with his chin for her to step back from the kitchen. "Go back to bed. I'll bring the cháo to you when it's ready."

"But you might not know where things are."

"I'm Kale's sous chef; I know my way around the kitchen now. I can manage."

She felt a shift in the air, a pause, an inkling to say more. Maybe this was a dream she'd wake up from soon.

"Then I'll stay on the sofa. In case you need help finding things."

Her friend-turned-boyfriend hummed in response as he turned to rummage through the cupboards. She lay back on the sofa with the throw all the way up to her chin. He was washing the rice, chopping the green onions, boiling the chicken, sprinkling in salt, doing a taste test, calling her name, kissing her lips—

Evie jerked awake, missing the calm of her dream. It'd be nice to wake and find a bowl of porridge waiting for her. Uber Eats would have to do, though. Her joints aching, Evie rose from her bed—no, *the sofa*.

The kitchen was empty. But there was cookware dripping in

the dish rack, and the rice cooker light blinked. She smelled broth and ginger root, and there on the counter was a steaming bowl of cháo gà.

 Evie: ♥

 Viet 😊

Two days later, when she felt much better, she sat on Kale and Tate's couch, knees to her chest. Her hood was up, engulfing her as she watched Việt filling up an electric kettle before dunking tea packets into two separate mugs.

Tate was washing the dishes, and his boyfriend was jabbering away while Lis listened, picking at a cake that Kale had made at some point, within the never-ending free time he had to perfect his art. He glared when Lis dipped a finger into the icing. Evie smiled as she watched them; this was what Saturdays were meant to be. This was where she was meant to be.

Only she and Việt knew the group's dynamics would be a little different going forward.

There was a shriek, and she jumped slightly, her head swiveling, only to land on Việt, who was cautiously making his way over with their tea. He placed the two mugs down, then sucked on the back of his pinky where some liquid must have spilled.

"That was very a high-pitched shriek."

"Oh, I'm sorry, I'll try to sound more dignified next time my skin is melting," Việt replied without any bite. He sank back down and passed the mug to her. Their fingers touched, and their eyes met.

Việt looked away first. He was cute when he was embarrassed, and she felt proud because she was the cause. And she might have shifted closer, a movement her boyfriend also noticed.

"You feeling any better?" he asked, trying for nonchalance.

"Yes, I just needed some rest."

Evie found her body angling toward his, until, without stopping herself, without *wanting* to stop, her head rested on his shoulder. She was warm all over, but it wasn't like the feverish sickness that had kept her in bed. It came from her chest, at the closeness of his face as he gazed down at her. His hood, which had been covering his eyes, slid off, and his hair stood up in a way that made her want to laugh.

Evie was falling for him all over again.

Suppressing a smile, she reached for her mug, and as the rim rested against her lips, her inner voice said, *Time for a show.*

Things in the kitchen were quiet. She didn't need to look to know their friends were watching their every move, likely confused at their newfound closeness, when she'd supposedly rejected their younger friend.

"Việt," she said.

"Hmm?" Her boyfriend blew on his tea.

"I like you."

It happened all too quickly: Kale cursing out Lis—"Did you

just elbow my cake?"—while Tate cackled, "Calm down, I'll clean up with a towel—"

Việt's eyes danced with mirth, purposefully ignoring the rising noise level a few feet away. "Really?" he said loudly. "Funny thing: I like you too." Quickly he lowered his head to plant a kiss on her.

That was unplanned. Evie might have squeaked, and when he moved away, she couldn't resist burying her hooded head against his arm, cheeks burning.

"*What is happening?*" Kale exclaimed. "I thought—Did you guys skip a few steps?"

"Stop! This is too cute—" Lis.

"BOTH of you, come on, let's give them some space—" Tate. Sounds of struggle followed. And plenty of protests. Perhaps Tate had held them back, arms outstretched. But Evie didn't care much. She and Việt remained in their own bubble on the sofa, eyes locked.

CHAPTER 34

VIỆT

He stayed late into the night at the apartment—and never left. The reason? Initially Kale offered them a place to crash after Lis voiced her reluctance to move after the festivities—more food, more drinks. And how could Việt think of going home after being this close to Evie, after having her head on his shoulder for most of the night?

Kale and Tate retreated to their bed, and the girls took the sofa while Việt slid into a sleeping bag. Lying close to Evie's sofa—Tate placed it there, not him—he summoned his courage to reach up to grab her hand. He held his breath as she played with his fingers before interlacing them. They chatted about everything and nothing, and it took an hour for them to finally fall asleep; that was fine.

What wasn't fine: Việt waking up flustered and sweaty. *Up* was a stretch because he couldn't lift his head, and he was now on the couch, wrapped tightly under piles of blankets. The girls were gone. And he was alone, with a small tickle in his throat and a body that felt overheated.

He tried to move again but was too weak, so he gave up until Evie sank down to her knees, bowl and spoon in hand.

He must be hallucinating. He must. Was she going to feed him?

Clearly last night didn't happen. Clearly there was no confession; he dreamt everything and was *still* dreaming.

"Finally you're awake. You became feverish overnight." She freed her hand to brush his hair out of his eyes, her touch light and caring. His fingers encircled her wrist. Her cool touch told him that this wasn't a dream, then.

"I'm sick?"

"Yep, it's your turn." She picked up the bowl and spoon. "This is the leftover porridge that you made. The others are out to restock meds."

"And you stayed behind?"

"Of course." She stirred the porridge, breaking eye contact. "I should be the one to care for you, right? Especially since I got you sick."

"Is that the only reason?" Blame his bold question on his feverish state or on his elation over the fact that everything—the reveal, the kiss, their intertwined hands—had all happened.

The spoon fell in the bowl. "Well also because . . . we're together now."

Ah, that sounded good. Her quick confirmation chased away

all his summoned boldness, a reaction that *his girlfriend* caught. "O-oh, we are," he stuttered. Evie's bashful expression morphed into one of mischief.

"Yes, we're boyfriend and girlfriend."

"Did you want to feed me? Is that why you tried to mummify me while I was asleep?" he had asked.

"What?" she said in mock outrage. "I was just *trying* to make sure you were warm enough."

"I could barely move my arms."

"You know what, never mind." She dramatically got up with the bowl and started walking away. Việt knew she was joking, but all rationale stopped working, and he got up to pursue her, when he tripped on the throw and—

THUMP.

Evie turned around and her mock composure broke. Here he was, on the ground before her . . . again.

"You good down there?" she asked, an undercurrent of laughter in her voice.

He moaned. "Just let me be."

Of course she didn't leave him alone. Accepting her offered hand, Việt pulled himself up and sat upright on the couch. It took another second for him to understand that she hadn't meant to spoon-feed him; she was only bringing it over to him. The broth was flavorful and savory enough that he kept eating until he had enough to warm his throat and ease its dryness.

• • •

The next time he came to, he wasn't alone because Evie, at some point, had climbed up, nestling close so that he was pushed against the sofa's backrest. Her upper body brushed against him in a whole new way, eliciting a barely contained moan. Ever so slowly, he placed his right arm over her. He wasn't sure if he meant to loosely embrace her. Or if it was to bring her closer, even in slumber.

Honestly, he didn't care, and he drifted right back to sleep.

CHAPTER 35

EVIE

"Have you been here before?"

"No, I haven't."

Turned out she could lie very well—maybe too well—because Việt just proceeded to open the restaurant door for her, and after giving the hostess his name, they were led to the main dining room.

Evie exhaled. This was fine. It was a nice restaurant, and she knew others went here on dates—even some anniversaries. How could Việt have known that she'd been here? It was silly for her to worry, so she tried her best to push all thoughts of her first date with Jake out of her mind. Việt had recovered from his sickness, which he definitely got from her, and now they were finally having their first date.

They ordered drinks first before looking at the menu. The options were dizzying—as if it was the restaurant's goal to tire them out.

"These options look great. What are you going to get?"

"Not sure yet," she answered quickly.

Back then she'd gotten the lasagna. Jake had gotten the tagliatelle, and she remembered thinking, *So that's how you pronounce it*, a word she'd only seen on the page but had never said aloud. And she had silently congratulated herself for *not* ordering it and therefore not butchering the word and embarrassing herself.

Việt said, "This one looks good. I think I'll get the—"

Please, *do not say—*

"—the tagliatelle."

Evie was cursed.

She couldn't hold it in anymore. "Việt, I'm sorry. I lied." Việt looked up at her. "I've been here before. On a first date."

The menu gently fell to the table. "Oh, I didn't know," he said evenly. "Sorry."

"Việt, it's fine—how could you possibly know that this was where me and—" Evie didn't even want to mention his name.

"If you're not comfortable, I completely understand. We can go somewhere else."

She grabbed Việt's hand, and he instantly quieted at her touch. "This date is about us. *Only* us. None of this is about Jake." She badly wanted him to believe her. Because, yes, she was thinking about Jake, but it was only a memory. She didn't miss him; she didn't want him to be the one sitting across her. She wanted Việt, and they could eat fast food if it came down to it. As long it was just him and her.

"I'll be right back," Việt finally said. His hand slipped out from hers and she felt bereft.

She should have said something; she was now a hundred percent sure that this date could not be saved.

It baffled her, how she would see her classmates change their relationship statuses every three months or so. Did they ever go through this? How was it possible to move on when you're surrounded by memories everywhere because memories stem from our senses—a touch, a place, a scent, a sound.

Now Evie felt she was better off in bed, in her pajamas, some mindless reality TV blasting from her computer. Việt had tried to set up such a lovely night, and she had messed it up.

A hand, now in her line of sight. She lifted her head. It was Việt; his face blank, but his eyes told a different story. They were alive—determined—like the moment before he confessed his feelings to her that night.

"Let's leave."

"But the bill—?"

"Already taken care of."

Well. Okay, then. She couldn't say no. She cautiously gave him her hand, let him hold on to it as she gathered her stuff. The waiter and the hostess looked confused by their quick exit, but still smiled politely.

Outside, vendors at the Davis Farmers Market were just starting to pack up; closing time was six on Wednesdays. She used to frequent the market to help Kale before their Saturday Sins meals, but she realized, with a slight tinge of regret, that she hadn't done so this year. Families walked away with plastic bags filled with their haul: crisp kale, bruisy red beets, sunset-colored pomelos. One Davis student carried persimmons in the well of his Aggies hoodie while a friend lugged away two cartons of apple cider.

Without realizing it, she and Việt ended up watching the same scene in silence.

"I used to watch *The Bachelor*. You know how they go on those lavish dates?" He chuckled. "When Bảo was planning his dates with your sister, I made silly suggestions based on what I watched, as if I knew what dating was like. But I also knew that the show had a limitless budget, and the bachelor gets a hundred grand as a fee."

Initially she was surprised he watched *The Bachelor* unironically, but now she was unsure where he was heading with this sentence.

"I heard Bảo and Linh had a good time doing pottery on their date," he continued thoughtfully. "But looking back, maybe he should have just asked Linh where she wanted to go. A date is about two people, after all." He looped his arm around her waist, and she relaxed against him, placed her right cheek just above his heart. "I should have asked you."

"I'm just happy to be on this date with you," she replied. He'd put on cologne, and it made her want to stay there, stone-still, wrapped up in his scent. Fresh water. Sun-dried wood. A forest's cool shade—sheltered and safe. Content.

"I know. I feel the same."

Evie smiled, though he couldn't see it. "Let's start over. Please?" she said, gazing up at him.

He stepped back so that he could face her. "Exactly what I had in mind. And I have a plan." He took her hand again. "Want to hear it?"

Her answer sprang in her mind before she even voiced it. "Absolutely."

Việt's plan, it turned out, was a picnic, and they would get ingredients from the market before them. When they crossed the street and came by the sign, his eyebrows went up, almost like he was asking, *Jake didn't take you here, right?* She only squeezed his hand in reply, and it was then that Việt was able to relax.

"I *might* have asked Kale for a favor while I was paying the bill," he explained as they searched for stands that hadn't completely packed up.

They were by a tomato stand. Việt bent over to pick up a bunch of tomatoes still attached by a vine. "Is Kale . . . cooking for us?"

"I'm the chef today."

Since it was nearing the end of market hours, not all the vegetables were fresh, some succumbing to the sunlight or the slight chill, but miraculously, the vendors somehow sensed Việt's determination and offered them the best they had left. With their help—including a thumbs-up from an elderly couple—they were able to add some basil, a baguette, fresh chicken stock, heavy cream, and various cheese to their bounty. Việt paid for everything, refusing Evie's help to the point that she had to snatch the baguette out of his arm. She laughed at his affronted look. Over one baguette!

The plan meant that Kale and Tate would vacate the apartment to let them do the cooking. When they arrived, the apartment left ajar for them, they stepped inside, and Evie's silent question found its answer. There, before them, was a picnic basket on the kitchen counter. Inside was a page from a UC Davis notepad:

Dearest Friends,

This is our sacred picnic basket that accompanied me and Tate on one of our very first dates, very early on in our courtship. Please take care of this precious item or I will never forgive—

Then it was Tate who scribbled all over Kale's first note and wrote, in his signature straightforward way:

Just bring it back next time you're here. And have fun.

"Kale's *very* lucky to have Tate," Việt said as he pulled out their market haul. He immediately reached for a navy apron by the sink and tied it around himself with a flourish, like he was some competing chef on a cooking competition show. He dumped the produce into a metallic bowl and placed it under a running faucet.

"The menu today is homemade tomato bisque with the freshest

ingredients that our prestigious UC Davis can offer. Accompanying this delicious soup will be the cheesiest of the cheesiest grilled cheese sandwiches—the best kind you'll ever taste. And all of this is portable." He gestured to the basket and a thermos that Kale had set aside for them. He rolled up the sleeves of his shirt. His hands rested on the counter. He continued speaking in his persona, "Miss Mai, do you have any objections to this meal, cooked by yours truly?"

He had lowered his voice to a pitch she'd never heard from him. And all of this, his sudden confidence, his stance, the way he *looked* at her, was, to put it simply, *attractive*.

"No, chef," she answered quietly, fighting a smile. "But before you begin . . ." She beckoned him with a finger, and he abandoned his persona, went around the counter, and stood before her. *Closer*, she gestured. Now Việt stood almost between her legs, arms caging her in. She was holding her breath; so was he.

He didn't say a word when she pulled him down by the collar. Not one word when she pressed her lips against his, and certainly not a word—because, of course, his lips were not available—when they lingered there, long enough to make Việt forget that the sink faucet was still running.

Việt: [snaps a picture of tomato bisque]

Bảo: CHEF VIỆT 😎😊😳😫🤤😩😫😕😣😭😎

Linh: who are you cooking for?!?

Ali: ^^^GOOD QUESTION!

. . .

Evie: [snaps a picture of tomato bisque]

Linh: OMG!!!!!!!

291

CHAPTER 36

VIỆT

"What did you use for the cream? Market?"

"Yes, everything was from the market."

"And did you *roast* the tomatoes and everything else? Or did you boil? Please tell me you didn't boil the veg."

"Roast, of course!"

"And then after that was when you used the immersion blender, correct?"

"Yes—but wait. Are we *still* talking about the meal? You're not interested in hearing anything about the actual date?"

"Oh, that." Kale waved his hand. "Fine. How was it?" Beside him, Tate only grinned at his boyfriend's flippant behavior.

But Việt knew the both of them by now—and knew they were very interested in it. After all, that was why, when they spotted him alone at the library, they descended on him like hungry vultures, his headphones were involuntarily removed, and the textbook he was studying from was slammed shut—eliciting the curiosity of the study group at the table opposite him.

So he told them everything. After Việt cooked the meal, he packed the food away and they held hands as they walked to the Arb, which was open all the time, and they eventually came to a spot not too far from where Evie first told him about her problems with Jake. And they talked for a while—from serious things, like Evie asking about his parents, to silly things, like the stretch of the cheese in the sandwiches. It was perfect.

Kale snapped his fingers, yanking Việt from his memories. "You didn't hear a word I said."

"We've lost him to Evie," Tate joked.

"Our boy's growing up!" Kale shouted. Tate laughed then, loud and clear. Now not only were students staring at them—even the front desk librarian fixed them with a glare.

Việt groaned. "Please. Go away."

The older boys relented, although Kale left Việt with these parting words:

"I want that basket back, okay? Or you're dead to me."

Not only did he return the basket, but before long, two months of being with Evie came and went blissfully. Truth be told, their relationship stayed mostly the same, but every interaction was imbued with newfound freedom. He reached for her hand anytime he wanted. After their runs, they used to go their separate ways, but now they traded air on top of the grass, their lungs limitless. She glued herself to his side when they watched TV at her apartment, and many times, he got lost gazing at her sleeping face against his shoulder. He loved the privilege of being Evelyn Mai's boyfriend, and he never wanted to take that for granted.

CHAPTER 37

EVIE

Pick you up tomorrow by your apartment?

Jake's annoyingly presumptuous text showed up, and it was a testament to how little Evie thought of her ex that she almost erased their last conversation from her mind. Maybe it was because her former relationship paled in comparison to her current one. The blushes and laughter with Việt came every day, and there was none of the anxiousness that plagued their first date. He took to heart that while it was not her first relationship, it was *their* first and theirs alone.

They still hung out with the Saturday Sins group, especially since the forensics competition was just on the horizon. Whenever Kale or Lis teased Việt too much, Evie joined them, then kissed him to playfully ask for forgiveness—only for him to demand lengthier reparations. She discovered her boyfriend liked to hold hands for no reason other than to feel her beside him. And just the other night, when she borrowed his yellow hoodie because she was chilly, she relished the heat that appeared in his eyes. She loved all the firsts she was sharing with Việt.

Evie should have deleted Jake's number but too late, he was reminding her that his parents were coming soon, with his soon-to-be sister-in-law.

She rang back, and her ex picked up right away for once. "I never said yes."

"Well, hello, Evie."

"There were no pleasantries in your text either."

Jake scoffed. "Look, all you have to do is come and chat a little—then you can leave."

"You're the one who said you never wanted to see me again. And other things. Why are you asking me to do this?"

"I can't stand the thought of it. My parents. My brother and his smug happiness. Especially since my life's been falling apart all over the place." A dig at Evie, if anything. "No, I don't mean that. I promise, it's really everything.

"I took you for granted. You were always there when I had to complain about them. You always knew what to say. And I felt like you were the one who understood me the most."

"Jake," she warned. The conversation felt much darker than she intended, and she wondered, as a person, if he was getting the help he needed.

"It would just help if you were there. So there's someone on my side."

Jake couldn't get himself out; he was stuck. She used to be that way, stuck in the easy, the familiar to the point it drained the color from life. Those colors only came back when she joined the clinic on her own accord, and understood she deserved to find self-fulfillment. That satisfaction stemmed from her choice and her choice alone. If Jake were able to choose how to live, instead of living under his parents' crushing expectations, would he be happy?

Flashing in her mind was an award ceremony during their second year, when his parents weren't in attendance. How cruel that his parents' absence could have just as much of an effect as their overbearingness on Jake.

Evie partly thought she would show Jake she found her own way; she was truly happy. The other part of her felt he needed saving, and because he wasn't capable of doing it himself, she was the next best option. Despite their bitter breakup, Evie didn't wish for his suffering.

"Jake, if I'm showing up to the dinner, it's only because we were once friends. But after that, I'm saying goodbye. To what we used to be."

He sighed in relief. "You won't see me again. I promise. Thank you. I really mean it."

She had to tell Việt; she couldn't lie about what she was doing. But she felt she wasn't explaining herself well. He faced her on her and Lis's couch. His eyebrows were furrowed as he listened to her describe Jake's family and their control over him—how that made her feel, even when she was dating him.

She fidgeted with her blouse's bottom hem. Which part would he react more to—the fact that Jake made this strange request or that Evie told him yes? She didn't agree because she still liked him; she had to make that clear at least.

"In case you were thinking it, my feelings for Jake are long gone," she blurted out.

His forehead smoothed out. Genuine surprise was behind his eyes. "Of course I knew that. I wasn't thinking that." He ran his hands through his hair. "Can you just explain *why* you agreed to go?"

"It's more like . . . I feel sorry for him. He's never had a good relationship with his parents. It's always felt transactional; they demand him to behave a certain way, to please the people around him, and he does all of that because he's used to it. He doesn't question it. And I wish he knew it didn't have to be that way."

"His parents sound vicious," Việt agreed. "It sounds like they ask more of Jake than they realize, and maybe they don't know what toll it's taking on him. You had front-row seats to it when you two were together, which must have sucked. And you're going to be in the thick of it during the dinner, probably."

Evie leaned her head on his shoulder, thankful for a solid place to rest. "Actually, I don't know if my presence will help. I just . . . I don't think I can sit here now, knowing what I know and not doing *something* about it."

"I can't say I'd go if I were you," her boyfriend eventually admitted. "But I trust you, Evie, and your heart. I just hope this dinner comes and goes quickly, and that years later, Jake will thank you for being there."

Evie melted against him. His fingers stroked her back up and down, soothing her, soothing them both.

After this dinner, she would leave everything about Jake truly in the past, and then she could move forward.

CHAPTER 38

VIỆT

"I don't know how you're okay with this, chief," were Kale's first words after Việt divulged his whole conversation. The both of them, along with Lis and Tate, were seated at the kitchen bar, unintentionally mirroring the very first time they'd all met.

Now, instead of feeling embarrassed or unsure of his place, Việt knew he belonged here. The way they immediately answered when he asked if he could come by and talk also said as much.

Việt's stomach sank as he absorbed his friend's words, saw Lis and Tate exchange a conversation's worth of glances. "Should I not be okay with it? I mean, it's not like—" He stumbled, then continued, "It's not like she still likes him romantically and wants to be with him."

"No, no, I don't mean to suggest that at all. We've watched Evie's relationship from the very beginning, and we know that ship has *fully* sailed." Kale paused. "Or sank."

"Semantics," Tate added.

"I think what Kale means is, we're sort of worried about you."

"I don't want to seem like I'm controlling her."

Lis let out a laugh, or a squeal, further puzzling Việt. Kale interpreted for her. "She and me and Tate, we're all thinking that you're so innocent."

He really couldn't tell if being innocent, in this situation, was good or bad.

Tate leaned in, resting his elbows on the counter. Like usual, he'd been quiet throughout the talk, but Việt understood he was just considering all sides, seeing not only what Việt couldn't see but also Lis and Kale's blind spots. "It doesn't seem like you were comfortable with her going."

"You're right." He glanced down. "This is my first relationship, and sometimes I really don't know how to act like a boyfriend."

If he'd asked her not to go, that was almost suggesting he didn't think she could take care of herself. From Jake's careless actions, from any hurtful comment that his family would likely make at the dinner.

"But you should have more confidence!" Lis insisted. "As her boyfriend, you're allowed to express how you feel, especially if you're uncomfortable. I don't think Evie would think you were acting jealous."

His head shot up. "Jealous? What do you mean by jealous?"

"You said nothing because you didn't want Evie to think you were jealous of her and Jake," Kale answered.

LOAN LE

Even though Kale essentially repeated Lis's words, Việt couldn't grasp their meaning. The words were fuzzy in his ears.

"Hold on. Banish our previous conversations. Việt, can you explain *why* you're uncomfortable with Evie going out to the family dinner tonight?" Tate asked.

His friends were good listeners, so he couldn't understand why they weren't listening now. "I don't want Evie to think that *I* don't think she could handle herself around Jake. Because I never liked seeing how sad Jake made her. I don't want her to get hurt in any way when she's with him and his family tonight."

"So," Tate said slowly, "when you say you are uncomfortable with this whole family dinner situation, you're not saying you're jealous?"

Jealous. He knew what that felt like—the pain, the helplessness, the discomfort while watching Evie touch another guy's hair, when he saw how affected she'd been the night Jake lied about being at the party. "No," Việt answered indefatigably. "I know Evie doesn't see him that way. We talked about it, and she said just as much."

"So you're just worried about Evie and how Jake and his family would treat her?"

Việt considered his friends and their odd behavior. "Why *wouldn't* I be worried? I'm her boyfriend."

Kale threw up his hands. "How can I say anything else to that?"

Tate straightened, removing his elbows. "This was intense for no reason."

"Really!" Lis sighed. Việt's head was swiveling between his friends, then landed back on the older girl. "We thought you were feeling bad

302

about yourself and were going to retreat, like you tend to do."

Ah. Well, he couldn't refute that observation.

"But you're going to be just fine. In fact, more than fine, if you repeat everything to Evie when she comes back tonight."

Việt was truly, truly lost. In his mind, he just hoped Evie was doing okay.

On his way back to Laben, he called his mom after she texted him to ask if he wanted a pair of Pumas that were on sale at Costco.

"Has Ba called you?"

"No, not yet," he answered, and he heard her sigh.

"It's okay," he replied.

"He is a coward."

"Have you and he talked?"

"Every day," she replied, annoyed. Việt was surprised—what did they have to talk about on a daily basis? "One time, he couldn't remember his doctor's name. And then yesterday it was to see if one of our clients knew we're delivering tomorrow. Once he was looking for his jeans. You know the ones he wore to dinners so that they wouldn't feel tight on him?"

By all accounts, this all seemed . . . normal.

"And did he eventually find the jeans?"

"He found them a half hour later! Trời ơi. He's useless without me," she said matter-of-factly. The line went quiet, and then he realized she was eating. Maybe peanuts or corn nuts. "He will call you soon. He wants to. But he is so stubborn."

"It's okay. I'm just glad it's going well. The divorce. That you're still talking."

"I don't think I will ever be free of him. In some ways, I don't want to be. Your father depends on me, but I realize I need him too."

Five minutes later, whether by coincidence or because his mother interfered, Ba texted him:

> The Dad: Ba dang o ngoai. Con o dau?

The instant Việt received his dad's text, he debated sending off a flurry of question marks but resisted. He jogged the rest of the way home. It was a perfect night to do that. He cut through buildings, ran through the space between two separate halls, and felt the breeze nudge him back, but he pushed ahead. His dad, for some reason, was here.

Right by the curb outside of Laben was Ba, leaning against the hood of an unfamiliar gray Toyota. He straightened once Việt came into view.

"My new car. Secondhand," his dad said in greeting. He shrugged. "Thought I should leave the other car to your mother." There it was, another reminder that the divorce was happening.

Việt tried to find his breath. "Ba, it's a six-hour drive. What the—why didn't you tell me you were coming?"

"Because I was afraid of changing my own mind. So I came here." Now that felt a bit truer.

"But *why*?"

"Your mother," he answered. That didn't answer much, so Việt continued to stare.

Ba glanced around as if his answer could be found there.

"Is there somewhere to eat?"

Burgers & Brew was the type of place his father loved: fast, efficient, and artery-clogging. Việt supposed, without his mother here, he could do whatever he wanted. If she *were* here, she'd slap the laminated menu against his father's shoulder to stop him from ordering an Angus cheeseburger and parmesan truffle fries. Then she'd eat a part of his meal herself, which was like—what was the point of protesting then?

But that wasn't going to happen again. Maybe ever. Việt tried ignoring the burning sensation in his chest.

Having ordered and without the menus to block their view of each other, Việt had to face his father. At first glance, he appeared the same—he wore a polo shirt, his glasses were still loose on his face, and they slid to the bridge of his nose as he checked his phone. But, and Việt could be wrong, it looked like he'd dyed his hair. And was he a bit thinner?

"You look . . . good," he said finally.

His father grinned. He leaned back and patted his stomach with both hands. "Ba mới bắt đầu Noom."

This was already too much. "So you talked to Mẹ," prompted Việt. "I didn't think you'd be talking to each other so soon."

"We are adults. We don't hate each other," his father replied.

"Ba want con to know that. And when it comes to con, nothing will change. Mình còn cha mẹ."

"Con biết rồi," he admitted. Out of all of this, he never doubted that they would somehow shed their parenting, as if it were all just an act.

"Ba Mẹ talked yesterday to figure out things. How the business will work. What things belong to Ba. What things belong to her."

"I don't even know where to begin," Việt said. He still had to process that his father had driven all the way here without any warning. He couldn't *not* ask questions. "Mẹ told me she asked for the divorce. Is that true?"

"Ừ."

"Were you shocked? Sad? How did you take it?"

"I have gotten drunk too many times with other friends who are divorced."

"Okay. That sounds . . ." Fun was not the right word, though Việt couldn't find another one.

"They complained about the same things as me. They were miserable. And now they are still miserable and have so many regrets, but they admit that they feel much freer. . . . Ba wished it happened sooner."

Việt swallowed hard. How much of his life did he regret?

"Not because a divorce was what Ba wanted. But because of con. Because you heard all the ugly things. All the time. No child should be placed in that situation," Ba said.

That was probably the most vulnerable statement Việt would ever hear from him.

"Ba thought we could make it work. But we failed. Ba failed."

Việt sensed that his next words would either open his father up or shut him down completely. "You and Mẹ . . . things just haven't been well."

"And here I thought you wouldn't have noticed. That we weren't as bad as I thought we were. The fighting." He glanced at his clasped hands, squeezing them out of comfort. Then he leaned back and crossed his arms.

"Ba còn thương Mẹ," Việt said.

His eyes cleared up, and the corner of his lip turned up. "Yes."

Yêu and thương. Growing up, Việt hadn't paid attention to the difference between those two words—or more accurately, the nuance. Yêu was romantic love, said between two people. It was that cinematic confession made after a desperate chase through the airport, the city streets, the train station. It was love that most people grew up thinking they wanted.

Thương could be romantic love, but more often it referred to platonic love and familial love. Việt heard it was somehow infinitely stronger than yêu. Thương was the love found in epilogues and all the untold stories that came after that.

It was the kind of love that remained after a divorce.

"And Ba will never stop caring for her or for con." His face broke, his voice clogging up with tears. But he didn't cry. He never cried. Though this was the most affected Việt had seen his father since he was nine. When he learned of his mother's passing back in Vietnam—deep into the night—and his own mother had to close the door to stem his tears. Ferocious. His sneeze was loud and obnoxious—but his crying was hurt, torturous, as if he were heaving his heart out.

Việt never wanted to hear that sound again.

He glanced down, swallowing hard. "I know. I know you will still love her. And me."

"Con a smart man. Must have got it from your mom."

The person saying this was the man who could calculate anything in his head. Who could measure the weight of a box in a few seconds. Who created a business from nothing and now had a dedicated client base who trusted him to deliver the freshest produce.

"Ba, you're smart."

"Ba didn't go to school."

"So?" Việt countered. "I'm still proud."

"Con . . . proud of me?"

"I am!"

His dad straightened up, puffed out his chest. "Ah, why wouldn't con be proud of Ba? Ta quan trọng. One day, Ba will be as big as Jeff Bebos."

Okay, that was a reach. His humility was evanescent. Việt held back a laugh. "You mean Jeff Bezos. And no, you shouldn't. That's not exactly a good thing to some people these days."

"What do you mean, con? Ba's now divorced, bald, still handsome. Just like Jeff Bebe."

"*Bezos.*"

At that exact moment, the waiter came by again. "Sorry, am I interrupting?"

Interrupting? No, it wasn't like they were having the first real conversation in eighteen years—capable of talking, at least—and his dad was telling Việt everything he thought he would never hear unless his dad underwent cultural surgery.

"Sooo, who had the BNB Burger?"

In between bites, Ba showed him pictures of his new apartment, which had almost no furniture, then asked about school and even the forensics team, which Việt figured he heard about from his mother. Việt explained it as best as he could, until he realized he was overexplaining—saying it wasn't available as a major, saying there was no concern about him switching majors.

"Does it make con happy?"

Việt nodded.

"Okay."

A word that wasn't strongly granting permission or showing support. Việt was grateful for any answer other than "You can't."

"Ba should go soon. Long drive."

The two stood once the bill was paid. At the last minute, Việt thought of Evie, and how she had been wanting burgers and fries. She was going to dinner with the Phans tonight, and from the sound of it, they were probably choosing an upscale restaurant. Which meant there might not be that much food to eat. He put in a take-out order as his father watched.

"Is con still hungry? Ba will buy more food."

"No, it's for a . . . friend."

"A friend." His father lingered on the word. Maybe he understood more than he let on. Maybe he just liked minding his own business. "It sounds like con a good friend."

Back in front of Laben Hall, they hugged goodbye. Hugged for real, no pat on the back, but with full arms around each other. A sudden emotion passed through Việt, and he couldn't explain it, or prevent it, and so he squeezed his father tighter.

"Ah, con will break Ba's back!"

They parted and his father grasped him by the shoulder again and squeezed. They held eyes for longer than Việt remembered them ever doing. His father looked as if he'd finally slotted in the last piece of the most grueling jigsaw puzzle and was now marveling at the full picture.

Wait, his dad didn't do puzzles, so maybe it was more like when his last Lotto ticket had all the right numbers and he was staring at them, realizing that they were indeed winners.

Anyway, Việt sort of felt the same.

"Good talk," Ba said. Then he gave Việt a thumbs-up.

It was cheesy. But then again, it was his dad.

It would take time for the surreal nature of this interaction to fade, but he was glad to see his father, to have this honest conversation, and he hoped this was the first of many. He lingered in the parking lot so long that grease started seeping through the burger's cardboard container.

CHAPTER 39

EVIE

Jake's dad had a movie-star quality like the leading men in her mom's dramas. These Korean, Chinese, Thai, Vietnamese men who would charm the leading woman with his words, tug them closer and closer with each witty remark, each compliment. His dad's back was ramrod straight; it was inconceivable to imagine him slouching on his couch after a long day's work, which was what her dad liked to do on his days off.

Evie knew she couldn't write off Jake's mother as a trophy wife. The beautiful, plastic-perfect woman, who would probably be gossiped about from the wolves who ran Little Saigon's social circles. From everything she gleaned from his phone calls home and his own words, his mother ran the house and her surgical room. Evie peered down at the woman's perfectly manicured hands, which managed to look both pretty and formidable enough to hold scalpels that precisely sliced through her patients.

The two of them had arrived in America before the war broke out; that explained their nearly accent-less English. They could have been mistaken for someone US-born.

Jake's parents didn't surprise Evie. What surprised her was the newly engaged son and his supposed gold-digger fiancée. They appeared . . . normal. Henry had dressed in denim jeans and an ironed light-blue long-sleeve and wore a class ring, while Mia, who appeared to be Evie's height, wore a periwinkle blouse and white midi skirt. Still tastefully dressed as the patrons in the restaurant, but not as stuffy. They had beamed when Evie took a seat beside Mia, with Jake on her other side. Luckily, he sat between Evie and the family matriarch.

"Wow, you are so pretty, Evelyn," the older woman said, smiling.

"Thank you. It's really nice to see you and Mr. Phan again," she responded.

"I was just telling her about the clinic," Jake said, eyeing her meaningfully.

"Congratulations on getting in," his father said to Evie. "Looks like you're on your way to a wonderful career in medicine."

"Yes, it's been rewarding to help others who wouldn't be able to receive help in traditional clinics. It makes me excited for the future."

"I have heard great things about the clinic from former class-mates," the father said. He cast a critical eye on Jake. "We thought he would get through, but even with all the tips I passed along" —

and *your name recognition*, thought Evie—"Jake was unable to get through."

Evie forced a smile. "Oh, but I know he'll get into another clinic or get a fantastic internship next semester; I don't see how anyone can turn him away."

Mrs. Phan's laugh was absent of any warmth as she responded, "Well, the clinic thought differently." Her harsh words dropped like an anvil, and no one spoke for a few minutes, everyone pretending to be engrossed in their meals. She glanced over at Jake; his shoulders were turned inward and he didn't look up. For the first time at this dinner, Evie felt a pang of sympathy toward her ex. He didn't deserve this treatment. No one did. "Well, Evie, your parents must be proud of an accomplished young woman like yourself. They'll be satisfied knowing you've found a vocation as noble as yours. Meanwhile, there are others who are just so lazy and amount to nothing."

Evie swallowed her desire to bare her teeth at the woman.

"I still have some college buddies who were involved in other clinics," Henry offered to Jake, clearly trying to cut off his mother. Next to him, Mia was staring at the tablecloth, hugging herself, making herself small. "If you want, I could ask them if they're open to an informational."

"Of course they would help, knowing that Jake is your brother!" Mrs. Phan chimed in, throwing Henry a proud look. She wasn't even hiding her favoritism, and Jake seemed to be fully aware of that. He only nodded at his brother's words.

"Henry tells me your store is managing to do well," Mrs. Phan finally said to Mia. A less cutting remark than the ones before, but still hurtful; she used *managing* instead of *doing*, almost suggesting that Mia was, somehow, impossibly, able to keep her store afloat.

"Yes, we have a great list of clients. Museums, schools, homeowners," she said. She was no longer wilted but proud. Evie noticed Henry grinning at his fiancée; they were adorable. "I hope you liked the water pitcher I made for your birthday."

"Ah yes. It is somewhere in the garage; I'm sure I'll find use for it soon."

It was painful to watch Mia dimming, as Jake's mother answered. Evie almost felt like she needed to intervene or redirect the conversation somehow, but Henry came to his fiancée's rescue.

"You should really use it. I have a similar pitcher in my kitchen; it holds a lot of water, and it looks great on my table. A work of art."

Mia blushed when the man took her hand and tenderly kissed the back of it.

A happy moment in the middle of what felt like the most miserable experience of her life.

"Well, someday, when I have a moment, I will find a good use for it," Mrs. Phan said.

The woman's cruelty sent shivers down Evie's spine. She peered at Jake—thought he might show sympathy toward Mia because he was familiar with his mother's cutting remarks. Yet, gone was his meek composure. An ugly smirk adorned his face. Glee at seeing someone who was not him, for once, taking verbal hits like a punching bag.

Evie couldn't breathe. If she sat here for another minute, she would no doubt get absorbed into this family mess. "Excuse me," she barely managed to get out. "I need to use the restroom."

In the locked bathroom, she leaned against the door for a good five minutes. She was getting texts from her friends. They were at The Green, looking so comfortable in normal clothes. She missed them. Her thumbs moved and she hit send on a text: I shouldn't be here. I want to be with you guys. Let's talk when I'm back?

In front of the mirrors, she breathed in and out, splashed some water on her face, then walked back out to the dining room. She came here thinking she was offering support to a former friend, but her presence—protected by the assumption that she had accomplished all the "right things" and therefore earned merit in the Phans' eyes—was hurting someone else. Jake was complicit in his parents' attitude, and she couldn't pity him anymore.

Evie needed to leave as soon as possible. The table's eyes were on her as she returned, undoubtedly questioning why she took so long. "There was a long line." Thankfully, the restrooms were out of eyesight, or else they would know she was lying.

Conversation stopped once she returned, though she couldn't tell if it was her doing or if another exchange had occurred while she was away. Jake's mother kept throwing glances at Henry, who refused to look up. His jaw was clenched. Evie watched as Mia reached over and rubbed his back, and his body relaxed at her touch. Meanwhile, Jake moved around his broccoli florets with his fork, his shoulders still up.

She relied on everyone's plates to tell her when dinner was nearly finished. Once all plates were cleared, she readied herself to pay for her part and escape. The universe had other plans; their waiter came by and asked, "Dessert, anyone?"

"Yes," Jake's father answered. "Let's see the menu."

Mia politely coughed and smiled sympathetically at Evie. At least she had some allies, as unspoken as the alliance might be.

Her phone vibrated suddenly, and she peeked down to check a message from Kale, in the Saturday Sins group.

Incoming.

"What?" she whispered.

She glanced up. Jake's parents stared open-mouthed at a sight behind her, so she turned and saw the waiter heading their way, leading two guests who looked strangely like—

Lis and Kale.

The two were dressed in the same outfits from the photo, though Kale also had on his apron because he must have been cooking.

"Evie, thank goodness!" Kale exclaimed, his natural voice booming. If their appearance hadn't gotten others' attention, his voice would. "We were looking for you *all over* school."

Standing just behind Evie now, he said, "Our class project—we lost some of the data and we need your help. Only *you* can save us, Evie!"

A little to Evie's right, Lis whispered, "Somewhat of an exaggeration, but . . ." She cleared her voice and projected, smiling at everyone seated at the table, "So sorry to interrupt your dinner, but can we steal her away? Like our friend said, we lost some important data, and we need to do well in this class, and we won't be able to finish our project without her."

As Jake's mother and father exchanged bewildered looks—Jake couldn't close his mouth—Evie caught Kale eyeing one of the dishes, perhaps dissecting each ingredient and wondering how he could replicate it at The Green. Lis jabbed him with an elbow.

Henry and Mia were trying to school their faces, but they probably caught on already.

Lis squeezed her shoulder, causing Evie to jump slightly. "Yes . . . I'm so sorry, but I think I have to go." She opened her purse and pulled out her part of the bill. "Thank you so much for inviting me to dinner, and please allow me to pay for my meal."

She turned to Henry and Mia. Even though they were meeting for the first time, and they knew nothing about each other, she said, with all the sincerity she had: "Congratulations. I really hope that you two will only know happiness together. Starting a new life, with just the two of you—that's so amazing."

"Th-thank you," Mia stuttered. And she gazed up at Henry, who smiled back.

Once they were out of earshot, Evie whispered to her rescuers, *"Thank you."*

"Don't thank us. Thank him." Lis nodded to the front. "He's waiting outside."

They rounded the hostess stand, but they weren't completely free. Footsteps followed them out, and Jake appeared looking uncharacteristically flummoxed. "Wait—what the hell, Evie? Why is . . ." He settled on his final words. "You're leaving?"

Jake's face fell—and that was when Evie saw *him* again. First-year Jake. The Jake who pulled her in by the strings of her hoodie and kissed her under the glow of Toomey Field. Who cried, only to her, when he learned about his father threatening his mother with divorce. Who sulked when he heard his parents weren't making it to his second-year awards ceremony because of other engagements. Who hated being compared to a brother who really did seem to love him back. That little boy was buried deep, deep down, and she shouldn't be the one to help him resurface.

It wasn't her place to console Jake anymore. Or her responsibility. She should never have agreed to *any* of this.

"I need you here, Evie."

"You really don't, Jake. You just wanted someone there to act as a buffer between you and your parents, but that's not my role. I can't be there to defend you. I can't tell them every good thing about you because I'm not your girlfriend anymore. No one else can do that for you." She inhaled. "You have to do it yourself."

Then she let her friends steer her away—and toward Việt.

It was weird to think that she might come to associate parking lots with Việt. Standing there, just as she had done that rainy day outside Chef Lê's restaurant, was her boyfriend. Evie rushed into his arms, breathed in his subtle scent: sun-soaked driftwood and fresh water from his cologne.

"Were you really worried?"

"No." He paused. "Yes, I was—well, I think Kale could give you the details." Mindful of the rain, he led her into the back seat of Kale's car.

"Right, all those tears and runny noses . . . ," Kale deadpanned from behind the wheel. From the passenger seat, Lis slapped him by the shoulder.

"None of that. But it was pretty fun how the moment he saw your text, he leapt up from the sofa." She grinned at her through the side mirror. "And then we hatched a plan. A ridiculous one, I know, and that's probably why Tate refused. He's back at home if you're wondering. Reheating food, just for you."

"Food?"

"I went out tonight with my dad." That was unexpected. Việt laughed, probably because of the incredulity on her face. "Yeah, I know, I'll tell you another time. More important, I got a burger for you, and fries. Mushy now, but with some time in the oven, they will be fine."

On cue, her stomach growled. Việt and her friends knew her stomach better than herself, apparently.

They would talk, she was sure, about everything: Jake, the dinner, even Việt's conversation with his dad—she didn't know where to start. All she could do was reach over and grab his hand. Hold him tight.

"Thank you for coming for me."

"I've said before: you care too much. But this is our way of showing you we care for you, too. I want to care for you."

As always, they ended up at The Green. They stayed glued to the kitchen bar, unconsciously mirroring their formation when Việt had first met everyone all those months ago. Except this time, the gap between Evie and Việt was far closer. She wolfed down her burger and fries, with Lis sneaking a few for herself; she knew she looked ghastly, yet her boyfriend, elbow on the table, cheek against his hand, was openly staring at her as if she were the loveliest thing in the world.

Once they were sated, a chain of yawning began. Tate, ever the night owl, let a drowsy Kale lean against him. He tilted his head, eyes probing the other couple. "You two probably had a night. Go home."

"Yeah, I know." Việt's palm was a whisper on her back. This time, she fell against him so that they were almost mirroring the other pair. "But we'll be okay."

Tate's eyes flickered between them, and whatever he found satisfied him. "Finally."

EPILOGUE

"Say 'Dada.'"

"Mama."

"No. 'Dada.'"

Philippe looked Chef Lê straight in the eye and smiled cheekily. "Mama."

"Oh yes, it's me, maman!" Saffron stole the toddler away from his father, kissing and calling him all kinds of French endearments.

At Chơi Ơi, friends and family gathered to celebrate the owners' only son's second birthday. Like Chef Lê, little Philippe was destined to be a social butterfly. He smiled at every guest, freely returned high fives, and kissed every offered cheek. And like his mother, he was dressed chic in a forest-green cotton jacket and shorts combo. His abundant dark brown hair, courtesy of both parents, was sleeked back.

Chef Lê feigned a wound to the heart at his son's betrayal. "One day, he'll call for me and not his mom. One day. Or else."

"Threatening your own son—nice," Việt deadpanned.

"Kid's not going to listen, I can already tell," Bảo joked, watching Saffron carrying Philippe back into the crowd.

Việt was touched to be invited to the celebration since he didn't think he was as close to the chef as Bảo and Linh, who stood right next to him. But the chef was someone who didn't understand the word *acquaintance*. There were strangers. And there were friends—nothing in between. Apparently, Việt's second visit to the restaurant during the winter break had upgraded him to the status of friend.

The R&J crew was back together again for the summer, and they already had plans to road trip along the California coast. Thankfully, Ali didn't volunteer to drive them.

"Where'd Evie go?" Linh asked.

"I don't know. I'll see where she's at," he answered.

"I still can't believe our baby's growing up. Even has a girlfriend!" Ali pretended to wipe away tears.

Việt rolled his eyes, though he couldn't exactly hide his smile. While the word *baby* was going too far, the last few months were a good measure of his growth. He'd begun seeing a counselor named Kim In-seo, whose gentle smile welcomed him each time he came for their sessions. She, like his friends, just gave him space to talk. Days passed quickly because of his and Evie's morning jogs and their Saturday Sins dinners in between his schoolwork. And when there were down days that not even a counseling session could quickly fix, there were exponentially more kisses and hugs from Evie—and food from Kale.

Wandering around the dining room, he spotted his dad, who was cackling along with the chef's father, joking about whatever Vietnamese men joked about when they were drunk. Việt's mother had to duck out early because she was going line dancing—of all things!—with her girlfriends. But his parents had spent a good fifteen minutes chatting. It felt odd watching them interact so casually; strangers would probably see them as nothing more than adults getting to know each other, and not a former husband-and-wife pair who figured out they were far better separate than together.

Việt was still trying to find his girlfriend, though.

The spring forensic science competition, just a few towns over from Davis, had also happened in a blur. At the end of it all, there were no roaring spectators, no celebratory pile of teammates waiting for him, Lis, and Kale. Just Evie, who kissed him the moment he got off the award stage, a flimsy bronze medal newly adorning his neck.

If he hadn't gone to Kale and Tate's party that September night, if he hadn't accepted Lis's invite to the forensics club, if he hadn't wandered over to the Dairy to meet the cows, there was a chance he wouldn't even be in Evie's orbit.

Now Việt left the dining room for the host stand. The sun beamed in so brightly, so cleanly, because the window, where it was once patterned with fingerprints and bird excrement, now shone spotless, courtesy of a meticulous cleaner. He focused on Evie, on the other side, who was chatting animatedly with an elderly Asian woman leaning on her cane, whose entire forearm was bejeweled.

Before the semester ended, Evie said she wanted to replicate the student-run clinic's efforts in Little Saigon. First she'd need to spread the word and gauge local interest. Perhaps this woman was interested or might even be a potential patient.

Việt palmed a business card in his jeans pocket. Chef Lê, by honest coincidence or stealthy interference, had invited a friend of a friend who was a forensic pathologist. He was Vietnamese as well and readily offered his card, told Việt to call. This small thing between his fingers was a promise, and he had to be sure he didn't lose it somewhere.

Sensing his gaze, Evie turned around. Their eyes locked. A smile bloomed on his face. She saw him, clear as day.

And he saw her too.

ACKNOWLEDGMENTS

Thank you to Jim, Krista, and the BFYR team for your patience as I repeatedly missed deadlines and ignored emails. (For example, I'm submitting this page late.) I'm thankful to my parents Dong Pham and Phung Le, my family, and my friends who politely asked about my writing over the last three years, then backed off because I clearly didn't want to talk about it. In the time it took for me to write *Solving for the Unknown*, I became an aunt to two girls, Amelia and Zoey, and every time I see them, I think of the wonderful futures they will have because their parents are my sister An and brother-in-law Kevin.

The second book is always hard to write, but the process allowed me to remember my college self. That Loan was not so great, especially during the third and fourth years. I felt lonely and sad and frustrated, and I wish I could have told her that 1) this will not be your biggest obstacle in life and 2) you're gonna get through it.

I created the Saturday Sins crew once I thought about my friend groups—the similarities that keep us together, the differences that make us interesting. Fresh on my mind are many friends I have lost, because of disagreements, because of my actions or inactions, or because of a tricky thing called time. But I'd like to say that they influenced my life and will probably never know it. Thank you to the two upperclassmen (Fiona and Nick) who made me feel like I belonged in the creative space. Thank you to the friends who understood that I disliked parties, yet gave open invites and accepted me with pure joy whenever I arrived on their doorstep.

I am still learning to be a friend. Thank you to writing friends who check in to see if I'm alive. Out-of-town friends who reach out when they visit the city. Friends who convince me to go to concerts and house me in their loft for the weekend (Hi Caitlyn!). I am grateful to the Sunday Runaround group chat—Clara, Eric, and Spencer, who, for some reason, don't kick me out of the group for not responding to their texts. I will try my best to treat you well.

Thank you for keeping me around and for letting me witness your extraordinary lives. I love all of you.

ABOUT THE AUTHOR

Loan Le is the author of *A Phở Love Story*, a YA rom-com that earned praise from NPR, POPSUGAR, Bustle, *Bon Appetit*, *USA TODAY*, and BuzzFeed. Her speculative short story appeared in *Firsts and Lasts*, a YA anthology that Penguin Workshop released in Fall 2023. She holds an MFA degree in fiction from Fairfield University, where she also earned her bachelor's degree. She is a senior editor at Atria Books, a Simon & Schuster adult imprint, where she acquires dark fiction. When Loan isn't writing YA novels, she's writing ghostly, dark adult fiction, baking sourdough bread and bagels, cash budgeting, and listening to BTS. Visit her website at WriterLoanLe.me, and find her on X @LoanLoan and Instagram @LoanLoanLe.